THE TOWER

Carol Ann Ross

1

COVER DESIGN by Chris Van Atta

Chris Van Atta

www.ArtSeaLove.com

https://www.facebook.com/ArtSeaLove/

ACKNOWLEDGEMENTS

Writing a book is never an easy task. It takes patience and dedication. It is most definitely hard word but work I find more fulfilling than just about anything else.

This book is exceptionally special to me because of the people I met while researching and writing it. They have become friends, lifelong friends, from whom I have learned much.

There is honesty in writing, with oneself and with those with whom you collaborate. Honesty is the stone on which true friendship is built. Thanks to those of you who have opened up your lives to me.

Thank you to Evelyn Hobbs, Randy Batts and Steve Midgett for your vast knowledge of the sea and the people who live the seafaring life. You will always be dear to me.

For technical support and other information I would never have considered I thank Patti and

Bruce Blacknight, Debbie McKnight, Bentz
Overstreet, Officer Chris Houser, SCPD, Detective
Hartsfield, SCPD, Stretch, Doug Thomas, Lou
Wilson and Marlene Bottoms.
Thanks to Connie Pletl for editing.

DEDICATION

To Joey

I became insane with long intervals of
horrible sanity.

Edgar Allan Poe

INTRODUCTION

Estelle pushed the stacked crates to the side, whatever they had once held had long ago been ransacked. She pushed again, harder, kicking her foot into the slats; they gave easily, the rotting wood splintering into soft shards.

A few curse words flew from her lips as she leaned against the cold concrete wall to peruse the splotched remains of paint jobs and renovations.

"So this used to be an observation tower in the 1940s." She tilted her head back, her long neck turning slowly as she studied the worn remnants of the three story tower, one of the last remaining artifacts from a time when Topsail Island was used by the military.

"So just what did they *observe* from here?" she questioned herself aloud. *Didn't Hank once tell me something about rockets after World War II? Something to do with bumblebees?*

"Shit, that was way before my time." Estelle shook her head. "These damn people around here keep living in the past--what did Hank want with this monstrosity anyway? It needs to be leveled."

Running a hand through her long hair, Estelle pursed her lips. Her eyes squinting as images of tapestries hanging from the sallow walls played in her imagination. "Kind of like a castle--sort of--I could do something like that with this thing."

She thought for a moment then shook her head no. "Hmm, not that. Something I could do, something I could turn it in to--I need to make money off of this thing. Sell it? Make it a house?" She sighed heavily. "They're all really big into the history crap around here, at least the local yokels are."

Her brow furrowed as she squinted once again in thought. "Hmm--restore it to look like it used to--all the old 1940s stuff, the rockets, all the shit that goes with this thing." She raised a brow. "Fifteen dollars a pop--no, twenty."

Estelle nodded and twisted her hair into a bun, stabbing it with a long wooden pin. She licked her lips. "I'll talk with the lawyer and see what he has to say."

Immediately laughter burst from her mouth, "Ha, a lawyer--me doing business with a *lawyer*. Now that's a far cry from Kentucky."

Estelle drew her mouth tight, unconsciously she balled her fists as her chest rose and fell. The image of herself as a little girl, her hair matted and tangled, her underpants soiled, sitting amidst the squalor of an old rundown three-room trailer flickered in her mind. She blinked the image away, her thoughts returning to the tower and of the man who'd given it to her.

It had been three months since Hank's death. He had left everything to her--the land, the beach house, the rental houses and the tower. Then there was the financial stuff, the stocks and annuities. She was set and had more money, more things than she'd ever had in her whole life. It was such a far cry from Kentucky.

Who would have thought that the little stick of a girl who once wore rags would have as much as she did now?

Her mind raced from one asset that Hank left her to another, thinking of its value, devising scenarios on how there could even be more.

Other men had given her *things*, left her things in wills but this time it wasn't just a bauble or few hundred dollars. Oh yes, the little house near New Bern was fine but it was not nearly as nice as Hank's home and not worth one-tenth of it either.

Compared to the beach house, the New Bern place was a shack. Regardless, there could be more. For Estelle there could always be more.

"I guess Hank was good for something after all." She grinned and for a single moment felt remorse for her old lover's death. It was an uncomfortable feeling and she brushed it away with the flip of her hand. "Sap," she spat the word, releasing it as if it were phlegm. "Just another male bastard."

Propping herself against a wall, she brought a thumb to her lips and sucked the tip gently. "Hmm, Theo could do something with this place. He's handy that way." She imagined Theo, her friend from Kentucky, the only person who had never wanted anything from her. She pictured his agreeable smile. Yes, Theo could always be counted on. "Theo will know what to do, how to make this thing look authentic. Then--" Estelle's eyes widened, her lips parted. "Ahh, then, once this place is an historical site, a real one--then, this community will welcome me with open arms."

"I won't need any of the things Hank left for E.J." Grinding her teeth, Estelle balled her fist once more. "No, that's mine. Why should that old bat have what is rightfully mine? Hank wasn't kin to her. She ain't his wife. She ain't his momma." Her eyes hooded, she muttered, "Someone's always taking from me."

Estelle leaned her body against the wall, sliding slowly toward the floor, then plopping down on the cold and sandy concrete, her legs sprawled child-like. She wiped an imaginary roach from her pants leg and drew her thumb once again to her mouth, a collage of images from the night she'd slit Mindy's throat flickered in her head like a slide show. "This time I won't make any mistakes. I'll take my time with Emma Jewel. That selfish hag is not entitled to my things."

Estelle's forefinger swirled the sandy floor of the tower attempting to create an image. "She's not my momma—she's nothing to me."

Pulling her knees to her chest, Estelle moved her forefinger across the sand designing the curve of a shoulder, the long lines of a back and waist flowing into the hips and buttocks. Her hand brushed away a bit of sand here, a bit more there as she drew the legs, slightly bent to the side.

Once again with the palm of her hand, she swept away much of the thigh and calf, replacing it with more sand she'd swept from the floor. It was as if she were attempting to fashion a puddle of some sort at the buttocks and thighs. Her fingers played in the accumulation, adding depth and flow.

Pushing a finger to her lips, she gently bit at a nail. "Hmm." She pressed swirled sand where the hair was and spoke, "His hand, Daddy's hand, will never rake its fingers across my pink skin—again--never, never."

Chapter One

It was a good thing--almost comfortable. Hank was gone now, dead like he needed to be. No need to worry about that bastard running his mouth. And as far as Don knew, Hank was the last who knew the truth, the last who could have told about him and the coke, the heroin, about Sarah and Reggie.

Don ran a hand through his thick blond hair as he drove southward into Surf City. His fingers touching the crew neck of his tee shirt, he felt the strands of his hair. It hadn't been that many years since he'd worn it high and tight, now the length made him feel a little younger, freer than his time in the military. Being an undercover cop had its advantages, he got to wear his hair like he wanted, wear more comfortable clothing, say sir to whom he pleased. He pulled his fingers through his hair once again, a couple more inches and he could wear it in a ponytail like he had in college.

Streaks of silver were running through his hair now but it blended well with his natural color. He even liked it. Carrie had commented on the silver, said she liked it, too. He smiled, thinking of her bright eyes and the night before when they dined as a couple at the Shrimp House. She'd even brushed it away from his brow, the tips of her fingers threading through the strands.

The young guys, the surfers, were all wearing their hair long, wearing man buns. He grimaced, shaking his head. He wouldn't be caught dead with one of those.

He pictured himself younger and chuckled at the one attempt he'd made at surfing and how now, at forty-five, he would feel even more foolish. "Shit, I'm too old for that nonsense. Who am I fooling?"

For a moment it *was* that good thing--almost comfortable, *Carrie could do that for me*, the thought was pleasing, almost healing, until he remembered Essa--Estelle, coming to the table at the restaurant and asking for their order. He cursed again aloud, recalling how she came on to him in New Bern, so blatant, so wanton. He'd wanted to throw her across the kitchen table, take her--or let her take him.

"That's what she wanted, she'd all but asked for it. That kind of woman prefers it like that." He paused, thinking of that day in New Bern, how she bent into the refrigerator, her legs spread. "Wonder if Hank ever mentioned me and Sarah to her, wonder if she knows."

He pulled the Dodge Charger into a vacant rental house driveway, thumped the steering wheel heatedly, his chest tightening as he thought of Estelle and how manipulative she was, how tempting she was, her long freckled legs, her broad mouth. Backing into the highway, he turned to go north toward Hank's beach house--Estelle's now.

She was irresistible, drawing him siren-like, drawing the darkest part of him. He thought of how she'd tried to lure him into bed in New Bern. A guttural laugh fell from his throat as he pictured the house there, how ramshackle it was. He laughed again and wondered if she would allow Hank's beach house to fall into disrepair as well.

"Maybe she'll kill another poor sucker whose home comes with weekly maintenance." his jaw tightened. *She's going to get away with it--with killing Mindy --with killing Hank. I know it. And nobody wants to pursue an investigation against her. They're just glad Hank's dead.*

"Well, I am, too," he spat the words loudly, self-consciously, justifying his angst, the ambivalence of why he was even cruising this section of the island, angering himself further. He thought of how unfair things had been in the last few years. How he'd been suckered into being a delivery boy for Sarah and how it was the one thing that had kept him from relaxing enough to pursue a relationship with Carrie, with his son Phil-- hell, with anyone. *It all could have been different.*

"This could have been my paradise." Hank's image formed in his head and Don thought of how some people get lousy hands dealt to them. Maybe he was one of those people. He shook his head. "Hank was a crazy ass wacko but maybe I'd be too if I'd lost my wife, my kid and my parents all within a couple of years."

Hank just couldn't figure out a way to turn that rotten hand into a winning one. Maybe he thought he was winning by knocking off all the drug dealers he could. "Guess that's why the chief doesn't want to pursue his wife--he figures she did all the dirty work for the town."

Slowing the Charger as he neared Hank's beach house, he drove past.

Yes, the lights were on. He drove a few miles north toward the tall span bridge and made a U-turn near the police station. Raising a hand he acknowledged Officer Hewett parked nearby in an unmarked police car; after turning, he headed back. This time he parked his Charger in the driveway of a second row house, a block north of Hank's. It was lined with palm trees and pampas grass, that ostentatious flora he had come to detest.

He knew this house was vacant. He knew pretty much which ones were and that would be most of them since it was now off-season, a month or more past Labor Day.

Hating the palms was one thing he had in common with the locals and natives. Like Morgan Simpers, he found them pretentious. Poor Morgan, last he'd heard, his wife had cut his allowance in half and made him sell the Baja. He was now driving a Kia, an old one, puke green. Don snickered as he pushed aside a stand of pampas grass and walked in the dark toward one of the beach accesses.

There was a crescent moon out. Thick cumulous clouds obscured it as they moved ominously in the sky. Don could barely make out the ocean but sparkling bits of silvery light reflecting off the water shined intermittently, showing off the sea and its movements.

But more than see it, he could hear it--the slow low roar of water as the small waves hit the shore. Even as it was, it called. Since he'd been a young Marine and visited decades ago, it had called. That's why he'd come back, hoping that he could capture those lost halcyon days. But now? What havoc had been wrecked? Why couldn't he leave well enough alone? All that he'd been praying for had come about, had practically slapped him in the face and what had he done? Ignored it, put it aside, letting some basic urges steer him away. *Let sleeping dogs lie. Let the bitch do her thing, just leave her alone. Go to Carrie,* He told himself as he stared at the windows of Estelle's beach house.

But there always seemed to be something pulling him away from good things, things that could bring peace. Why couldn't he just be happy with Carrie? He knew she'd be his in a moment. And he did like her. Love her? Yes, as much as he was capable of loving. And wanting that comfort? Wanting the good things in life? Maybe that was too easy.

Like his old friend, Lev, had told him, it seemed he had to throw away whatever good things came into his life, as if he was afraid or didn't deserve them.

Breathing a heavy sigh, Don looked toward the dune where Hank's beach access would be. The shining lights from the house illuminated part of the porch and gravel driveway below. He watched a figure cross the large plate glass window--Estelle. She wore only a tee shirt covering her torso, her long legs, bare and strong strode across the room. Moving to the window she pressed her body against it—her limbs spread askew, her breasts pushed against the glass. Her head tilted back, the thick long hair cascading past her shoulders. Don watched as her fists beat the thick hurricane glass of the window, her mouth open in laughter. And then he saw her look his way, her eyes steeled, seeming to look straight at him. He ducked low into a dune. "No way she knows I'm here."

He watched as she walked to a nearby cabinet, retrieved a pistol, opened the sliding doors and aimed it at the closest streetlight. He heard the pop, the tinkling of glass hitting the pavement and then the house was washed in darkness.

His eyes adjusting to the blackness, he caught glimpses of her as she rushed down the stairs, across the paved strip of roadway and toward the stairway across the dunes. In a moment she was above where he rested in the sand. A cloud passed and the moon silhouetted her body.

"I knew you wouldn't stay away. I know you want me. I know things--Hank told me things."

And there it was, the answer he'd been dreading. Hank *had* told, maybe during one of his drug induced moments. *Hell,* Don closed his eyes for a moment not wanting to have to move forward. But then why had he come here tonight if not to find out if Estelle knew about him? He'd guessed she probably did, why else would she be so wanton, so blatantly sexual with him. She wanted something and it sure as hell wasn't money--he had none.

"Tell me you're here." she pulled the shirt over her head, tossing it to the sand.

He heard her move another step down the stairway and pictured her unclothed body. He could smell her scent amidst the salt air. He stood to meet her, staring into her eyes. Moving a step closer he felt as if he were marching to his own death.

A weak attempt to feign indifference was swept away in seconds as she pressed herself against him.

His hands grabbed her buttocks, jerking her closer, as she wrapped a leg around his torso.

****

"You're such a bad boy," Estelle cooed. "And you like it."

She licked her lips sensuously. "For a cop, you're pretty good."

She caressed his thighs. Finding the distorted flesh of a wound, she ran her fingers over it. "I wondered when you'd come around," she said as she rubbed Don's muscular calves with her foot.

"Why didn't you take me in New Bern?" She licked her lips again. "I know you wanted it."

Don turned away.

"Hung up on that little burnt out cashier, oh yeah, waitress now, huh?"

He glared at her, not speaking.

"I guess she's okay, if you like that sort of thing. No excitement, dowdy little small town girl, not much there, if you ask me. Day in day out she stands her ass before customers at that damn restaurant and lets people treat her like shit. She'll let you treat her like shit, too. Ha! You're treating her like shit now--cow eyed for her and screwing me."

Estelle rose, she stood facing Don, "Men, you're all alike, you think with your dicks."

Don watched her cross the bedroom floor; her body was perfect, loose in the right places, taut everywhere else. He felt himself stir, angry that he felt so aroused by her still. He sat up and reached for his trousers, catching her reflection in the mirror. *She's a damn murdering bitch*, he reminded himself, standing to search for his shirt.

"Leaving?" In a moment she stood before him, her fingers threading through his chest hair. She tugged lightly on it. "Let's go again," she whispered, running her hand to his thigh and finding the ragged flesh again. She rubbed her fingers over the red and jagged scar and then to the matching spot behind his knee. Lowering her face, she ran her tongue along the raised cicatrix, its numbness surged into pinprick bits of pain as he watched her bite into his skin.

Don relaxed back onto the bed, as Estelle touched the scar again, pressing her fingernails into it, gently at first then intensifying the pressure. Her eyes held his as she bit down on the tissue, drawing blood.

"What the hell are you doing!" He lifted her forcefully from his body. "That's too much! You're too much! You're sick!" He rose, wiping the blood from his leg, "What in the hell am I doing? You?" he studied her as if seeing her for the first time. "Shit, what have I been thinking? You killed Hank and Mindy. Who else? Who else have you sunk your damned teeth into?"

He pulled his pants on then placed an open hand on Estelle's chest and pushed. "You whore."

"I'm the whore? You're the one who came here tonight. You're the one who pulled me to you, your hands were all over me - *you* were all over me. I didn't hold a gun to your head."

"Screw you," he said as he grabbed his shirt and headed for the door.

"Remember, I know things. I know about all the damn dealing you've done, all the damn people you've sold drugs to--Sarah, Reggie. I know. I could ruin you. I *will* ruin you, you arrogant shit." Estelle's voice grew louder and louder, distorting as it grew more and more shrill. "I'll tell Carrie, that sweet little nothing you dream about--you're perfect little nothing cunt, you and she can have your perfect little life, but not if I have anything to do with it."

Don turned to the growing shrillness, Estelle's face grotesque with anger, red, her eyes now narrow slits, spittle hung from the corners of her mouth as her arms flailed angrily, her body jerking with each word as she screamed.

"Screw you, I hate you, I'll get you and your little bitch, too!" She cackled the last few words, then laughed.

"Leave Carrie out of this," his voice, calm, carried the weight of a threat. "I *will* see your dead body, if you touch that woman." Don watched the transformation, Estelle's lips curling at the corners, her eyes widening, her body relaxing.

"Now, that caught your attention, didn't it? Threatening Miss Perfect made you stand up and notice, huh? Made you get angry didn't it?" She laughed. "You don't want anything to happen to that little innocent, no, naive gem--

the one that holds your hopes and dreams. The one that's going to heal you and make you a *good* man."

She paused, her nakedness now blatantly unappealing to Don.

"Is that what you want to be, Detective Belkin? A good man?" She sat on the edge of the bed, her shoulders erect and broad.

"What's so great about being good? What's so great about her? I'm a lot prettier than she is --nicer all over." Her hands caressed the contours of her body. "I don't understand why you'd pass *this* up for *that*. She's boring, no excitement there. Oh, I know what it is...she's the kind of woman you can take care of. That's what you want-- a woman you can take care of. That's what will make you a good man, someone you can take care of."

"You need someone to take care of *you*--a mental ward--you're nuts." As the last words left his lips he realized they were the wrong ones.

Estelle came at him, her fingers arched to scratch at his face. He grabbed her wrists, she kicked at him, and he moved rapidly to block her. She fell to the floor.

Estelle's laughter pierced his ears. "Come on now." Pulling her arms back, pulling Don in to her she wrapped a leg around his torso. "Come on baby, you like it, you want it!"

"I don't want you, can't you get that through your thick head? I can't stand to have you touch me. Stop!" He jerked her body against the floor. "What do you want with me? Why are you--"

Hissing through her teeth, Estelle's body grew limp. Her brow furrowed, her lips tightened as she cocked her head to the side. "What is it men see in women like Carrie? She's nothing, I mean, look at me. I'm non-stop. You ain't getting anything better than this, and I'm good. You know I'm good and you liked it. You liked it a lot. That dowdy little bitch has no--"

"You don't know anything about her," Don interrupted, still holding her wrists.

"Poor little divorcee, hubby didn't do her right," she whined the words. "She told me all about that last summer when you were in New Bern thinking about banging me. So, I *do* know her and shit, everybody's got a sob story. *You* have a sob story, and I bet it's a pretty good one--those fucking scars on your body." Estelle barred her teeth. "What's your story, Detective Don?"

She scowled and turned her head. "You don't know pain - that little wimpy bitch doesn't know pain - she's all bent out of shape because she had a bad marriage and because Hank dumped her. Big deal. It happens to everybody. Now you, and those reminders of war, those nasty ass scars on your legs, what's that all about? Is that why you have no relationship with your son, the ex-wife, can't start one with that dowdy bitch?" Estelle spat. "Hank told me about her, how easy she was, how needy she was."

"Hank was an asshole and there's always an asshole around to take advantage of good people."

"If they're stupid enough to put it out there, then they deserve it." Estelle pushed against his hold and grinned.

"People like you, like Hank and others who think that way are evil; you're selfish, hedonistic users. You manipulate people to get what you want and you make me sick."

"If someone is going to let me manipulate them--well, that's not my fault."

"It tells me you prey on goodness; you take advantage of people who give. At least there was a method to Hank's madness. He wanted revenge for the love he'd lost. You want everything--you want to see people squirm, bring them to their knees, take away their hopes, their future. Carrie isn't ruthless like you. I despise people like you." He felt like slamming her into the floor, his chest heaved. "Carrie doesn't take, unless the door is opened for her."

"Then why haven't you opened it?" Estelle spat. "Still not sure if you want all that goodness?"

He studied Estelle's supine body, covered in sepia freckles, the broad mouth, too broad now, like a marionette mouth. He felt disgusted with himself for having allowed a creature like her to pull him in. She was right, he did think with his dick. He eased his hold on her. "So, what do you want? I have no money--none to speak of and I know you like men who can afford to buy you things, give you things. What is it you want from me to keep your silence?

"To make sure you don't try to hurt me, I'll need certain things from you. I could have told you earlier that I knew what you and Sarah

Chambers were up to--and the other things Hank told me. But I had to get you in the sack first."

"Cold, calculating bitch." he released his hands from her wrists and stood.

She slowly rose and padded to the bed, rubbing her wrists. "I think the phrase is like you said earlier, manipulator, master manipulator."

Estelle raised an eyebrow as she reached for a tee shirt and thong. "I'm good at that, always have been and I learned all about that kind of shit when I went to college." She slid him a scorned glance. "Yeah, you thought I was just the V-girls' bimbo cousin, didn't you? That my IQ was around eighty at best? Ha, well, I am their cousin. Their father's stepbrother was my daddy--I'm the cousin from Kentucky--no blood kin, though. None of their stupidity runs in my veins.

"Still, in some way, I am related to those would be Kardashians!" She sneered as she leaned back on her elbows, her legs sprawled again as she lay on the bed. "I went to the University of Kentucky, got my BA in Psych. Did some vocational rehab counseling for a few years. That's when I learned how vulnerable people are, men especially, and how they believe what you want them to believe. How they'll walk into a door simply because you asked them to. "

She rolled her eyes. "And I'd say you're still fucked up from Iraq. You saw some stuff, maybe even did a few things you'd like to forget, but can't. Am I right soldier boy?"

"You don't know what you're talking about and I don't give a damn who you're related to or where you went to school. It means nothing to me. *You* mean nothing to me. Just tell me what you want."

"Protection."

Chapter Two

"Protection, the bitch wants protection. I'm the one who needs protection. She's the one killing people, not me." Don's hands tightened on the steering wheel as he pulled from the vacant driveway.

A mottled gray and silver sky barely lit the morning, he switched on his dims and pressed his foot hard on the accelerator, steering the Dodge toward North Topsail. "What in the hell am I supposed to do?"

He turned right, before the North Topsail Police Station, and headed to the end of the island; it was a long drive of mostly vacant rental houses. He slowed and passed them, consciously endeavoring to slow his heart rate. He breathed in, exhaled-- the self-loathing for having spent the entire night with Estelle competing with the desire to forget it.

Pulling into the island parking lot, or what was left of it from the last storm, he swung his legs out of the car and walked toward New River Inlet. Already a few fishermen were poised with their rod holders and chairs, casting lines out into the waters. "Hell, it's not even seven o'clock," he mumbled.

Don could feel the damp salt air, laced with coolness, against his arms. He glanced toward the ocean and horizon, the misty morning limiting his view and hiding the colors usually so prominent and vibrant. It felt fitting to be surrounded by grays and muted colors, even the breakers curling and releasing their spray seemed drab.

How long he walked, he wasn't sure, but the sun was nearly straight overhead by the time he circled back and made his way toward the Charger. He couldn't even recall all he'd thought about but it had left an uneasiness coupled with the gnawing empty feeling in his stomach. He stopped at Sea View fishing pier, ordered a burger and fries, and headed to his own house in Surf City.

Slouched on the sofa, he flipped through channels--old movies, news shows, reruns of 70s sitcoms, talk shows. "Would the audience like to know if it's Henry's baby?" The emcee thrust the mike toward the crowd. A roaring "yeah" filled the room and a broad smile played on the emcee's face.

"Garbage." Don pressed the off tab and threw the remote against the wall.

She was on his mind, Estelle. Images of their raw sex taunted him, leaving him with the same sick feelings he'd been wrestling with for the last few years. Their images, Sarah's, Reggie's, Milton's--even his own son's, lodged in his head and would not leave. "Damn it all to hell." He slammed his fist into the wall.

His cell phone buzzed; he checked out the lighted display--Carrie. He let it buzz and watched the message icon light up. He wasn't about to talk with her now, not after being with Estelle. His fist slammed the table.

He showered, drove to the IGA and bought a twelve pack of Bud and a pack of Pall Mall then sat on his porch and smoked nearly half a pack before crumpling the remainder and tossing them into the trash. He felt his stomach rumble, he ignored it and watched the reddening sky turn to indigo and them starlit black.

Exhausted, he let the loneliness sweep over him. What was it - what was the answer - what could he do to stop all the messed up thoughts going through his head?

Don picked up the bottle of beer from the table and slung it across the room. It shattered, spewing beer over the wall and chair beneath it. He picked up another, cast it though a window. The crackle and tinkle of glass filled the air. His hand reached for another; he stopped, gathered his keys and strode to the Charger.

Slamming the gearshift into reverse, his tires squealed as they adjusted into first. His foot pushed then eased quickly from the pedal, tapping the accelerator, keeping just over the 35 mph limit, then over 40 and back down until he reached the Onslow County line.

He sped to 55 and moved past the Brass Pelican, Ocean City, Surf City Campground and toward the bridge. An unmarked car watched as he sped forward, he glimpsed a waving hand.

Envisioning him and Estelle together on her bed, it was as if he could still taste her, he wanted to spit her out. He wanted her away from him, with no ties whatsoever--erased from his thoughts. *Get rid of her* screamed in his head. Getting rid of her would make all the bullshit go away.

He could make it look like an accident.

The thought played in his belly for a moment—Estelle taking flight from the bridge, Estelle sailing into oblivion, Estelle's bloated body washing ashore, Estelle's throat cut, her wrists slit. There were people in Sneads Ferry he knew who could make Estelle disappear, he wouldn't even have to get his hands dirty.

He toyed with the idea a few seconds more, letting the images of a dead Estelle rest in his mind's eye.

Filling his lungs with air, he exhaled slowly again and nodded his head in acquiescence, acknowledgement that he was no longer capable of killing. The war had seen to that.

It took hate to want death and he had never been able to initiate hate. Not in Iraq, not here. The temptations had always been there. But he had never wanted to know that depth, never wanted to submit to that level of malevolence.

Estelle was close though. He could easily hate her. But what he hated more was what he'd allowed himself to do.

He'd known dirt, scum, who wallowed in hate, wore it like skin—their own selfish indulgences gone askew leaving them unrecognizable and twisted by hatred, the worst drug of all. He wanted no part of that.

No, simply hating or killing a bad thing wasn't the answer, but someone had to stop Estelle. There had to be a way of shutting her up, a way to save himself without destroying himself in the process. He felt the tension raise to his shoulders as his jaw tightened; he passed the North Topsail Police Station to approach the high rise.

Suddenly the center of the bridge was there and for a second, a split second, he could have taken flight. The ethereal thought found his bones and for that nanosecond he relished freedom—freedom to hope without any "ifs," freedom from uncertainty, freedom to be sane. His mind raced before easing his foot from the pedal and slowing to 90, then 70 and into Sneads Ferry.

Easing into a filling station, Don pulled his car next to pump five and switched off the ignition. Relaxing the tenseness that had built in his body, he sighed heavily and watched as patrons entered and exited the convenient mart doors. He stared at the lighted numbers on the dashboard and subtracted and added the needed hours and minutes to get the correct time. It was past ten. Where had the day gone?

He admonished himself for not bothering to even fix the damn clock—another reminder of how little he cared about anything. His friend Lev would say, "You like making things hard for yourself."

It was true; he procrastinated over things he knew could be easier and the things that could have brought the most joy. How in the hell had he made it in the Marine Corps for twenty years with that attitude?

I wasn't like that then. He sat numb, his eyes studying people opening and closing the store doors. A few men held them open for women. Most smiled back, thanking them for the politeness, a few didn't.

Don watched two off duty Marines enter the store. They, like all military, had that recognizable posture, the squared shoulders, straight back, aloofness—confidence and awareness, the most recognizable traits of all.

Once a Marine, always a Marine. He, on the other hand, endeavored to mask his physical appearance to some degree, putting on a few pounds, wearing looser clothing, the longer hair, sleeve tat on his right arm. Pride disallowed anything more.

Another young man, still in his fatigues, approached the store, held the door open for a woman and turned, it seemed, to look directly into his eyes. Don lowered his gaze quickly and the sobering scene of his last week in Iraq burst from nowhere and squalled in his head.

The man stood before him, his hands raised high above his head. Clasped in one hand was a grenade, around his shoulder hung an M-4 Carbine.

"Tell him to drop his weapons," he'd yelled to the Farsi interpreter. "Tell him now!" A dozen other Marines stood poised, aiming their weapons to fire at the man. Don heard the interpreter yell the words.

"Tell him again," he screamed, "Put your weapons down!" His voice boomed toward the Arab man simultaneously with the interpreter. He motioned with his own weapon for him to drop the rifle. The man shook his head no and grinned.

Had the Arab reached for his weapon, had he moved his hand to dislodge the grenade in the other?

He must have. A barrage of bullets rattled from all dozen of the men's rifles. The smell of gunfire filled his nostrils. What else was he supposed to do? He and the others had done the right thing. Hadn't they?

The man lay on the ground in pools of blood seeping from the scores of holes covering his body. Later, Don would calculate that his weapon had discharged nine rounds into the enemy.

The Iraqi fucker was the enemy. Don nodded, reassuring himself, blinking himself back to reality as he watched the young jarhead, the one in the fatigues, exit the store.

They'd just come from a string of raids that had begun earlier that morning, sometime after midnight. Apache helicopters hovered overhead lighting the area while someone blasted in Farsi ordering the occupants of the homes to put their weapons outside their doors, to come out with their hands raised.

How many homes had they raided? Forty or fifty—it had been a lot. The families would be huddled together—questions asked— misinformation lead to other raids, it was a frustrating never ending task that led them in circles, lead to nowhere and lead to some loosing their moral compass. That was it, morality changed—but it was war and no pansy ass sympathy was going to be tolerated, unless you wanted to be the one lying on the ground in your own blood riddled with bullets through your own face and torso. He didn't want to be the one dragged naked through the streets, his genitals severed, flung aside, food for mongrel dogs.

The blare of a horn woke him, jarring him to consciousness; he exited the car and walked boldly, like the Marine he was, to the store entrance.

****

Paula pushed against the piling, her boat gliding across the water like a toy as the bow faced open water. Quickly she reached to turn the wheel, her fingers squeezing the throttle, as she motored away from the marina and out to the Intracoastal Waterway.

A tall red marker to her left indicated she was in deep enough water to maneuver; it had been years since she'd run aground and that had been before the depth finder and when Micah had been in her life fulltime. The man was always in her thoughts—somewhere. She'd loved him since diapers.

Tittering a girlish laugh, she recalled the last time they'd been together—the fishing poles, getting her blouse caught on a hook and how Micah had dislodged it along with her capris and panties. It was always fun, no matter. Love or no love, he was true. Their bond was cemented; constant as the rolling ocean they both drew their passion from.

She'd seen him online, pictures of he and his wife posted occasionally. They lived in Asheville—the other end of the state. But he still owned a couple of beach houses on the island and visited, a few times a year at first, then more frequently in the last three.

Their affair, this new one, had started innocently enough, playful, and then what they'd shared so many years before, rekindled. She'd never stopped loving him. And he admitted he'd been wrong to leave so long ago.

The question was if she could accept things as they were, or if she should wait and how long. More often than not she knew those things didn't matter. He felt right. The world was right when he was with her. But it had been months since his last visit and she was in one of those moods where she doubted his love.

Lev, he was no Micah, but she knew he liked her, was *gaga* for her and it had been a long time since any man had given her that kind of attention, opening doors, helping her carry things, kissing her in public. He adored her, at least he acted like he did. And she liked that. It had been too long since she'd been adored and she needed that, too.

"He will be fun," she said. "And Micah--" She shrugged, not daring to dwell for long on that intimacy. She picked up her cell and called to invite Lev for an evening cruise, he jumped at the chance.

They motored slowly toward the cove, a secluded place thirty minutes away. Standing at the helm, Paula felt his eyes on her, him studying her, which felt nice, too.

Twice he stood beside her, reached his arm around to pull her close.

"Not now," she teased ordering him to sit in a chair near the gunwale.

Ten minutes later, he rose again, wrapped an arm around her waist and kissed her neck.

A breath escaped her lips as she turned away. "The cove is only a few miles more."

He kissed her neck again, moving his body tighter against her.

It was fun dissuading the man, then leaning into him, feeling him tense as she touched him.

Loving was fun, why had she deprived herself of it for so long? Hungry for closeness, tired of loneliness, Paula initiated the intimacy quickly as she dropped anchor and hoped the man wasn't going to fall in love with her.

****

"Well, hi there. Didn't see you come in." Paula lied as she stood in line to pay for gas. She'd seen Don, parked by pump five when she pulled in, he seemed lost in thought. She hoped to avoid him, she hoped he wouldn't ask about Lev. Their boat trip was no one's business.

Don and she stood silently as they both waited in line, stepping forward as patrons made their requests and left the store.

"So, did you enjoy your crab bisque the other night at the Shrimp House?" he asked.

"Yeah, it was good, must be new on the menu. Glad you suggested it." She waited awkwardly in the stilted silence, knowing that if they were there much longer Lev's name could come up. She looked into Don's face and grinned, he grinned back.

"Seen Lev around?"

What was she supposed to say? She felt color come to her face as she turned her back to him and shrugged, "Yeah, earlier today."

"Oh," He moved a couple of steps farther in the line of customers.

Paula handed a twenty to the cashier, "On pump seven," nodded to Don. "See ya."

That was odd, Don thought, watching her as she opened the glass door. *But then Paula has never been one to yak it up—always been sort of distant since I've known her.* He stepped to the counter and paid the cashier; exiting he watched Paula pull away in her red Camaro.

She was a strange bird, in some ways unapproachable—not a particularly pretty woman. The opposite of what Lev usually set his sights on, he always chose the sweethearts, the lookers. There had to be something special about this woman, *maybe she*…Don chuckled, an intimate image of the couple flashed through his mind. *Who knows?* Don thought. *It isn't any of my business.*

He slid into the Charger and pulled out onto the highway behind Paula. Adhering to just below the speed limit, he watched her tail lights grower dimmer in the distance.

His thoughts drifted back to Iraq and the Arab standing before him, holding weapons. He could see the thick lashes of his eyes.

He blinked his own and recalled the night with Estelle. The thought left him feeling weak and overwhelmed with guilt; he shook his head, wishing he could erase what he'd done—not just her, but everything.

Were these things just another way of pushing the knife in a little deeper into wounds that had never healed—another way to propel himself away from the kinder, more pleasant components of life? Maybe he was becoming one of those twisted and distorted by hate.

The thought sent a chill through his body and he considered the events, choices—the wrong ones and how they plagued him since returning from his deployment in the Middle East where distinctions between right and wrong, good and bad were clear. Unlike here, home, America, where despite all the flag waving, the thank you for your service platitudes, he felt disliked, judged, especially by certain factions whose cursing gazes hid behind smiles.

The unfairness of it all astounded him. *We keep you safe. We bleed for you, give our lives for you—die for you.*

Where was right and wrong? Rules of engagement—*damn rules of engagement.*

They were there, the sensors said they were there—the enemy.

Everyone knew the building was full of them. Why not use what we have, what we had, blow the fuckers to Allah and their seventy-two virgins? "What the hell do I want with a virgin?" He laughed aloud, focusing on the dim red lights in the distance.

"No, we can't do that." He spoke aloud to himself. "We have to get out of the vehicle, make ourselves vulnerable, get our asses shot at, because there might be a civilian among the enemy—what about--" His blood ran cold as the names escaped him. The faces had not. "The boys, young perfect men blown away so

America won't offend people who are killing us—maybe I'm no better."

Unwilling or unable, he couldn't decide which, he had refused to help his ex, Maggie—he'd sent Phil away, ceded any authority to that bullying dealer Seth Milton, those were his sins, things he now found himself being swallowed by. Allowing the brutish depth of self-loathing to posses him—Estelle was the manifestation. It was easy to take her, to hate her, to hate himself—to wallow in the muck where it was comfortable.

This is about as low as I can go without blowing my own damn brains out. What am I going to do? He rubbed a temple, messaging the ache that had been steadily growing. "Estelle isn't a real woman, not real flesh and blood, she's Satan incarnate. What does that make me?"

Carrie was the light, the hope. There was still a longing, still a flicker of desire for the person he had once been or dreamed of being. There was still a part of him with dreams, unequivocal expectations and plans that tugged from somewhere.

Her image came to mind; the hint of a smile curling the corners of his mouth. Even the thought of her brought calmness to him, a peace. He wiped the beads of sweat from his forehead and leaned back in his seat and let the dim red lights fade into the distance.

Carrie held the mirror, the question was: could she face his demons with him? Or would she hate him?

He picked up his cell phone and pressed the numbers to the police station. "Tell the

Chief I'm taking a few days off—maybe more—anything earthshaking comes up, give me a call." He listened to dispatch remark and joke, nodded and set the phone on the passenger seat.

Pulling onto the grass, he turned the car around and pressed hard on the accelerator as he drove toward the back gate of Camp Lejeune in Sneads Ferry. He swerved to miss a cat crossing the road then slowed to the speed limit.

Again Estelle's image rose in his mind. "He begged me to take his life. He begged me to end his pain. But I couldn't, I loved him so." Estelle's eyes had been pleading, damp, and sorrowful.

"Bullshit!" Don blared recalling their last conversation. "What a liar. Her mouth moves, she lies."

"I did a good thing. I helped him. When he dropped all that Dilaudid and told me to take him to the sound, I did. I just thought he was going to cool off but then he brought out the razor."

Estelle had reached for Don, reached for him to comfort her as she told the story, the made up story. Even then it had made him sick—all the lies. Everything seemed like lies now.

Across the bridge the lights of the guard house to Camp Lejeune glared. He slowed to a stop and flipped his wallet open to expose his military pass.

Chapter Three

It was shorter going through Lejeune to Morehead City and the VA clinic there. Where else could he go? He wanted to get somewhere quickly.

One of the other officers on the force had mentioned the place to him, a place where vets could seek help. He'd even given him a suicide hot line number. Had the officer recognized a look? Did he wear that look like a badge? Why didn't everybody see it?

At the time he was annoyed by the concern. How dare anyone assume he couldn't carry the weight.

I guess I'll have to give Estelle credit for one thing. Screwing her made me hate myself enough to realize I do need help.

He searched his memory for the exact words the officer had said, he couldn't recall them. All he remembered was that Officer Randall recounted how therapy had helped him focus, helped him realize he was not the guilty party—that he deserved a normal life, that he was a worthy person.

Don clung to the thread, the one that could lead to the light at the end of the tunnel, to some normalcy or peace, anything besides the self-loathing he was living.

It was desolate, driving through the base at night, tall pines stood tall, their shadows reaching along the two-lane road; intermittent access signs to different zones where young men trained reflected against his headlights as he drove along. He remembered training at those places over two decades ago when he'd first joined.

The world was crisper then, as he recalled, but then those images were from his youth when he was full of idealized reality and dreams of seeing the world.

Brownsville, PA could not offer him what he wanted, excitement and adventure. The Marines could offer that. He was ready to sign up, excited about the future and all that it held. But his father had other ideas and talked him into going to college first, getting the degree that he'd never been able to attain.

Don listened, took the old man's advice. It proved to be good advice that Don had never regretted until lately. How often had Don considered how different his life would have been if he'd simply risen through the ranks, started as a grunt. Maybe even chosen a different major in college.

No one could see the future; no one knows how a war will affect you or how, before you realize it, important things have become twisted and you find yourself avoiding the things you thought you wanted. Life certainly wasn't what he dreamed it would be as a teenager or even as a younger man.

****

Eye Movement Desensitization and Reprocessing Therapy, EMDR, that was what it was called. It sounded hokey to him. Doubts resurfaced immediately when his counselor mentioned it but he nodded, ready to try anything.

He recounted the one incident that imaged in his mind more than the others. And how after unloading nine rounds into the rag head he and the rest of his squad fell under attack.

A sharp sting ripped through his body armor and into his thigh, exiting the other side. He buckled and fell to the dusty ground. Stunned but not immobilized, he reached for his rifle and sat upright, squeezing the trigger, aiming at places where he heard movement and saw flickers of cloth. The enemy was well hidden in the small village they'd raided.

Twice he felt the zip of a bullet fly by his head. The third one blew into his helmet, knocking him backward and over to his stomach. Dazed, he watched the slaughter of his buddies as Al Qaeda forces overran them with barrage after barrage of firepower.

He heard a string of pops, yelling in Farsi and he waited for the inevitable. His eyes closed he prayed for Maggie and their new son.

Then there were more pops, more rapidly. The sounds of grenade launchers and heavy assault rifles filled the air. It was chaos, bodies hitting the ground, running, screaming. From some access point the rapid popping clipped at windows and doorways, rooftops, some zinging past or near him, some thumping quickly into the dirt.

Then there was silence. Silence—all but the sound of his lips parting to breathe air.

Don lay prone on the ground, his hands covering his head; he heard the dull drop of boots as they edged toward him. He waited to see whose boots they were and from the color, he knew he was safe.

Still lying on the ground, his eyes strained to see just who was standing beside him.

"Hey dickhead," Lev Gass nudged him with a boot. "Lay there."

Don heard the rapid pops again and then there was silence once more.

Of the twelve men in his squad, he and two others survived.

Chapter Four

Carrie stepped gingerly to the table, water glasses atop the tray. She settled them before the two customers and asked, "May I take your order?" then smiled gently.

One of the women rolled her eyes. "Can't you see we haven't even looked at our menus yet?"

The younger one reached across the table and patted her hand. "Mother, she doesn't know any better." She looked up to Carrie's face, her lips moved, dripping condescension. "Dear heart, give us a few more minutes, please. We've just came in from a long day's journey and are so tired." She stressed the 'so.' "You have no idea how tired we are, come back in a few minutes will you please? Thank you now, sweetie."

How tired they are. Carrie fought the urge to tell the women off, she nodded and turned toward the kitchen. *They don't know the meaning of tired.* She pushed through the swinging doors. "My feet are aching, my back hurts, I have to put up with arrogant bitches like *you.*"

"You talking to me?" Sammy asked, grating a block of parmesan cheese atop a plank of mahi mahi.

"Oh, sorry, Sammy. No, I'm talking about those two women I've been trying to wait on for the last half hour. They're sitting there yacking it up. There are other people in the restaurant, there are other people I have to get orders from and wait on." Carrie blew a heavy breath and pursed her lips.

"Still planning on quitting?" Sammy asked.

"I don't know. It all depends on Paula and if she's serious about me working on her boat—if she gets a bigger one—if she can find a cheap enough slip to rent—if she can drop down to part time at the bridge."

"That's a lot of 'ifs'."

"I know, but I wish she'd find some things out quickly. The next asshole who complains about the clam chowder, is going to have it on his lap. I swear I wish Blythe would take it off the menu. Nobody likes it."

A waitress stuck her head in through the swinging doors. "Hey, these two women say they'd *appreciate it* if you'd come get their order—they've been waiting over forty-five minutes."

Carrie's jaw dropped open, "Can you believe that? I just came from their table." Grabbing the tray she stormed from the room. "I thought all the assholes left after summer."

"They're moving here now," Sammy called after her. He chuckled, "Maybe I'll spit in their order for you Carrie."

****

Before she'd even rounded the bend in the lane to her home, Carrie could hear Joey and

Bella yapping. Joey was unmistakable, loud and sharp. Bella added her high little voice intermittently.

Carrie wondered if the neighbor's cat was back in the yard again, taunting her little dogs, crapping in her yard, peeing on the shrubbery.

Shaking her head she recalled the last time the orange tom had been in her yard, he had jumped in through a window and sprayed the back seat. It still smelled despite her effort to scrub the musky stink away. On some days, hot days, she swore she could still smell the disgusting, feline odor.

Rounding the bend, her step quickened as Carrie spied the faded gray Charger parked in front of her cottage. Don leaned against the hood, his arms resting by his side. She hadn't seen him in over two weeks. He had texted her once though, telling her he missed her.

Her heart racing, Carrie fought the urge to run to him. She walked slowly, casually as if he was merely a friend.

Don turned, watched her as she moved toward him and smiled. "Saw your car, thought you might be home."

"Decided to walk to work, save a little gas, nice day." She smiled back, walking into his outstretched arm and leaning into his body. She always felt comforted by his embrace, always letting her mind drift to that place where there would be more. Yep, there was no doubt, she was in love with him. The ache she'd been feeling quelled, she wanted to hold him tighter, bury her face against his warmth. Her head swarmed with thoughts of the game, the one she didn't want to play. Not letting on, not seeming too eager. She pulled away. "So, what's going on?"

"Nothing much, just thought I'd stop by and see if you have any plans for this Saturday."

He could have phoned for that, she thought. *Yep, he wants to see me. That's a good sign.* "Anything special, flying me out to Cancun for lunch?" she teased.

He shrugged, catching up with her as she climbed the few steps to the porch. "A friend of mine is letting me borrow his boat, thought we'd take a day trip to Beaufort."

"Friend with a boat, huh? That sounds like fun. Yeah, I'll go."

"Can you get off Saturday?"

"And miss a boat ride to Beaufort? You bet, I'll find a way."

He held the screened door open while Carrie fit the key into the lock, followed her closely and waited as she set her purse and bag of groceries on the table. His hand on her shoulder, he turned her to face him, "I want to see you more often."

"Well, we are going to Beaufort--"

"I know, but what I mean is--" Gathering her in his arms Don brought his face to hers. "I want you in my life all the time."

****

"This is Paula's boat." Carrie turned quizzically to Don. "She loaned you her boat?"

"This is Lev's boat, he bought it from Paula. I spent all day yesterday scrubbing the hell out of it to get the fish stink out. What do you think?" He beamed waiting for Carrie to comment.

"It is the cleanest I've ever seen it." Carrie grinned. "Is she getting another one?"

"It seems so," Don chuckled.

"Hmm, doesn't make a lot of sense to me. Her father helped her get this one. Lev must have offered her a lot for her to give this up."

"He did. And there's more to come." He teased.

"What do you mean?"

"This thing is a good thirty years old and is worth somewhere between twenty-five and thirty thousand—he gave her fifty."

"She took it?"

"Yep. He told her he had a friend who was interested."

"Are you the friend?"

"Hardly."

"Anyone I know?"

"He just told her that so she'd sell it to him. He had something drawn up—"

"So he lied to her."

"Sort of. He's just trying to help her out."

"She's not going to like that."

Don shrugged, "I've never been able to tell Lev what to do when it comes to women."

"Well, if it's Paula, then he's got a death wish, because she'll hate him for it."

"Just between me and you and the pilings, he's going to surprise her with something pretty soon." Don helped Carrie onto the fishing boat, cast off the lines and pulled away from the dock. The air held the familiar winter nip.

He wrapped an arm around her as he steered between the red and green markers of the Intracoastal Waterway. Keeping the speed at around ten knots, they motored slowly northward enjoying the natural scenery, dotted with houses and little docks fingering out into the water.

It was the first time she'd been beneath the high-rise bridge in North Topsail. From the highway it had always seemed narrow and unimpressive. But from the water it was spectacular and she could hear the hum of tires as cars drove overhead.

Something so simple and so pleasing warmed her and she turned to Don, watching him guide the boat from one marker to another until they reached Beaufort.

Don edged the boat into the slip at the marina, Carrie jumped to the dock with a line in tow and wrapped it around a cleat. She secured the forward line as well.

"So what have you got in mind?" She asked teasingly.

"I could use some lunch." Don patted his stomach. "Then we'll check the town out." He drew her to him. "Spend the night on the boat and see what else we can find around here tomorrow."

"I like this relaxed style of living." Carrie kissed his cheek.

"We'll have to do this more often."

They finished their peck of raw oysters and headed out to examine the little town of Beaufort, North Carolina.

****

He had changed, no not changed, but had become the man she'd seen glimpses of, the one who'd been there for her after the ordeal with Hank offering understanding and compassion. He could have taken advantage of her vulnerability but he hadn't, instead, he'd been a friend. And that was something she needed desperately at the time.

He felt truer, relaxed and was willing to trust himself. She felt it in the touch of his hand, the reassuring glances and his willingness to open up, to trust her with truths about himself. At least that was how Carrie felt since Don's return.

He'd explained the EMDR, the therapy he'd been taking at the VA hospital. And he told her about Iraq—opened up to her as if he'd known her forever. He was trusting her. That meant he loved her and he'd told her that, too.

As they lay together in the V-berth, Carrie watched his face, at peace, a slight grin curling his lips. She rested an arm next to Don's, watching his chest rise and fall, his lips releasing shallow breaths. She liked laying this close—not touching, only feeling the heat from his still sleeping body. Appreciating him for who he was, awed by his strength to open up to her, torn inside for the things he'd endured.

Wanting to touch him, Carrie resisted and basked in the nearness—it was all so unabashedly stimulating as she studied his arms, the hollow of his belly, and the rise of his hips. She slid a leg as close to his as possible without touching; she felt emboldened, secure that this man was not playing games, that he truly wanted her.

She grimaced momentarily, thinking of her last sexual encounter—Hank, and how uncertain, how nervous, how vulnerable she had felt the whole time. The image drifted quickly away as she continued pouring slowly across Don's full lips, the fine lines of his face, a childhood pox mark near his temple, the thin fine stubble of his morning beard. She felt her breath quicken, consciously she slowed it and felt the breathing deepen as Don turned to face her, his eyes drawing her back to the place they'd been hours before.

Chapter Five

Estelle sat on the top step of the beach house. Her knees bent, she pulled them close with her arms. Gazing out to the ocean she watched the few people bundled warmly for the cool winter weather as they strolled along the shore.

Her face scowling, she shook her head. "Damn fools, why in the world would someone want to walk out there? All that sand, I can't stand it. Gritty crap gets in everything." She stood and headed back inside.

There was nothing beautiful about the beach to Estelle. There was nothing beautiful about any place to her. She'd become numb to just about everything except the adrenaline of the game—manipulating someone, anyone. And then the image flashed in her head, washed over her, bringing immediate realization that what she needed was acceptance.

She may have been poor white trash in Kentucky but here she was somebody. She owned stuff, lots of it. "People should respect that. They should respect me."

What else? She thought. And she wondered just how she could become more important and accepted by the town.

"Last you called, you said you were in your late husband's beach house. How's that working out for you?" Theo leaned his long thin frame against the front porch banister, strewed a handful of chicken feed across the yard and watched the hens scurry to peak the grains.

"There's memories, of course," Estelle sighed into the phone. "I miss him. I've packed most of his things and have given them to the church. I'm sure there are many out there less fortunate who would appreciate his clothing."

"Cut the crap, Estelle. You? Church?" He strolled toward the hog pen and emptied the bucket of potato peelings and corn cobs into it. "I ain't that stupid." The tall lanky man sauntered back across the yard, scattering the chickens as he made his way among them.

"Yes you are," she retorted. "You are that stupid—always have been."

There it was again, the demeaning remarks. He didn't want to let her know they hurt him. Theo sloughed off the barb, trying to act as tough as he'd told himself he would.

"I called to ask you a favor. I know I can count on you, Theo. You've always been there for me." Pausing, Estelle waited for a reply. A few moments passed without one. "Do you think you can handle doing me one more favor?" Her voice was harder, more urgent, and somewhat demanding.

"Uh huh." He nodded endeavoring to keep up with her and the tough "I don't give a damn" attitude that always intimidated him. Still, he struggled to stand up to her. "I've been on to you since we were five years old. If you're not going to get something out of someone, you ain't going to bother with them—me included. So what do you want now, Estelle?"

"Theo, how dare you talk to me like that, as if I don't even care for you. It's not true. I love you."

"You got another man already, I bet that's it. You have another man on the horizon and you need me to fix him up with the doc. Right?" Theo shook his head. "The one you just had ain't cold yet. Knowing you, you probably drove the poor bastard to his death."

"Theo! Where do you get off talking like this to me? There is no new man. How horrible of you to say so. You've never been so—so accusatory. You're really starting to hurt my feelings."

Was she or wasn't she lying. Theo wasn't sure. He heard the whine in her voice, it tugged at his heartstrings, but there had been times—"Sorry Estelle, I don't know when to believe you, I don't know—I'm just—it's just that you told me your husband slit his wrists, that he was on some kind of drugs and committed suicide—right? That's what you told me, Estelle. And then you've never been one to go very long without a boyfriend." Opening the barn door he set the bag of feed inside.

"Theo, I can hear those chickens raising hell. Are you feeding them now?"

"Yeah."

"And that really hurts my feelings. I call you 'cause I miss you and here you are feeding the chickens. I bet you're not even listening to half of what I say. How about giving me your undivided attention? It's me, Estelle. I'd like you to pay attention to me when I'm talking to you."

"I just put the feed in the barn, right now, I did it right now, Estelle. You got my ear all by yourself. Okay?"

"Okay, that's better. I was saying, I really miss Hank and that I'm sad he's gone. Can't I be sad for five minutes? Won't you give me that? Why all the judgmental stuff? Hell and shit, I do miss him—sort of. Damn, he left me all this stuff, a beach house, boat, land, rental houses. I won't have to work another day in my life. I have to be sort of sad for someone who left me all this."

"Um, huh, well, sorry. It's just that I don't know if you're happy or sad about your husband dying. You told me one time he hit you and then another time you're telling me 'bout how you loved him. Sometimes I talk to you and you're all giddy and happy sounding and other times, I could swear you sound like you've been crying. Sometimes I think you're gonna reach through the phone and grab my neck like you always used to. I don't know, Estelle, I don't know. But I'll be there in a minute if you want me or need me for anything. I've always been there for you."

"Yes you have, Theo, and I appreciate all your care and concern." Her voice faded for a moment before speaking once again. "How's the play house you've been working on?"

His eyes twinkled and voice jumped. "This one is better than the last. It looks just like a little southern mansion, just like Tara in the movie Gone With the Wind."

"You were always good with your hands, Theo."

The complement seemed warm and sincere and it soothed his worries, calmed him, reassured him that the little girl he'd known since a toddler still loved him.

"That's kind of what I wanted to talk with you about."

"You need a dollhouse?"

"No," she scoffed.

"You need a real house. You want me to build you a real house. I don't know if I can do that or not."

"Not exactly, Theo."

He could hear the impatience in her voice.

"You sure are lucky. Your late husband left you a house and that guy in New Bern gave you a house."

"A shack, compared to all this, that was a shack." She paused for a moment, scrunching her brow. "But I don't need another house, Theo. Hank, my sweet late husband, left me a tower."

"A tower?"

"Yeah, a flipping tower. Some monstrosity from the dinosaur era."

"What kind of tower? Rapunzel, let down your golden hair?" He chortled apprehensively.

"Rapunzel, my ass. Now knock it off—I'm serious. He left me this three story tower, some old piece of shit, but we can make it into something really spectacular. What do you say, Theo? I need you."

"Okay, tell me about the tower. What about it?"

"I think it was built in the '40s and was used for some kind of missiles or rockets. Been vacant since then."

"One tower?"

"Hell no, they're all over the island, but most have been made into private residences. I'm thinking we could renovate it into--"

"He left you more than one?"

"No, stupid. He left me *one* tower, but there are several on the island."

"You're confusing, you always do that, you say things without fully explaining them. You are really confusing sometimes, Estelle."

"Damn, you're dumb, shit for brains. He. Owned. Only. One. Got that? Did I say it slow enough for you that time? You'd get confused putting on your socks. Damn, why do I bother with you? If your brains were lard, you couldn't grease a skillet."

"I'm not dumb, Estelle. I wish you'd stop saying that. I just don't have the education you do."

A long silence ensued. Theo could hear her slowly exhale. He knew that silence, that fettered breathing. It meant she was angry, fuming, struggling to keep herself under control. The breathy sigh he heard next, meant that she had. She spoke, "Come visit me, honey. I need a friend. I need someone to help me renovate the tower and you're so good with building things. I believe you would have been an excellent architect if only your lousy parents would have let you go to college."

She sighed softly. "Help me Theo, help me make decisions about construction. I have ideas." She paused again adding tremulously, "But I know yours are better. I need you, I need you to be strong for me, Theo."

He'd heard those words before, in the same trembling voice, as an adolescent, as a teenager and as she grew into womanhood. Though the words had remained the same, with each phase of her growing, they had come to be enunciated differently. Once innocent, then manipulative and conniving, but they always worked their power over him.

Once again he acquiesced to her wishes. He would always give in. He knew that about himself. He'd known since he was a teenager and watched her playing in the mud in front of her home—watched her toddling about her father's house, cockroaches crawling along her little legs, she reaching out to touch one before it scuttled away.

He would always give in to Estelle. And would always help her with anything, even if it was wrong. But there was no wrong when it came to Estelle. "When do you want me to come?" Theo asked eagerly.

****

"This is where you'll stay." Estelle opened the door to a spacious room, windows built high toward the ceilings to let in light. The sills came to Theo's chest and he imagined how difficult it would be for a shorter person to even see out of them. His eyes widened, awestruck by what he perceived as luxury--the chocolate colored duvet spread neatly on a blonde four-poster bed, the matching chifferobe and bed-side tables.

Carved conchs sat atop an octagon shaped mahogany table situated near the entrance to the bathroom. He looked up at the windows again.

Estelle grunted loudly, "I know what you're thinking. Don't ask me why. Hank designed this thing, and for the life of me I have no idea why he put windows up that high."

"I know." Theo raised his eyebrows. "It's so people can walk around in their underwear in here without being seen from the outside."

"That's what they make curtains for, dumbass."

"With windows like this, you don't need curtains." Theo retorted, his mouth drawn tightly.

"Shit, you're so dumb. " She caught the pained look on his face, the sagging shoulders. "Aww come on now, why are you so sensitive all of a sudden over stupid stuff? We always joke around like that. Right? I say you're dumb and you tell me how smart I am. Isn't that the way it's always been?" She paused, studied his demeanor. "But you haven't said that even once to me since you've come. Have you Theo? You still think I'm smart, huh?"

He nodded his head. "Yes, you're smart, but I'm getting kind of tired of hearing you say I'm dumb. Emily says—"

"Who is Emily?" Estelle's eyes widened, she stepped closer and grinned.

Theo's eyes drifted to his feet. "I talk to her sometimes."

"Talk to her? What about? Where did you meet her? Is she a girlfriend, Theo? Does Theo have a girlfriend now?" Her voice sing-songed.

His face reddened, his feet shuffled about. Not daring to meet her eyes, he nodded his head. "Sorta."

"What is she like, Theo? Is she short and plump? Does she like to cook?" She patted his stomach. "I bet you like to chow down. I bet she likes that, huh?" Estelle smirked and poked a finger into his soft belly. "What do you say, Theo?" She watched his face redden.

Theo changed the subject quickly. "I knew going to college would help you, Estelle. And see what all it's got you now. I'm proud of my baby girl. Yes sir, I'm proud as a peacock, you going to college and you being so smart." He reached a hand to touch hers.

Instinctively Estelle jerked back, took a deep breath then curled a finger around one of his. "Uh, well, I guess you're wondering when I'm going to pay you back all that money you paid for tuition and—"

Theo grasped the remaining fingers in her hand, squeezing gently. "Oh, no, no. Estelle, that's not what I meant. I—uh, I'm just glad you're doing so well. I ain't never and will never make you pay me back any money I spent to get you through college. You are so smart, you'd have found a way to go even if I hadn't have dipped into my savings to help you."

Estelle's eyes slid to the ground, her breathing quickened slightly as she eased her hand from Theo's and stepped toward the bed. Leaning back on her elbows she sprawled her body and tossed her hair to the side. She watched Theo study her, unable to mask any reactions or emotions, then lower his eyes.

"We're not blood kin, Theo, and you know it would be alright with me." Stretching her neck Estelle arched her back. "It would be okay Theo."

Basking in the attention, the disturbing feeling she knew she evoked in Theo, Estelle patted the bed. "Come on, sit down with me."

He sat down near the end of the bed.

"Why so far away?" She reached to grab his upper thigh, tugging, encouraging him to move closer.

Theo knew it was wrong. Wasn't it? Estelle was so like a daughter, he'd half raised her from a toddler with her alcoholic father absent most of the time. There was no mother. He wondered if the old man had ever touched the girl. She'd never mentioned it. But there were times when the old man made references to her allure, to her sexuality. Still, she'd never complained or accused her father of anything salacious.

From adolescence Estelle had toyed with men, had used her sexuality to get what she wanted. And she was doing it again now to him, grabbing his thigh, kneading her fingers into his soft flesh, he could feel them through the denim jeans he wore.

"Naw, Estelle." Theo rose abruptly from the bed. "I'm just fine standing."

She frowned, cocked an eyebrow and pursed her lips. "Your damn stomach bothering you again? You going to shit your pants again, Theo? That's kind of sickening, you know."

"I can't help that. It's, it's the Crohn's, you know that."

She slid her eyes away from him and grunted. "Yeah, yeah, I know. But it's still kind of disgusting." Estelle pushed the hair away from her face, her voice softened. "I'm sorry but you hurt my feeling when you don't want to be next to me." She lifted her eyes to his, sat upright and reached a hand to fondle him.

"No! No, Estelle, this ain't right. You're, you're like a daughter to me." He abruptly pushed her hand away from his groin.

"But I'm not your daughter."

"Why do you want to," his words stumbled from his mouth, "to do *that* with *me?*

"I love you Theo. I bet I love you more than Emily—that's her name isn't it?"

"What do you need another woman for?" She rose and stepped closer. "I want you to move out here. Sell that nasty old farm and live out here with me by the beach."

"I like the farm, Estelle. I like Emily."

"Emily, pfft." Estelle's lips broadened into a grin. "That's it. Emily has stolen you away from me, hasn't she?"

Theo shrugged.

"Theo, you've given me lots of things. You got me through college. If it hadn't of been for you I'd be working at some shithole in the mall or some bar. I owe you." Caressing her breasts with open hands, Estelle flashed her eyes at him. "Don't tell me you haven't thought about it, you lying shit. I've seen the way you look at me sometimes."

His face flushing in anger, Theo words burst from his mouth, "So—I'm human, and you're a damn tease, a whore." He wished he could have taken them back. But he knew they were true words. He knew Estelle was one of those women his mother had warned him about. She liked sex, she was one of those nymphomaniacs he read about in the magazines he kept hidden beneath his mattress. He stepped back farther from her and lowered his eyes. "No, I'm in love with Emily."

"You're in love? Love?" Her head twisting to the side, Estelle's hooded eyes studied the man before her. "I don't know about loving anybody else, Theo. What about me?"

Theo's face reddened. "I love you, too, Estelle, you're my little girl. I love Emily, well, you know. It's different and you shouldn't be grabbing me where you shouldn't be. Now, I know what you're doing. You've been doing it forever, teasing me—and you need to stop, it ain't right, Estelle. I'm—I'm like a father to you and--" His face flushed and his eyes met hers. "I guess you act like you do because you had no momma to tell you right from wrong. But you ought to know better by now."

Estelle rolled her eyes. "You're too serious. And I'm just playing." She slid her eyes sensually over his body.

"You play mean, Estelle. I don't want to play like that anymore."

Tilting her head sideways, Estelle scowled. "You're no fun." She shrugged. "No matter, I don't care. You've gotten old and baggy anyway."

"I'm only staying for a few weeks and then I'm going back to the farm. I'm having Christmas and New Year's with Emily." He blurted the phrase and waited for the response, one he expected to be cruel and ridiculing.

Estelle's eyes fell sharply, then slid just as quickly to the side and finally reached his. "That will be just fine, Theo. If Emily means so much to you, then you should be with her. It's about time you found somebody. Men like you need a little woman around the house."

"She loves me. We've even talked about getting married and having a baby."

Again Estelle's eyes darted away, again she focused them quickly back on Theo's. "I think that's just what you need, a baby. You have always been like a father to me and look how well I turned out." Her lips stretched into a smile. "You know, maybe around February she can come and visit—stay with us until you finish the tower and then you two can get married in it. What do you think of that? I'll even spring for the wedding—pay for the whole thing. Emily can toss the bouquet from the top of the tower." She leaned in and kissed Theo on the cheek. "Yes. This is such good news, Theo. I'm happy for you." She yawned and stretched her arms high. "What a day, what a night. Think I'll hit the hay." She leaned to kiss his cheek again. "See you in the morning."

Theo watched as Estelle exited the bedroom. He blew a breath from his mouth, elated that Estelle seemed so pleased about him and Emily. He was confused still about her initial behavior, but he told himself he shouldn't, it was typical Estelle.

He patted himself on the back for standing up to her, thinking that perhaps that was what had prompted her generosity to him and Emily. "Maybe she is changing. Maybe now, she'll treat me differently, maybe have some respect for me."

Since her move a few years ago to North Carolina, life had most definitely been easier. There was less nagging, less tension and less feelings of inadequacy. Even the Crohn's had begun to lessen.

Emily became his new confidant, his closest friend and within time, his lover. Theo was not used to having lovers. The few times he'd been with a woman were paid encounters and they always left him feeling ashamed.

He felt comfortable and wanted with Emily. There was no manipulating, no cruel accusations, she didn't tease him about his Crohn's disease or other physical short comings.

Resting against the bed Theo thought of how life would be different when he returned to Kentucky. After this job for Estelle he would make Emily his priority and they would live together on his farm happily ever after. The thought warmed him as he fell asleep.

Chapter Six

The picture was a bit blurred but Estelle could make out the features and figure of the woman Theo was seeing. Emily was almost as she'd imagined, plump, her hips broad. Her drab, mousy brown hair hung loosely to her shoulders, an elastic band held it away from her face.

Her small and close-set eyes were dark brown, almost black. The upturned nose was almost too small for her face and her small mouth was thin, without shape. "Damn she looks like a freaking mouse—ha—little mousy."

The girl stood, posing next to an oak tree, her stout body dressed in a knee length plaid skirt and green blouse, a cardigan hung loosely over her shoulders. Her shoes looked to be too big for her feet. "Consignment store rags," Estelle snorted.

"Just what I thought, white trash, common white trash. Probably lives in a trailer—I'm certain of it." Estelle drew her thumb to her mouth, she bit hard, then sucked tenderly on her bruised skin. She looked again at the picture of Emily. It could have been her. It *would* have been her if it had not been for Theo being in her life. Where were Emily's scuffed knees? Her torn open blouse?

"Theo's old enough to be her father!" Holding the photograph firmly, Estelle tore down the center, continuing to tear until the photo was in bits.

****

"This is a better picture of Emily." Theo stood on the skirt of the tower holding his phone; he scrolled across the photos. "Don't you think? The one I gave you was taken a few months back and Emily has lost a few pounds since then. But to be honest, I don't care what size she is, I love her."

"I thought you could do better than this." Estelle pushed the phone away from her and wrapped her arm around him, "I mean, she isn't really fat—I guess—just plump." She felt Theo pull away and quickly added, "More cushion for the pushin', huh?"

"Oh geez, Estelle." He glared reprovingly at her and groaned.

"Okay, okay, I'm just saying, she's a bit on the chubby side but if that's what you like, if it's what you want, then go for it, honey."

"She's coming for a visit in February and I don't want any nasty remarks from you. I don't want to hear anything about what you think of her appearance. Looks ain't everything, Estelle."

"Well, I know that, Theo." She pressed a finger into his soft belly. "Just look at you, a string bean with a pot belly."

"It's things like that. You say the meanest things and then you--"

70

"And then I what?" Estelle pushed her body against his, her open palms caressing his chest.

Theo slapped her hands away and stepped back. "It's stuff like that. You use me and twist everything to something dirty. I wish I'd never come here."

"Really? Never come?" her eyes squinting, Estelle flew at him, her hand drawn back as if to slap him.

"I—I don't mean it like that. It's just that you're cruel to me and—you *exploit* me."

"Ah, a new word, *exploit*. Who taught you that one? Emily? Emily's been teaching you a lot of things lately."

"I've told you, she treats me nice. She doesn't put me down or laugh at me."

Her eyes shifting from Theo to the picture he still held on the phone, Estelle folded her arms across her chest and turned away to face the ocean.

"You're mad now. Sorry, Estelle. I don't want to hurt your feeling, but I need to tell you the truth. Emily says I need to tell you the truth. I love Emily, Estelle. I hope you can learn to love her, too, and she can be part of our family."

Estelle continued starring toward the ocean, unflinching, stoic as if she had not heard his last words. But she had and they had cut like a knife. Theo had hurt her, this being she'd known her whole life was pulling away and she felt the separating physically as if it was tearing her skin, her organs, away from her body.

She was going to teach him about love and pain, she'd promised herself that almost from the first time he'd spoken of Emily.

The envy boiling in her blood, Estelle could not fathom Theo's love for anyone else. He would have to be punished and be taught about separation and loss.

Chapter Seven

Theo opened the cooler and pulled out a beef and provolone sub and a Sun Drop soda pop. He relaxed onto the metal folding chair and chewed, perusing all the work he'd accomplished since having begun work on the tower in November.

He looked down at the black and white photo lying on the floor of the tower then raised his head to study the work he had so far completed. Yes, he was getting there. The tables were in the right places, the tracking equipment, though not functional, looked just like the photo.

A man in Fairmont said he had a couple of old chairs from the 1940s that were exact matches for those used back then.

One of the first things he'd done was build the stairways and now they were exact replicas of those that once stood in the towers.

Nodding, as he chewed on the sandwich, Theo smiled to himself. He was proud of what he'd done. Surely Estelle would be, too.

The tower would be completed by April, he was positive. It would be perfect. It was just the time when he and Emily were planning to marry. Now, he just had to convince Estelle to let him take a couple weeks off for Christmas and New Year's.

It had been nearly two months since he'd seen his Emily. He missed her terribly, though they spoke on the telephone at least three times a week.

At first, Estelle seemed annoyed with the calls. Theo had considered there would be jealousy, that Estelle would automatically dislike Emily and he was right. But after their last conversation her attitude had changed— she seemed more accepting of the fact that he and Emily were a couple and she commented almost daily on how happy she was that he'd found someone to love.

Theo had set things straight, as far as he was concerned. He'd put his foot down after decades of giving in to Estelle. It eased his conscience that things were now as they should be. He would have hated to have to choose because his choice would have been Emily.

****

"Now dear, I don't want you to breathe a word of this to Theo. You can't tell him I'm coming and you can't tell your family either."

"I don't have any family."

"No children?"

"Didn't Theo tell you? I lost my baby—my daughter." Emily sighed into the phone, "That's how Theo and I met, at Doctor Bledstone's. He's in Altonville. Isn't that funny? We both drove out of town to the same doctor, it seemed like kismet, us meeting. Well, we're

74

both seeing him for depression but the funny thing is, since Theo and I have been seeing one another we're not depressed anymore. I don't think I—we've been happier. I thought surely Theo would have told you."

"Not a word, but don't let that worry you one bit. I'm sure he didn't think it was important to tell me how you met. But one thing is for sure, now he talks non-stop about you. It's Emily this and Emily that."

"We have become really close and he understands so much about my baby and how my husband, Justin, left and oh, he used to call me fat and lazy and he blamed me for the baby dying. It was so horrible and then--"

Estelle listened as the woman droned on and on about her former husband, about the love between she and Theo, how it had to be destiny for them to have met while both were being treated for depression and how this and how that.

She allowed Emily to continue, the plan forming in her head, coming together like pieces of a puzzle. Already Emily adored her, she was listening to her spilling her guts, confiding in her.

As she spoke into the phone, Estelle imagined Emily, her pudgy and pasty body lifeless, her brown drab hair, limp against her face. *Maybe I'll buy her something from Wal-Mart. Maybe I'll fix her face—a little mascara, some eye shadow, a little lipstick.*

Estelle's nostrils flared as the image burned in her imagination. Step One was complete—gaining her confidence, it would continue to grow once she met the girl in Kentucky.

75

"Justin even called me stupid but Theo says I'm not, and I know I'm not and Theo has helped me--"

Blah, blah, blah, Estelle mouthed, *you are stupid*—the fingers of her hand making talking motions. *It will be a joy to shut this bitch up.*

"Well, honey, you just don't worry about what some silly man says about you. It's Theo to the rescue and I'll be over there in a few days and we'll sit and talk about this. I want to help you two as much as I can and I want it all to be a surprise for Theo. He has been such a warm and caring figure for me my whole life."

Skeptical at first, after hearing Theo talk about Estelle before he left for North Carolina, Emily had thought she was manipulative, bossy and cruel. But now, Emily understood the pull he had to her. She was nice, she was understanding. Maybe Estelle just needed to be loved. Maybe she, too, was in need of understanding and patience. Just now, on the phone she had sounded so nice, so caring. That was it, Estelle just needed to be loved and accepted.

She and Theo could do that for Estelle, give her the love she needed, and then they'd all be happy.

Chapter Eight

Christmas had come and gone. Theo made the trip to Kentucky to see his beloved Emily. As far as he knew everything was right with the world—his world and the two women in it.

In fact, Estelle seemed overjoyed about his and Emily's relationship. Not one frown, not one scowl or condemning word had she uttered since early December when they'd had the conversation, the one where Theo felt he'd set things straight.

Now January, he looked forward to the visit from his sweetheart the following month. He anticipated a friendly if not joyful meeting between the two women in his life.

Lifting his head from the Field and Stream magazine, he smiled as Estelle entered the living room.

"I have to go to New Bern for a couple of days Theo. Think you can take care of things for a while?" Estelle slipped her arms through the sleeves of the Burberry jacket and settled a tan beret atop her head. "There may be a buyer for the little cottage—sure would love to get rid of it."

"Now? You're going now?"

"I just got the call from the Realtor. It's not going to be any bother is it?"

"No." He settled the magazine in his lap. "It's no problem at all, Estelle. I'm sure there's plenty of food in the fridge and I know how to work the television. I think I'll do just fine."

He noticed how when she leaned in to kiss his cheek, she avoided bringing her body in close. In the past she had used any excuse to rub against him, her hugs were long, conforming her body to his, and normally she teased with her eyes or tongue. Lately she had done none of these.

I must have really had an effect on her when we talked last. Does she finally understand that she can't play with me anymore? He thought as she drew her body away and straightened the little beret.

"Good luck," he called, as her hand grasped the banister and she stepped down the stairway.

"Be sure to find out as much as you can on the four musketeers and anyone else that sounds interesting." Estelle called back. "Get me the low down on these yokels, honey."

He shot her a puzzled look.

"Oh come on now, you know who I'm talking about." She turned and stepped toward Theo. "The cop, the bridge tender bitch and—while I'm gone. It'll give you something to do."

"Oh, yeah, I know, I will. Don't worry."

"Check out the bars, the locals will rattle your ears off talking about people. You'll find out what size underwear they're wearing." She laughed gaily.

He liked seeing her look so carefree; it was a characteristic he seldom saw in his friend. He laughed back at the joke and watched Estelle descend the remaining stairs then backed from the driveway.

The doctor seemed surprised as he walked into the examination room. The chart had read Mrs. Estelle Butler. But there was no mistaking the Estelle he'd become so familiar with over the last several years. This was Estelle Reardon, the woman who'd opened up a whole new world to him. She sat perched on the examination table, her dress drawn up around her thighs.

The shock wearing off, Doctor Bledstone forced a smile to his face. "And to what do I owe the pleasure?" he asked, slowly scanning her, attempting to appear casual and even glad to see her thumbing through the pages of the file, his eyes rose to meet hers. "Butler?"

"My married name."

"So when do I get to meet the lucky man?" Bledstone asked, wary of his patient, of her motives for seeing him.

"That would be kind of difficult, doctor. Poor Mr. Butler passed away last year."

"Oh." his eyes shifted. "Sorry to hear that, Estelle." He walked closer to her. "How are things going?"

"Swimmingly," she smirked. "I love my new beach house."

He smiled, nodded his head and sat on the adjacent stool facing her. "Just like old times, huh? You coming here for an examination you don't really need." He shook his head. "What can I do for you? Usually you just call me if you need something."

Doctor Bledstone, like all men, hadn't been able to resist Estelle's youth and sensuality when he first met her. She teased him on her first visit over two decades ago, aware of the wanting in his eyes.

She responded to the lingering touches of her thighs during exams, to his closeness as he spoke to her. And when she bent to unzip his trousers she watched the pleasure it brought to his face. He was so easy. He was putty in her hands.

Back then he was pliable, eager for the new kind of sex Estelle introduced him to, things his wife, a former Miss Bluegrass, would have never considered.

The Bledstones, along with their three children, lived in the finer part of town. He was president of the Rotary Club and attended Luxton Methodist Church regularly. Citations for outstanding work in the field of medicine lined the walls of his office; he was a pillar of the small community.

Estelle introduced him to things he'd only fanaticized about and soon he found himself writing false prescriptions for testosterone, just to keep up with her appetite. Not long after that, Estelle initiated a meeting with Gail from Lexington. Gail introduced the fine doctor to a discrete swingers club just forming in nearby Altonville.

But Estelle did not attend the parties; she preferred sex with individuals over whom she held power, controlling a man's guilt and his wallet.

The doctor's family would have been appalled to learn of his extracurricular activities, and so he wrote prescriptions for Estelle whenever she needed. He didn't question the Dilaudid and he came to not care about the illegal implications of Estelle's requests, he simply prescribed the drug to her as if she were a patient. Though rare, the patient list grew to include out of state patients.

Now Estelle was here, in his office. He wondered what she wanted and if there would once again be demands for silence.

"You have a patient, a little squatty, mousy girl. She needs a prescription."

Chapter Nine

Estelle spotted Emily immediately as she walked into the bus terminal in Luxton. She looked just like her photo, her face, pinched, even more mouse-like than in the picture.

A broad grin spread across the little mouse's face as she jumped up and down in the small waiting room. She waved a homemade "I'm Emily" sign as if she would have been hard to find, as if she were in an airport terminal. Estelle endeavored to control her disgust at the rube-like behavior as she walked to greet her.

"So you're the famous girlfriend, I've heard so much about you. I'm so happy to finally meet you." She held her at arm's length. "And you do look just like your picture." She bent to hug the woman, drawing her close. "In fact, you're the only thing Theo wants to talk about."

Estelle had the gestures down pat. She'd even practiced them in the mirror at home, the look of happiness, warmth, hugging as if she meant it. She was being sure to lavish attention on Theo's girlfriend, just enough to convince her of her sincerity—just enough to have Emily trust her.

"These are for us later tonight, after we eat one of those scrumptious dinners you cook, the ones I keep hearing Theo talk about." She handed a pink box tied with a white bow to Emily. "Eclairs, I bought them at the sweetest little shop on the island. They were fresh yesterday when I bought them and I didn't even open them on the bus ride here." Estelle's eyes widened as she licked her lips, relishing how easily the lies fell from them. "Yummy, I can't wait to dig into these."

"But I already made something for dessert tonight."

"Oh." Estelle scrunched her nose. "We can have both. After all, we're celebrating your wedding."

Now it begins, she thought, kissing Emily's cheek, *the little game of cat and mouse.* Estelle felt the adrenaline as she tingled with excitement. *Watch the mouse, just watch the mouse until it feels safe, until it forgets to be on guard.* She had written the steps to convincing Emily of her sincerity and of how her visit would culminate. Estelle cursed herself silently for having left the note pad in her nightstand with the steps, but she knew them anyway. She'd memorized them.

"Are we going to Theo's farm?" She asked enthusiastically as they walked to Emily's car. She hugged her once more. This time more tightly.

Emily nodded. "Yes, I tried to clean the place up best I could. You know it's just a plain old farm, nothing fancy."

"Oh, I remember it so well. I used to visit there as a kid. I practically lived over here." She threaded her arm through Emily's. "I bet you've dolled the place up a bit, you just seem the sort who likes pretty things. Theo was never much of a decorator."

"A little." Emily blushed. "I made new curtains and painted a couple of rooms, but you know how men are, they don't pay attention to the way things look. I don't think Theo would mind one bit if I hadn't done a thing, but it makes me feel better to have the house looking cheerful and clean. You'll see when we get there." Emily slid Estelle's suitcase into the back seat then settled herself behind the wheel to drive the twenty miles to Theo's.

****

The house did look different. Where there had once been loose broken shutters, there were now freshly painted ones. The yard was not strewn with old tires and lumber as before, but was neat and orderly. Flower beds filled with seasonal flora stood against the barn and sides of the house. Even one of the now leafless maple trees had a circular flower bed around its base.

"It really looks pretty in the spring when the crocus and daffodils come up. And then after that I usually have pansies and vinca plants."

Estelle nodded, "Yes, it does look a lot nicer than the last time I saw it. You've done well, Emily."

The inside of the house looked different, too. It was more airy; gone were the dark heavy drapes, shears replaced them letting light and sunshine enter the once darkened living room.

"This is one of the rooms I painted." Emily led the way into the kitchen. The bright yellow walls blared as the women entered through the doorway. "I just love yellow."

"I can tell that." Estelle said casually.

"I know I could have gone with a softer yellow, maybe a pastel, but I really like yellow." Emily caught Estelle's eyes and tittered. "You see, Estelle, I really have been busy since Theo has been away. He's going to be so surprised when he gets back—after we are married."

Now Estelle was sure. She would follow through with her plans. How dare *they* make decisions without consulting her. How dare Theo make a decision with Emily only. It burned her to the core and she felt the heat rising to her face. Her skin puckered with bumps as she felt Theo's betrayal sink into her pores. Catching herself glaring at Emily, she quickly turned the reaction to a bright and broad smile.

"I new you'd be happy for us. I sort of had my doubts in the beginning, you know, when Theo first talked about you. I was so worried that you'd be jealous."

"Jealous? Heavens no." She patted Emily's hand and thought how the girl, the little mousy girl wasn't going to be a problem any longer. How dare they, how dare Theo make plans to go back to Kentucky. Theo hadn't even mentioned that.

Sniggering, Estelle thought of how those plans were so much minutia, so irrelevant in the scheme of things. She touched Emily's arm as her eyes scanned the room. "Oh, how sweet, Theo is going to be so impressed with all the pretty little things you've done."

86

Throughout the rest of the day, Estelle placated Emily, oohing and ahhing at one thing or another, praising her for working so hard on the place. At super time she raved about the corned beef and cabbage, and the pineapple upside down cake.

When they both had changed into their pajamas, Estelle commented on how cute Emily looked in hers then implied that something more sexy would be needed for their wedding night. She adopted the "girl friend" attitude she'd watched on television shows and read about. In a way pretending was fun but it soon became tedious and boring. She struggled with the small talk.

"Oh, you don't know how hard it's been being so tall." Estelle sat cross-legged on the king sized bed and reached to the plate of chocolate éclairs between her and Emily. She bit hungrily into one. "There are hardly any men at all taller than me."

"I think you're lucky. At least you can eat what you want and not worry about it bloating you out like a watermelon." Emily shifted her legs to a more comfortable position and tittered, then took a dainty bite from her own éclair. "Thank you so much for coming to visit me. It means a lot."

"Think nothing of it. Theo has taken care of me nearly all my life and this is the least I can do for him. But I don't want you to say a word to a soul. You haven't said anything have you? You haven't said a word to Theo about me coming out here? If you have then the whole deal is off. I won't buy you a thing." Estelle's eyes were firm as she feigned a light hearted giggle. "I really don't want him to know I'm helping you pick out your gown. I want it to be a surprise."

"Oh Estelle." Emily grabbed the woman's hand and squeezed gently. "No, I haven't said a single thing to him. It's just our little secret, yours and mine. I think all of this, you visiting and spending time with me, is making us closer. You are so wonderful, thank you."

Estelle grinned. "My pleasure. You know, when Theo told me about you, I was so happy that he had finally found someone sweet and nice—someone to love him like he needed to be loved." Estelle touched a napkin to her lips and stuffed the rest of the éclair into her mouth. "Yummy, I just love these things. Come on now, eat up. I bought these for you, you know."

"I really shouldn't. I did have a piece of cake after supper."

"Oh, it was just a little one. I watched you, you cut the tiniest piece."

"I want to look nice for Theo when we get married. I really shouldn't."

Her bottom lip protruding, Estelle whined. "Come on now, I brought these all the way from North Carolina and believe me they are the best you'll ever have. After eating this, you have me mailing them to you." She urged Emily to take another bite of the éclair, and watched as she popped the remainder into her mouth. She pointed to another one.

"That one has more chocolate than the others and another one is not going to make any difference. And besides, this is a celebration." *Yes, little mouse, you can trust me.* "Come on now, eat up and enjoy."

Sucking her bottom her lip, Emily took the éclair and bit daintily from the end.

The cat enjoys playing with the mouse, come on little mousy. Estelle watched Emily's small dainty mouth open wide to bite from the Éclair. "Geez, Emily, that was such a tiny bite, take another." Nodding, she added, "Have you and Theo selected a date?"

"Sort of. We're thinking about the middle of April."

Estelle nodded.

Lowering her head, Emily wiped her eyes, a tiny whimper sounded from her mouth. "I couldn't believe it when Theo drove up to the farm in that truck this Christmas." She raised her eyes to meet Estelle's and spoke earnestly. "He was so proud and so grateful—I— and the necklace. You shouldn't have spent the money. I know it must have been expensive and I've never had a real gold necklace or anything else made out of gold—real gold." She giggled and wiped her eyes again. "It made our Christmas so special, Estelle. You'll never know how much it means to us."

Estelle closed her eyes, warmth settled over her, she basked in it for a moment before wiping her own eyes. "I was happy to do for him, and for you." *The cat bats the mouse again—oh this game is so much fun.*

She'd bought a truck and a necklace, the least she could do, and an impressive touch, she thought, to gaining the couple's trust.

This added dimension of stringing victims along satiated her beyond measure. She knew the climax was going to be explosive.

Maybe it was so titillating because it was Theo. Could he have been holding her back all along? Estelle pondered their relationship. Certainly if he'd loved her all those years, he wouldn't put another person before her.

As she thought, she grinned, watching Emily's mouth chewing and talking at the same time; a finger wiped away a smear of chocolate frosting. Estelle stifled a grimace as she watched the woman reach her tongue to her lips.

How despicable was this piece of nothing—this rodent. How could Theo be attracted to someone like her? How could he choose Emily over her? Estelle scowled and drew her lips tight.

"Is something the matter?" Emily asked.

"Oh no, I think my leg is falling asleep, I just need to switch positions again." She lied again, enjoying the falsehood, she giggled girlishly.

The plan was in motion. As it had been with Hank, Jeff, her own father and Theo's parents. The plan. Everything was working as she wanted. But this one was even more delicious. And it was so easy. She had the power, no one would ever be on a par with her. Estelle relished the feeling of superiority. Each time it was easier, each time it was better.

This time every detail had been considered. She had planned perfectly. As she'd discovered there were nuances to murder—to this one especially. People's routine's changed, environments changed. What if Emily had refused to even eat the éclairs? What if Emily had told Theo? All these things had to be taken into consideration to make events move along smoothly and look as natural as possible.

Estelle praised herself for the planning—planning well—so unlike things with Mindy.

With her she'd been in too much of a hurry. She would have never considered killing Mindy, she had nothing against her and the girl had nothing she wanted.

That plan, or lack of one, had been sloppy. And that sloppiness resulted in the death of a young person who, though meaning nothing to Estelle, jolted the community. It seemed Mindy was missed more than Hank. How was that possible? She was a little nothing. Hank's family was rich. He owned all that land, had all that money—and Mindy was common, she didn't have a pot to piss in—she was a nobody.

But how was Estelle to know the figure wrapped in the old afghan wasn't Emma Jewel? How was she to know the little nothing meant so much to so many?

*Emma Jewel, E.J. She screwed that thing up for me. Mindy's death is **her** fault.* Estelle smirked.

E.J. was another loose end she needed to tie up. The old cow had one third of what rightfully belonged to her. If only that bitch of a daughter hadn't put her momma in her will. And why didn't Hank take his mother-in-law out of his? Things would have been less complicated.

Estelle reached her hand to caress Emily's, she smiled gently. "You are such a pretty girl."

She imagined E.J. before her, chewing on an éclair, dying, retching, in pain like she should be for taking what belonged to her. *When I get back, I'll take care of that old bitch.*

Estelle nodded to Emily, watching her mouth move, her lips smiling as she blabbered on about Theo and marriage—blah, blah, blah. She studied Emily, how she crossed her legs, how her short round fingers touched her lips or pulled her pajama bottoms over her dimpled knees. She was pudgy, just like in the picture Theo had shown her, but she did possess a kind of femininity, her brown hair falling in soft waves around her chubby face. She looked soft, her complexion porcelain and pristine, her movements poised, her pinky always extended as she lifted the éclair to her lips. Above all, it was Emily's innocence that exposed her vulnerability—the most feminine quality of all.

Understanding Theo's attraction to her was not difficult at all. Estelle reached to touch Emily's arm. "Are you going to wear a white dress?"

Emily drew her shoulders high and tilted her head back, she laughed breezily. "Oh yes, I want the works. I want a beautiful gown with beads and lace, but not too fancy. I want it to look like something worn in the forties, the hay day of the towers. You know, sort of flared at the bottom. And I want red roses for my bouquet. I want a ring bearer." She glowed, leaning toward Estelle. "I didn't have those things with my first husband. You know, we *had* to get married and then the baby died."

Waiting for the usual condolences from the listener, Emily examined Estelle's face, her own puzzled expression prompting Estelle to whisper, "I'm sorry for your loss."

After a moment, Emily continued detailing the gown, the flowers she wanted, and the pictures. "I want you to be my maid of honor, Estelle. It would mean so much to me."

Estelle was tired of hearing how much things meant to Emily. *What is that supposed to do for me?* She thought, patting the girl's hand, watching her take another bite of the éclair, searching for the telltale signs of the drug she'd laced into the éclairs. *When is that damn Dilaudid going to kick in?* She thought. "It means a lot to me, too," Estelle smiled, adding to their conversation.

"And I guess Theo has mentioned to you that we would like to have the wedding on the tower, rather than in front of it? It will look so retro, along with my dress. And Theo's going to wear a black tuxedo."

She noticed the flushing of Emily's skin, a first sign that the drug was doing its job. *Maybe I should have bought her the gown first, I could have dressed her in it—very dramatic with a note attached to the bodice. "Oh, Theo I couldn't face you anymore. I don't deserve you."* Estelle's eyelids closed partially as she thought *rave on little mouse.*

Emily's excitement bubbled as she touched her face and gestured. "Oh, I can't wait. It's going to be so wonderful. I've got the most wonderful man in the whole world."

Will little mouse ever shut up? Maybe I should have added another capsule to the mix. Estelle fidgeted, uncrossing her legs and repositioning them. She tilted her head, exhibited a half smile as she noticed Emily's face flushing even more. "Huh, he really is a wonderful man." She leaned in to the conversation, feigning curiosity as Emily talked on and on.

"Gee whiz, it's getting hot in here." Emily fanned her face.

"I'm comfortable but if you're hot I could open a window some."

"No, no, if you're all right, it must just be me." She smiled weakly. "I never thought anyone would love me ever again. I'm so lucky." She touched Estelle's arm. "None of this would be possible without *you*."

Estelle pursed her lips and lifting her head, grinned. "Really?" She paused. "But you and Theo have this all planned. I can see that."

Emily fanned herself again with her hand. "I'm still warm. Are you sure you're okay?"

"Feels fine to me. Maybe it's all the excitement and all your talking about plans. You're getting yourself all excited." Estelle patted Emily's hand again, rubbing the pudgy fingers softly.

Fanning herself still, Emily continued. "Theo and I talk about our wedding all the time on the phone. He's been saving his money—now and then he'll buy me something, some little thing to show he loves me. But that's all—he says it makes him feel good."

"Umm, Theo is a generous man. He used to buy me things, too, when I lived here."

"You were like his daughter, that's what he told me."

The statement bit into Estelle, she quickly responded. "Oh, it may have started out like that, but--" she saw Emily's jaw drop a bit, her eyes widening and thought once again of how

94

fun it was to toy with the little mouse. "But I'd say it was more like a big brother." She sighed, "You know, Theo paid for my college. Did you know that?"

Emily nodded. "Yes, he told me—said you were so smart it would have been a shame for you not to go. And he told me how you used to work in Vocational Rehabilitation before you married Hank, when you still lived here in Kentucky." Her eyes drifted downward. "I'm so sorry you lost your husband. I know how much it hurts to lose someone you love. You never get over it, it sort of hovers over everything in your life."

"I miss him very much." Estelle dabbed a finger to her eyes as if to wipe a tear.

"We all react differently to sorrow and loss. Theo says--"

"He says what? Differently, how?" Estelle scowled.

Raising a shoulder, Emily once again looked downward. "I just mean that everybody is different."

"I guess Theo told you a bit about Hank and me."

"Well, yes he did, and I know that despite everything, all your problems, you two loved each other. I can tell. You are too kind to--" Emily bit again from the éclair.

He's told her. He's told her about me—I bet she and Theo talk about me all the time. Stupid—she's stupid. They're both stupid. "You're right about death hovering; I will never forget Hank's passing. I've come to understand his pain and rather than judge it, I accept pain."

95

"Those are wise words, Estelle. You are smart, just like Theo says."

"Umm." Estelle watched Emily rub her stomach and wince. Releasing a slow moan, she licked filling smeared around her mouth.

Poor little mouse, Estelle continued listening as Emily droned on about the impending nuptials.

She managed to stifle a titter, thinking how disappointed Theo would be when his fiancée would not answer his phone calls and how distraught he would be when she did not show up as expected in February. Would he be so sad that he couldn't complete the tower by spring? Would the Crohn's become more acute? Just how would the death of his beloved Emily affect him?

She loved the suspense, though she had an inkling that Theo, because of his sense of obligation, would have the tower completed on time. Her eyes closed for a moment as she pictured Theo, shoulders slumped and teary eyed. She cocked her head to the side and frowned. "I hate this time of year, it's so cold."

Holding the end of the nibbled éclair, Emily took another bite and patted her stomach. "I shouldn't be eating this. My tummy's so full now and it's rumbling. I feel hot and sweaty, too. I just don't feel good."

Estelle watched tiny beads of sweat appear along Emily's hairline. *The cat watches the mouse. Its tiny lashes flutter and its dark shining eyes look helplessly.* She grinded her teeth together, watching, waiting, the adrenaline pulsing in her veins. *Now, now. Do it now!* The thought screamed impatiently in her head.

"I just love the necklace you got me for Christmas." A finger delicately touched the gold heart around her neck. "You didn't have to go to all that trouble."

Fidgeting, frustrated by the nonstop yammering from Emily, Estelle nearly spat the words. "What good is money for if not to share it with friends?"

"Estelle, we really want you to be part of our family." Emily yawned.

"Uh huh," Estelle watched the sweat trickle down her brow.

"Ooh, I knew I shouldn't have eaten this second éclair, I'm feeling a little dizzy, sort of nauseous. Gee, I feel so sleepy, too."

"Oh, it's just all the excitement over your wedding and talking about Theo—and you coming to Topsail. You're just all worked up, honey." Estelle patted her hand.

"I feel so tired, so sleepy," Emily nearly whispered.

"Just relax my dear. Just lie back on the bed and try to sleep."

Stretching her legs long, resting her head on the pillow, Emily searched Estelle's welcoming face. "You're so nice. So sweet." She extended her hand for Estelle to hold. "I hope I feel better soon. I just feel—feel so--" She moaned lowly.

Estelle watched her body release its tensions, moving into the state so familiar with one on Dilaudid, relaxed, limp, lethargic. She pinched Emily's arm, rolling the skin back and forth, there was no reaction from Emily.

Estelle tugged sharply on her hair, pulling out several strands, again no reaction. Emily was where she needed to be, like Hank had been, not caring, not afraid, not feeling anything at all, compliant in every way.

Lying next to Theo's girlfriend Estelle whispered, "Relax and take a nice long breath. It will all be better soon." She stroked Emily's hair and the side of her face. She smiled, thinking how right she had been in the description of Emily. "Yer jest a simple, needy, lil ol' farm girl, ain't ya?" Estelle whispered mockingly. She touched Emily's limp tresses and jerked a finger through a tangle. She studied the cheap clothing closely, the obvious hem of her skirt. She poked a finger into her soft thick belly—"Pillsbury Dough Girl, humph, yeah, you and Theo would have been some match." She shrugged and resumed stroking the woman's hair, then touched her face with her fingers, feeling the up turn of her tiny nose, the thinness of her lips. "Little mousy."

Rubbing her hands along the light brown fuzz of Emily's arms, Estelle felt the unfamiliar burning of tears. Her body jerked convulsively a few times before she reined in the strange feelings.

She continued stroking Emily's body, her neck, her breasts and belly—her thighs, calves. Estelle continued touching, caressing Emily, languishing in not sexual pleasure but in sorrow and tenderness—as if the girl could have been her.

She had once been that girl—poor, dirty, stupid. As a child she'd been mocked in school, ignored and shoved aside. Just like she imagined Emily had been.

Feeling her chest heave a sob, Estelle strove to keep control, to stop herself from crying. She bit into her lip, she could taste the blood, it calmed her and she closed her eyes and smiled warmly, kissing the girl's cheek and petting her hair away from her brow.

With a finger Estelle whispered, "Your momma will feed you worms in the morning— now fly away little bird."

Pressing against her, she kissed Emily's lips lightly then touched them with her fingertips. Estelle reached into her pocket, and drew a brown plastic medication bottle from it, shook the contents and closed her eyes again.

It began so easily, the opportunity had been thrust in her lap. First, finding the brown plastic bottle of Dilaudid in the pocket of Theo's jacket. He'd offered her the zip up parka one chilly afternoon after visiting with the Cornbys.

At home she found her father once again drunk and belligerent, ordering her to fix his meal and to wait for him in her bedroom. How convenient it was to "season" the steamed cabbage. And how satisfying it was to watch her old man reel, to sweat and drift into an uncaring, unfeeling state of being. He became so very relaxed, zombie like. Now, Estelle had power over him and she liked that very much.

She walked him outside, arm in arm. Him stumbling over his own feet, until she released him to fall face first into the deep puddle in the rear of the ramshackle house they occupied. He made no sound, no attempt to right himself.

There was no struggling at all. It amazed and pleased her.

Later she laughed, realizing that three or four pills would have done the job, rather than the seven she used. She wondered if the four left in the bottle would be enough to take care of both Mr. And Mrs. Cornby. They owned one hundred and twenty acres of farmland and Theo was the only heir.

Theo liked doing things for her, spending money on her. He bought her nice clothes, at least nicer than she'd ever had. And he bought her little pieces of costume jewelry she requested. Nearly all of the money he received from his weekly allowance was spent on her.

Estelle had heard his parents complain about the gifts and the money. And she was aware that she was welcome at their home only because of Theo.

Yes, things would go more smoothly with the old couple out of the way.

Executing her father's death had been so easy—no pain for him or for she. She liked the way Dilaudid worked on her old man, making him so pliable and easy to persuade. Estelle could see how the drug could help her achieve things she'd been unable to before. Sex went only so far when it came to controlling some people.

Estelle closed her eyes, thinking of how far she had come from the squalor of her childhood, of the people who had stood in her way and how much she now enjoyed having power over those who had once seen her as low class trash.

She pressed a cheek next to Emily's, her long luxurious hair shifting to rest against Emily's shoulder and the pink chenille bedspread. She smiled softly and studied the pinched brow and look of discomfort on the woman's face. "You are gone away little trash girl. No one will ever look down on you again."

Chapter Ten

Sidling up to the long wooden bar, Theo waved a hand at the bartender, beckoning him to take his order.

It was not a busy night at Gerard's, the young bartender nodded to the girl he was talking to and walked toward Theo.

"Miller Lite." Theo nodded. "And send one over to the lady sitting alone in the corner."

"I can tell you right now, mister, she's not going to accept it. Save your money."

"I'm new in town, just trying to meet a few people. Anything wrong with that?" Theo asked nervously.

The bartender shook his head. "Sorry but I think she's taken."

"Married?"

"No."

"What does she do for a living?"

"I think she works the bridge."

Theo's eyes narrowed. "They let women do that?"

"Buddy, they let women do just about anything. Where have you been?"

Theo chuckled. "I guess you're right about that, women are doing all kinds of stuff these days." He looked curiously at the young man. "I'd still like to get to know her, she looks sort of nice. What do you say?"

"She doesn't like beer." The young man smirked.

Theo twirled the bottle against the bar, "Kinda highfalutin? Sorta homely to be so high and mighty." Theo sneered. "And she ain't got no boobs, does she?"

"Hey, Miss Paula is a good woman, don't say anything bad about her around me."

Theo nodded. "Okay." He stuck his thumb to his mouth and chewed on a hangnail. "What's she drink?"

"She's been drinking Grand Marnier, with a little ginger ale and lime."

"What kind of drink is that? What's it called?"

"Beats me, it's just what she gets when this guy she's been seeing is with her."

"He ain't with her now." Theo blurted.

"He will be, it's Wednesday. He'll be here and then you're going to regret buying a drink for Miss Paula. The drink that she isn't going to accept anyway."

"What is Grand Marnier, anyway?"

"It's a liquor, a fancy cognac. This guy she's seeing is the one who orders it for the both of them. If he didn't I don't think she'd even drink."

Theo paused, quickly studied Paula, and turned back. "Send her two. Tell her it's compliments of an old friend—oh yeah, what's this man's name she's waiting for?"

"Levi—Lev—something like that."

"Last name?"

The young man shrugged. "No idea."

Theo watched the bartender carry the drinks to Paula's booth, watched him turn to nod his way. Theo smiled and nodded back.

He watched Paula shake her head as the young man slid the drinks back onto the tray.

Slowly Theo walked over to the table, placing a hand on the shoulder of the bartender. "No need, buddy. Leave them here. Just give me a minute."

Endeavoring to look boldly into her eyes, Theo wrestled with his nervousness and extended a hand. "I'm John Graves, a friend of Levi's. I heard he's a regular here, I'm passing through for a weekend of fishing and I thought I'd check up on my old buddy from Iraq." Theo stood, a beer in one hand, the other thrust into his pants pocket. "This was his drink, got me hooked on it and I reckoned he probably did you, too. Am I right?" *I said it just like I rehearsed.* He thought, relaxing a bit, proud of the accomplishment.

"Hooked on it?" Paula eyed the Miller in his hand. "Then why the beer?" Her voice sarcastic and accusatory.

He guffawed and looked at the beer in his hand. "Well, uh, it kinda too early in the day for the hard stuff, I'll stick to my Miller. I just wanted to give my old buddy the best. This young fellow here says you're his girlfriend— and what a pretty one you are." Theo watched her brow pinch. "Anyways, he said Levi should be in any minute."

The word girlfriend was an uncomfortable term, one Paula wasn't sure she wanted to be associated with when it came to Lev. She looked away and raised a shoulder.

The man's loose stance and casual clothing hung comfortably from his body. He was a tall man, well over six feet—thin, a bit slumped at the shoulders. Normally she would have felt no threat from this man with the homey mid-western accent and the open face. He appeared friendly enough. But there was something, a bit of nervousness about him. She sensed the *something*, and Paula had come to trust her senses.

The "pretty" remark had annoyed her somewhat, but then that could have been simply mid-western politeness. Southern men and mid-westerners did that sort of thing. It was nice, even if it wasn't true. Even Lev lavished her with flattering comments and terms of endearment.

Still, there was something about this tall gangly man that bothered her, maybe it was how he referred to Lev as Levi. She'd not heard that before. Don, whom he'd known even before joining the military, had never called him by that name. Sometimes, he called him Gass, Lev's last name, but usually it was Lev or *asshole*. She smiled at the banter the two often shared. "Lev Gass, is that who you're looking for?"

"Ah, she smiles." Theo smiled back, mistaking the gesture and the information for permission to move closer. He motioned to sit in a chair.

"Hey, no sitting. No, Mr. Graves. Lev is going to be here any minute and I'd prefer if you waited for him to—" She lifted her chin, a broader smile crossing her lips. "And here he is."

Lev's bulky frame neared, his shoulders squared even more as he eyed the tall figure at the table. The man towered above him, still,

Lev walked into his space and inhaled deeply. "And you are?"

Theo apprehensively reached his hand out to Lev. "Graves, John Graves." The name rolled uneasily from his tongue. "Well, ain't this embarrassing. Mister, I was told that Levi Lafarge had a place here and was running a charter boat out to the Gulf Stream. Levi and I were stationed in Iraq back in '02. Looks like I made me a mistake. Sorry 'bout that." He chuckled, his eyes darting about. "The lady here says your last name is Gass and you sure as hell don't look like my old buddy." He snorted.

Cautiously, Lev shook the man's hand. "Levi LaFarge? Never heard of him, he's not around here as far as I know. Sorry buddy. Looks like I'm not your man."

"When the bartender told me you was drinking Grand Marnier, I thought for sure I had the right guy. That's all Levi ever drank." He laughed again, placing a hand on Lev's shoulder. "Levi LaFarge, nope you sure as heck ain't LaFarge, he was a bit scrawnier. I bet nobody messes with you, man."

Lev grinned, he too felt something odd about this so-called friend. He was sure that this was some sort of attempt to ferret information; he waited for the lead-in to gather some other tidbit.

"Levi's from Michigan. Where are you from?" Graves stammered.

Lev's lips tightened, as he stood tensely before the man, not bothering to answer.

Theo forced a trembling grin and countered, "Well, I guess I'll leave you two alone. Sorry to

107

intrude and the Marnier is on me. Enjoy, and sorry for the intrusion." He bowed slightly and turned to exit the bar.

Like Don, Lev had been CID in the military. His senses were keen, sharp, he could spot a lie a mile away. Scrutinizing Graves, immediately he knew he was an imposter. If this man was gathering information on him or Paula he was new at it. And for sure, he wasn't gathering it for himself. He was doing a job for someone. Lev chortled at the feeble attempt of the stranger to attain information.

Theo brought his thumb to his teeth and chewed on the broken skin around the nail, pinpricks of dried blood dotted his soft flesh. Drawing his shoulders in tightly, his hooded eyes studied the graveled path leading to his truck. "Shit," he muttered the word angrily. "I don't know what Estelle expects me to find out about these people. They seem just as ordinary as the folks back home. And why has she got to know all this stuff for?" He stuffed his hands into his worn jeans, his lips drew into a lopsided sneer. "Man, she sure was an uppity ol' bitch."

"That was strange." Lev pushed gently against Paula, encouraging her to allow room for him to sit next to her. His lips brushed gently against her cheek. "How long has he been hanging around?"

"Only a few minutes. Glad you came along when you did. He was starting to give me the heebie-jeebies. I think he's fishing for something."

"Yeah, something isn't right with him." Lev called to the bartender who once again smiled and excused himself from the girl he'd been talking to at the bar.

"Another round?" The younger man nodded to the untouched Marnier's on the table.

"Yeah, that'll do. But tell me, have you ever seen that man before, the one talking to Paula?"

"Hey, how you doing?" Ignoring Lev, the young man turned his attention to Paula

"Hi Troy." she smiled.

"Sorry."

"That's okay."

"I told Dad you've started coming in here and he told me next time I saw you to say hey—so hey from Micah."

Paula grinned. "Tell him I said hey back."

Turning his attention back to Lev, his face grew more solemn. "Never saw him before in my life." He shook his head. "Strange dude asked me what y'all were drinking. Wanted to know your name, wanted to know all kinds of things about Miss Paula."

"What did you tell him?"

"Not much." He grinned. "Isn't your name Levi?" Troy smiled.

"Lev."

"Hey man, we've never been formally introduced, I thought it was Levi. And Miss Paula's never been one to kiss and tell," he chuckled.

Lev grabbed Troy's hand, pumped it a couple of times, "Detective Gass."

"Ah, a cop. You're one of those Meet the Cop guys, huh, 'come have a cup of coffee with the local law enforcement.'" The bartender's head bobbed up and down as he spoke through his broadening smile, "I ought to do that sometime. Meet and greet the local men in blue." He stepped back, eyed Lev for a moment. "Hey where's the blue? You undercover?"

Lev grinned. "Not today."

"Well, it's good to meet you Detective Lev Gass. I'm Troy Conway, surfer extraordinaire. Just doing this gig to--"

"Nice meeting you Troy. Bring us another round of Marnier and take these back." He nodded to the now watered down drinks on the table.

"Miss Paula, I'll be sure to tell Daddy you said hey."

Paula grinned and nodded and waited for the inevitable question from Lev—*just who was Troy's dad?*

"Childhood friend," she offered before he spoke. Micah's image burned in her head, his warm eyes searching hers.

"Who?"

"I thought you were going to ask me who Troy's dad was."

"I assumed he was an old friend, you know everyone around here. No big deal. Right?"

Paula nodded. "No big deal."

"What I want to know is—who's this hokey hick, John Graves, and I don't believe that's his real name for a minute. He wants something."

"Said he was waiting to see you. That you two had served in Iraq together."

"Well, we know that was a lie." His lips tightening, Lev tensed. "You noticed how nervous the bastard was, didn't' you?"

"Nervous as a cat."

"I'm not Levi Lafarge, he knew that before I walked in here. That bastard has never been in Iraq and he's never served in the Marine Corps."

"How do you know that?"

"Trust me, I know what I'm talking about. Pansy-ass couldn't find his ass with both hands. He's nosing around for someone, that's for sure." His jaw tightening, Lev eyed the doorway. "The bastard's got to be at least fifty. And the name Lafarge. Wonder how long it took him to come up with that one?" Lev paused for a moment. "He's new at this. Someone put him up to it. He wanted to talk with *you*, get information from *you*. Didn't you notice how he acted when I came in? He wasn't here to see me."

Paula shrugged. "Maybe you made him nervous. You are sort of intimidating."

His face stern and drawn, Lev asked, "What did you tell him?"

"Nothing, told him to take his damn drinks back and I think I said your last name. Shit— I'm sorry."

"Don't worry about it. You didn't mention anything about what I did for a living, where I come from. How'd he know I was in Iraq?"

Paula rolled her eyes. "Not hard to figure. Look at you. The only thing you're missing is the uniform. You have Marine written all over you. And, guessing your age, I'd say you might have been in Iraq or Afghanistan." She shrugged. "But how am I supposed to know all this?" She asked, annoyed.

Rubbing the tension in his neck, Lev settled closer to Paula. "Missed you."

She smiled and took a sip from the Marnier. "We saw each other yesterday."

"I still missed you." Lev reached into the pocket of his jeans, withdrawing a small box. "Open it."

Her fingers poised on the edge of the table, Paula glanced apologetically to Lev. "You shouldn't be buying me things Lev. You hardly know me."

"What I know, I like." He pushed the box closer to her. "It's no big deal, just a little something I thought you'd appreciate."

Paula pulled the top from the box, her eyes widened. "I thought you said it was no big deal. This had to cost a lot, Lev. Now, I really don't want you spending money on me. At least this much."

"Try it on." He pulled the pendant and chain from the box, dangling it in front of her. "I know you like it." He chuckled softly. "When we were talking about sea turtles the other day, you got so mad. I just thought this was appropriate. I knew it was just what you'd like—to wear a sea turtle around your neck."

Paula touched the gold turtle, its shell a collage of fiery blues, greens and rose colors.

"That's Australian opal, pretty, huh?"

Paula nodded. "Yes, it's beautiful. But I really don't wear jewelry."

"That hurts my feelings." He touched her wrist. "Where's the bracelet I gave you? I was sure you'd like that—with the T and I hooking.

It's a Topsail Island bracelet. I thought for sure you'd like that."

Lev stood, the pendant in hand, and placed it around her neck. "This is perfect on you, too. Please accept it."

She rolled her eyes. "I don't know what to say."

"Say, ooh baby and drag me to your boat."

"You're something else." She shook her head. "No, it's too much, Lev, I really can't accept this. I don't even know you that well."

"But you're going to." He held her hand to his chest. "I really like you a lot Paula, I've never met anyone like you, and you're different."

Maybe, she thought, *maybe he will be good for me—keep my mind off of Micah.* Lifting her eyes to meet his she nodded. "Okay, just this and no more. I mean it, no more."

****

"Gass, origin—German, Jewish—Gasse" So the little Lev Gass is a Jew—a German Jew. Wonder if he had family that were in the concentration camps." Theo scanned the computer screen slowly, scrolling down, perusing information about *Gass*.

He scrolled down again and checked the time in the corner of the computer screen. "Damn, it's three o'clock in the morning. I hope Estelle appreciates all this work I'm doing."

"The Arizona Daily Sun." He said the name aloud and leaned closer as he scrolled from one screen to the next. "Gass—Marines—blah, blah—blah—Marine." The photo was of a man who looked to be in his sixties. The resemblance was there. "Must be his father." He gnawed on the thumbnail of his right hand and the skin around it. "Criminal investigation and—neighbor, geez, his neighbor, sure does have a lot to say." He pulled up Facebook and typed in the name.

Chapter Eleven

Don pulled into his parking slot at the police station and walked the stairs leading to the chief's office. He would tell him about Estelle— tell him everything he could involving her. She could say whatever she wanted, tell him about being involved with Sarah and Reggie. Hell, at this point Don didn't give a damn. Regardless of what Estelle told the police or anyone, it came down to his word against hers.

The fact was, there was no evidence linking him to Sarah, to Reggie or anyone else. He would tell things, all things, but he would tell it his way.

Even if Hank deserved what he got, even if the island was better off without him, Don was going to prove that Estelle killed him and that she killed Mindy as well.

"That little girl did not deserve to die," he spat the words as he knocked on the chief's door. Hearing the grunt from the other side, he turned the knob.

"Finally back, huh? Have a nice vacation? You're not getting paid for this one detective. You're lucky it's off-season and the island is dead, not even a shoplifter so far." Chief Moore lowered his head and rolled an unlit cigar from one side of his mouth to the other.

"She killed Hank and she killed Mindy."

"Estelle Butler, Hank's wife? I assume that's who you're talking about."

"Yep, that's her, the bitch."

"Damn hot bitch. You done her yet?" Moore slid a glance to meet Don's eyes.

"Yeah, I did her a couple of months ago."

The chief leaned back in his chair. "I was kidding. You're not."

"I've got a shitload of stuff to tell you. You ready to listen? Want to go for a ride?"

Rising from the chair, Moore pulled on his cap, "I guess we're going in your Dodge."

"Yep. I know it's clean."

Don drove to the end of Old Landing Road, stopping just before the water's edge. He rolled both his and the passenger side windows down and pulled the key from the ignition. He could feel the breeze, laced with the chill winter months always brought.

Breathing in, he perused the sound, it was like glass, the water reflecting the clouds above. White sticks jutting intermittingly from the water marked oysters beds. In the years he'd lived at Topsail, he had seen only a few men out on their flats boats, solitary souls plying long tongs to gather the crustaceans. He'd watched as they maneuvered the tongs and placed the contents on the table built onto the bow of the boat.

He imagined those men had the strength of weight lifters. He marked it in his mind that oystering was one of the things he'd have to try before he left this world.

Sitting quietly a moment longer, letting the calmness the water always brought seep into his bones, Don cleared his throat. Preparing to speak, reassuring himself of the scenario he would paint for the chief. He reminded himself that anything else was his word against Estelle's.

"This is where it all began."

"True confessions?" The chief grunted, lighting what was left of his stale cigar. "Must be serious stuff." He blew a ring of smoke out the window.

"Something like that." Don nodded. "When I was new. I'd been here only a few weeks, maybe a couple of months—" He turned his gaze to the chief. "Seth Milton, remember him? Remember that asshole?"

"Yeah. I remember him. And you're right Milton was an asshole. I was glad to see him leave. He was always cocky and always had a snide know-it-all attitude."

"He got me into this shit, brought me out here one night. Reggie Bourne came motoring up in a skiff, held me at gunpoint, threatened to make me the criminal, unless I started helping out."

Moore leaned back in his seat, listening. He studied Don for a moment. "Milton left not long after you got here. If I remember, you and he were patrolling this area regularly." He bit into his cigar. "So, he held you at gunpoint, huh? Why didn't you come to me?"

Don shrugged. "I was new. Wasn't sure what to do and I was fresh out of the Corps, out of Iraq—sort of confused and wasn't sure if you weren't a part of it, so I went along."

"Idiot. You know I'm going to have to--"

"I'll deny everything," Don started, "but just hear me out first. Look, I know I screwed up. I know I'm shit—was shit. So give me a chance to make this right. I'm telling you, I didn't have much of a choice, they were threatening to hurt my kid."

"That's why you sent him off to military school?"

"Yeah," Don lied.

Rolling the cigar between his lips, Chief Moore scratched his chin and pulled at the loose flesh there. "Where was it Milton said he was going after he retired?"

"Florida."

"Yeah, that's right." He nodded. "Hmm, I remember now, he said he was going to buy a fishing boat and charter tourists out to the Gulf Stream. I think he said something about Fort Pierce."

Searching his memory, Don shook his head. "I know it was Florida, but I don't recall him ever mentioning Fort Pierce. You sure about that?"

Moore nodded as he lobbed the cigar remnant into the water. "Yep, kept yammering on an on, had a couple brochures laying around his desk and I think some guy called about a fishing boat he had been asking about, one he saw on Craigslist." The chief eyed Don curiously. "And you're telling me he was involved with distributing drugs?"

"While I'm getting things off my chest, I'm not really fond of people throwing butts in the water—fish swallow them, fucks up their insides."

"You're telling me about drug deals and murder and now you're worried about the damn fish? Are you sure you're not nuts?"

"Nope, I just like fish."

The chief grunted. "Okay, so what else about Milton?"

"He and Reggie—a shipment came in once a week via Reggie and the skiff, right here. He came from the north. Could have been Sneads Ferry, could have been anywhere along this coast. But since he was only in a skiff, I doubt he was from very far away."

"You never found that out?"

"I didn't want to know. I'm telling you, I didn't want to do this, I was *encouraged*—I guess you might call it."

"Yeah, right."

"Reggie always had a small package with him, maybe the size of a cigar box. They catered to a small clientele—doctors, lawyers and Indian chiefs. The big dogs here on the island. Milton delivered it to Chambers and when he left for Florida I took over his job.

"Sarah distributed the stuff to her *friends*. The little bit she had left over she gave to Reggie who would cut it down and sell it cheap to his buddies. They argued over that all the time. She didn't like him cutting it down and she didn't trust his so called buddies. She called them riffraff."

"So Hank killed Sarah Chambers because she was dealing?"

"No, he had that dick Mick do it."

"The fake English dude."

"That's the one, the weirdo that wore the Hawaiian shirts."

"Yeah—and he killed Bourne too?"

"Yep. Mick did them both and then Hank killed Mick."

"Well, we know how crazy Hank felt about drug dealers. Why didn't he kill you, too?"

"I don't know. I think he understood that I'd been dragged into it. That I wanted out."

"And he killed Sarah and Reggie so you wouldn't have to be a drug dealer anymore." Moore grunted sarcastically. "Nice guy, it all sounds so warm and fuzzy and very convenient for you."

"That's the way it happened, sort of coincidently. I sort of benefited from Hank's murdering and besides, before I ever caught on to him, he and I were buddies, kind of. He took me fishing occasionally."

"Humph, again—pretty convenient."

"It's the truth."

"Sarah and Reggie are both dead, that dick Mick is dead and so is Hank. Anybody who could testify against you is dead."

"Exactly my point. Why would I be telling you all this if I didn't want to?"

"I'm guessing that Estelle knows, that's why. Hank told her. Right? And she's riding you."

"Yes, she brought it up. She says she'll tell you all about me if I don't keep the police off her back. I don't know how she expects me to do that. If you have any suspicions you'd be on her ass, regardless of what I do."

"She's stalling for time." The chief said, pulling another cigar from his pocket.

"That's what I figure. I think she wants E.J."

"Most likely." Chief Moore sucked strongly from the Corona and continued. "As far as we could tell, last year when Hank bit it, she was clean as a whistle. We checked her out."

"But you don't know her. Estelle's out there in la la land, got her own agenda, her own psycho way of doing things. I'm sure she's playing me until she no longer needs me."

"I need evidence." Chief Moore growled.

"Look, I don't have to do this. I could quit, move away. If I lacked the conscience I could have her killed or do it myself. Because I really believe she murdered Hank and Mindy and who knows who else. But I want out of this, I want…"

"I know what you want."

"Then you believe me?"

"I'm not saying that. I'm saying I'm willing to give your side of the story a chance." Chief Moore sucked his teeth. "There is something about her, Estelle. She comes on really strong—too strong." The chief stepped from the car. "Glad I'm a happily married man," he chuckled. "I think she'd wear a normal fellow out. You normal?" He grinned.

"Don't remind me. She's not one of my more shining moments."

"I had my suspicions about Hank from the beginning—her killing him." He kicked at an oyster shell and turned to Don. "But then there were no witnesses, he was full of Dilaudid, he had a prescription for it, and that stuff will knock you on your ass—makes you not care, not feel."

"That's just it. Hank was always clean as hell. He hated drugs—remember? That's why Sarah's dead—and Reggie and that weirdo Mick. He absolutely hated hard drugs."

Pulling the cigar smoke into his lungs, Chief Moore began, "I didn't like it down here when I first came. My wife nagged me in to taking the job. I was working in Chicago, got shot and she said it was either me or the job."

"You must love her."

"Yep, she's a good woman." He held the cigar between his thumb and forefinger, rolling it slowly, watching the gray smoke coil in the air. "I've come to like this place. It's small, and I used to think the people were rubes." His lips wrapped around the Corona again. "But that's not true, it's quite the opposite. I like them, I'm glad my wife talked me into coming here." He walked back to the car. "There's good people here."

Don nodded. "Yeah."

"The Dilaudid Hank had was prescription. He had bottles of the stuff, legal, it wasn't like he was buying heroine or crack from a dealer. He was getting this stuff from the pharmacy."

"Hank would have never taken anything like that. Believe me. Estelle has someway of getting the stuff."

"The script said some doctor in Kentucky."

"She used to be a LCSW for the state of Kentucky." Don said.

"Counselors can't write scripts."

"Did you check out the doctor who wrote the prescription?"

"He's clean. Had a file on Hank and everything," Moore answered.

"We need to take a closer look at this doctor. Somehow he's supplying her. More than likely she got Hank hooked on the stuff,

122

and he ended up not knowing whether he was coming or going."

"Of course, you know she did us a favor."

Rolling his eyes, Don leaned against the Dodge. "Everybody is glad Hank's dead. But I'm telling you, he was really fucked up, he didn't know if he was coming or going."

"Shitty place to be." Moore sucked the cigar loudly. "He called Estelle, Essa, right?"

"Yeah."

"His dead wife was Emma."

"Yeah. Pretty close, wouldn't you say?"

"I think she was working him, turning herself into Emma. E.J. mentioned she heard him call Estelle, Emma, one time, that time she went to New Bern. In his condition, if he was being doped, he wouldn't be hard to manipulate. You know he was over the edge for his dead wife."

"That's what I heard."

Don nodded. "Poor slob, there are parts of his life that I feel sympathy for. If he'd gotten some help or—"

"If frogs had tails they wouldn't bump their asses." The chief grunted.

Don chuckled, "Okay then, it's settled. You're going to give me some time to figure this out. I'll get Estelle and I'll prove she's a killer." He raised an eyebrow, "I have my suspicions that Hank is not her first. I want to go back to New Bern and Beaufort and do a little snooping around."

"I'll keep a tail on her and that string bean she has staying with her," Chief Moore said. "Do you know anything about him? Is he doing her?"

"I've got no idea. This is the first I've heard anything about it."

"Some fellow showed up a few days ago. Lev didn't mention anything to you about it?"

"I've been out of town."

"There are phones."

Don shook his head. "No, Lev never mentioned a thing to me. If I know him, he knows all about the dude by now and either there's nothing there or he figures he can handle whatever there is by himself. I'll ask him about it."

"Do that. So when are you leaving for Beaufort? Or is it New Bern?"

"Smack dab in the middle."

"Umm."

"I'll leave in a day or two. And you're going to give me time--"

"Two weeks, that's what you get to find something concrete, something we can work with, before I start wondering about your motives."

"Why don't you have a talk with E.J. Rosell? I bet she knows a lot more than she thinks she does. That old woman is a fountain of knowledge when it comes to just about anything around here."

"I'll look into it."

"I believe Estelle meant to kill her the night Mindy was murdered."

"Haven't we established that?" The chief grunted.

"Have we? I don't see anybody doing anything about it." Don clenched his jaw, grinding his teeth. "Estelle mistook that girl, all bundled up in E.J.'s afghan and hat, for her. I don't think Estelle kills for the fun of it, I think she has a motive and the motive is money or stuff, something she thinks she needs and wants. She feels justified in killing her victims. Mindy had nothing for her, but remember, E.J.'s daughter, Emma, left her property in her will. Stuff that would have gone to Estelle. Estelle wants it. She thinks it belongs to her. Hell, it was nearly a third of Hank's estate."

"Someone told me they saw Estelle at one of the towers a few weeks back. I assume that was Hank's."

"Yes, he owned a tower. Now, I wonder what in the hell she is planning to do with that."

"Tear it down?"

"No, the word around town is that she's going to renovate it to 1940s, make it look like it did in the day."

"Why in the hell does she want to do that?" Chief Moore scowled again, biting into his cigar.

Pulling himself to sit on the hood of the Charger, Don laughed. "I think it has something to do with not feeling like she's trash anymore. Yeah, she's all about the money, but our murderess wants respect. She wants to be accepted. At least that's what I got from her the night I was doing things I shouldn't have." He faced the chief. "That's one sick puppy. She thinks she can buy her way into being one of the big dogs around here."

"That's why you think she's overhauling the place?"

"She knows how the locals and other long time visitors feel about them—not that she gives a damn about what they think or even the

125

towers. She wants to get in their good graces." Don pursed his lips, gathering his thoughts. "Sometime before the tower renovation is finished, she's going to kill E.J. or try to, you know, get her out of the way."

"Not if I have anything to do with it. I like that old woman. Reminds me of my Momma."

"You had one?" Don scoffed.

Chief Moore studied Don for a moment, he nodded his head. "You have a pretty good bead on Estelle, stick around, call who ever it is in New Bern you need to talk to."

Don grinned, "No, I need to go there. The V-girls aren't going to say anything over the phone. It's a vanity thing to them, they like an audience face to face." He chuckled. "Sometime you're going to have to meet these chicks."

"Yeah, I've heard about their show, must be a laugh a minute." The chief cleared his throat. "Regardless, if you don't come up with something in two weeks, I won't give a damn about anybody's vanity."

Chapter Twelve

"I'm here. You asked me to meet you here, so tell me what this fabulous thing is you want me to see?" Paula shut the door to her Camaro, stood and studied the line of vehicles at the marina parking lot. She caught a breath as she spied Micah's yellow Hummer. Her eyes scanned the marina, hoping to catch sight of him.

"You can make payments." She heard Lev say as he reached for her hand and tugged, drawing her to the slip where a weathered but sturdy forty-foot Holland fishing boat was moored. "It's for you."

"What do you mean, for me?"

"The boat is for you and knowing you, you won't take it as a gift, so you can make payments on it." Lev's grin spread across his face, his eyes beamed as he drew Paula to him. She pulled away, her eyes once again scanning the marina for Micah.

"I did a lot of work trying to find out just what kind of boat to get you." He took her chin in his hand, turning her face to his. "This is the best, I know, I asked around."

"You're nuts. People don't go around buying other people boats. And I know about my boat, the one you overpaid me for. There was no buyer, you lied to me. I hate that."

"It's no biggie, Paula. I'll find a buyer. In the mean time, I have a couple of friends that are enjoying it. Don took Carrie out on it a while back."

"Bullshit."

"I just wanted you to have what you want, what you need, a little sooner than later. What's wrong with that?"

"You should have been up front with me. You're manipulating me. I don't think--"

Lev shook his head. "I'm not manipulating you, not really. Look, you can make small payments or no payments at all. Anything you want. Okay? I set people up in businesses all the time Paula, it's what I do."

She crossed her arms. "You don't get it, do you? You keep the damn boat."

"What in the hell am I going to do with it? You're the fisherman or fisherwoman, whatever—and I bought it for you. You're always saying, 'if I only had a bigger boat.'"

Paula studied the boat. It was just what she needed. At least another ten feet longer than the one she had before. It offered a much longer and broader deck area and a bit more cabin for nights when she wanted to stay aboard.

She turned to scan the lot once again for Micah, she spotted him talking to one of the fisherman at the far end of the marina, his hands gesturing as he spoke.

He turned her way and nodded. Paula felt her face tingle as she struggled to focus attention on Lev, the Holland—her head swimming in confusion.

Why had Lev, this man she hardly knew, bought her a fishing boat? She felt herself anger as she considered her options quickly.

Even the money he'd given her for the old boat wouldn't be half enough to purchase the Holland out right, she'd still owe him probably another thirty-five or forty thousand. Paula's mind raced. Did that mean having to continue a relationship with him? Was he going to expect *things?*

She had learned that when a man gave expensive gifts, he always wanted something in return—always. Whether it was for her to look the other way, to dismiss certain things or to allow certain favors, whatever, accepting gifts usually meant there was going to be some kind of price to pay, eventually.

Lev's eyes twinkled, his lips curved in a perpetual smile as he talked about how the boat would allow Paula to truly pursue her livelihood. She'd have the potential now to quit the bridge-tending job.

In the mix of her thoughts and Lev's voice she saw Micah turn and begin walking toward her, nervously she blurted, "I can't, that's all there is to it. Now, go away! I won't take something from you and have you expect me to love you for it or fuck you for it."

"Damn, you don't pull any punches do you?"

"No. I don't pull punches. You're not even that crazy about being on the water. You get seasick, remember."

"The Intracoastal works for me."

"This boat was made for open water, Lev." She turned away, angry about the words she knew she had to say. "I can't do it. I can't take something from you--"

"I said you could make payments."

"So what happens when we aren't *boyfriend and girlfriend* any longer?"

"Maybe--"

"Doing this makes it even more difficult. I'll always feel like I owe you."

"Don't be silly."

"Don't be silly? Shit Lev, you can't buy people—my affection. This makes me resent you for thinking maybe you can."

"Hey, just because I want to help you out—it would be a business deal."

"It would be business if we weren't, you know—screwing."

Lev smiled and shrugged.

"You're just so flippant about it."

He stuffed his hands in his pockets. "Look, I like you a lot—maybe even more."

"You don't know me. You just like the *idea* of me."

He looked stunned by the accusation and stood motionless as Paula continued.

"Who turns down a boat?" Lev asked.

Paula rolled her eyes again, adding a frustrated sigh. "Get serious, Lev. Your reputation, the way you flirt with everyone, the girls drool over you and for the life of me I don't understand why."

"Ouch."

"Sorry, I know you're Mr. Personality, you like schmoozing and you're good at it and to be honest I never understood your interest in me."

"You're dif--"

"Oh, don't start with *I'm different*. I know I'm different, before long you'd get tired of how different I am. You're used to a *different* kind of

130

woman and I can't and won't compete with other women."

She crossed her arms over her chest. "I won't lie and say I don't appreciate the attention. But in all honesty, Lev, I don't love you. And I don't think I ever will."

Paula watched the teasing smirk on his face droop, his chin drop against his chest. Instantly she felt remorse for her words. "I like you a lot. The intimacy is…nice but I've seen you in action, I've seen--"

"Forget it!" Lev turned and walked toward his car. He pulled out of the marina, gravel flying as he sped down the exit.

Paula watched, still confused, hurt in a way for having to be cruel. She stood numb, oblivious to the call of her name.

"Hey! I've been yelling at you. You didn't even hear me. What's up?" Micah called as he walked toward her. "I heard there was a nice fishing boat docked here. I had to take a look at that." He touched her shoulder as he passed to view the boat. "Damn that's a fine looking vessel." He eyed the Holland, pulled on a line to bring the boat closer to the floating dock and rubbed a hand along the gunwale lines. "This is mighty nice, just what you need." He walked toward Paula, a broad grin stretched across his face.

"It's not mine."

"What? It's all over town that your boyfriend bought this for you, that's why I drove over— had to take a look at it."

"He's not my boyfriend and I don't love him."

"Okay." His eyes stared into hers. "But I could never give you anything like this." His hand slid across her shoulders. "Paula, you don't need to pass something like this up." He leaned down to kiss her forehead. "Obviously this man is crazy about you and so what if you don't love him. Maybe you try?"

"He's not what I want, he can't offer me what I want."

"It's a damn nice boat, Paula."

Standing stoically, Paula held her breath, fighting the hurt and tears she knew would fall so easily later. Why couldn't she just roll with it, continue seeing Lev, sleep with Micah when he came to town. Then she could have her cake and eat it, too. She turned to Micah angrily. "I don't need you to tell me what I need in my life."

"I'm sorry." His arm around her shoulder, Micah pulled Paula next to him. "If you don't love him, you don't love him and that's all there is to it. Right?"

She nodded.

Micah's hand traced from her shoulders and rested at her waist. "Been a long time Paula, want to talk about it."

"No."

He kissed her mouth gently. "I'm sorry about last time. I shouldn't have gotten so angry. I know you only want the best for me."

"You're married, Micah."

"That never stopped you, never stopped either one of us before."

He was right about that. And now was just the time when she needed to ache. She had just hurt someone, she was hurting. Why not punish herself, why not pleasure herself, with the only person she loved?

Being with Micah was just too sweet, too perfect. She'd wanted him her whole life and shared so many things together. They times, good and bad, had cultivated understanding into the very heart of who she was. Nobody saw her the way Micah did. She knew that.

Paula glanced in the rear view mirror of her Camaro, Micah drove casually three car lengths behind. She felt her heart racing, anticipating the lovemaking. She pulled down the long dirt path to her home and waited as Micah parked behind her. Clasping hands, fingers intertwined, they rubbed against one another as they entered the home and walked the familiar route to Paula's bedroom.

He was the only one she allowed to see her cry. The only one with whom she felt no restraints. The only one with whom the intimacy was truly lovemaking. There was no one she trusted more, no one who knew her more.

Their intimacy was the best. He was patient, in control, maneuvering her to climax after climax. She saw the pleasure in his eyes drinking in her convulsive responses as he moved within her. Yes, it was worth it. Yes, he filled her so completely. And yes, finally she held him again.

****

"What am I going to do with it now? I can't return the damn thing. What do you say

Carrie—work your magic. That crazy friend of yours turned me down. But I bet she'll work with you. Come on now." Lev teased, even in front of Don, he teased, cajoled, he was certainly a salesman.

"Lev could sell ice to an Eskimo," Don smirked. "Watch out Carrie."

"What do you say? It's a good deal and I know if you have the boat, *Ass on Her Shoulders* will captain it. I think she just needs a buffer between us."

"I don't know anything about running a boat. I don't even have a captain's license." Carrie turned to Don. "I think your friend bit off more than he could chew."

"I think you're right."

"If she won't captain it for you, find someone else. There are plenty of fishermen around here that would jump at the chance to run that boat."

Carrie nodded. "You're right about that, but let me talk to Paula first."

"This might be just the opportunity you've been looking for to get away from working with the public," Don teased.

"Okay, smartass. You have to understand, I know absolutely nothing about boats and fishing. I've only been out a few times with Paula."

"Did you get seasick?"

"Hell no, I have a stomach like an iron skillet."

"Well, this is your chance and mine, too, I think it's a good investment," Lev stressed the words.

"Lev is an entrepreneur. He's owns part of a gift shop in Sneads Ferry." Don spread his hands on the table and slid a glance to his friend. "What is her name?"

"Gladys, I'm just helping her out." Lev shrugged. "I help people out."

"You help women out," Don chided.

"What's wrong with that?" Lev laughed. "Gladys couldn't have done it without me."

"And she was a little appreciative, right?"

Lev sipped from a bottle of water. "So?"

"And there's a girl in Wilmington. What business did she open?"

"An art shop," Lev answered. "She's a very creative chick."

"I bet," Carrie groaned. "No wonder Paula didn't want to go into business with you"

"Those days are over and Paula is different. I've never met anyone so independent, so gutsy—she makes me feel—"

"Are you in love with her?" Carrie asked.

"I'm sure of it. No one has ever made me feel like she does."

Don nudged Carrie's leg under the table and shot her a skeptical glance.

"She'll come around. You get her on that boat, Carrie and you two start pulling in the fish and the money and she'll come around."

"I really don't understand you," Don said. "Your family is loaded; you're loaded. What do you need this for?"

"The challenge. I love seeing something come from nothing."

"First you join the damn Marines, nearly lose your life in Iraq."

He turned to Carrie, "Asshole here has a medal of honor and another medal for bravery. He not only saved my life but two other guys' lives."

"I'm impressed," Carrie nodded.

"Not to mention, Asshole lives off of the crappy pay he gets from his military pension after twenty years of service. Correction, the crappy pay supplements his inheritance or whatever it is he gets every month."

"Dad invested wisely." Lev dropped his eyes, smirked and shrugged.

"I'd say, if you can drop fifty or so thousand for a chick."

"Paula's no *chick*," Carrie and Lev spoke simultaneously.

"Excuse me, for some woman who has shown no sign that you mean anything to her." Don retorted sarcastically.

"She's always been picky," Carrie broke in. "I've only known her a few years but in that time I haven't seen her with anyone at all. And she's a little closed mouth about relationships. The only time she mentioned a man in her life was a couple years ago, seems she had a thing with Hank one time."

"From what I understand Hank had a *thing* for anything in a skirt," Don chortled.

"Paula doesn't talk about her life, she's not a real social person."

"Lots of the local people keep to themselves, you never hear much from them."

"That's because *you* and the rest of the damn transplants don't do anything to become part of the community."

136

"What the hell is that supposed to mean? I fell in love with this place twenty years ago. I'm on your side, Honey. And I'm a damn detective. I'd say I'm part of the community."

"Ever have a beer with any of the locals, ever go to any of the events around town? No, you live here, arrest people, snoop on people and then decide you're too good to share your time with them—to really get to know them. You know, detectives, they're not as stupid and backward as you think. There is an honesty and wisdom here that poets write about and you're too damn arrogant to see it."

"Hey, wait a minute." Don placed his arm on Carrie's shoulders. "I'm with *you*, and you're from around here."

"I don't count. I'm from Florida—gives me a unique perspective."

"Don't fit me into that 'transplant' box with all the rest. I'm nice to everyone," Lev added sarcastically.

"Oh, I just think it's all about getting laid for you, Lev. It doesn't matter where anyone is from for you. And as for Paula, I think the reason you want her is because she doesn't think you walk on water. You're to her what all those other women have been to you over the years—a piece of ass," Carrie chided, and continued, "You're a player. You want women to fall in love with you. You like the attention, it feeds your ego. You don't even consider that you are hurting them, or maybe you don't even care. Nevertheless, it's all about you. Well, Paula didn't fall in love with you, not even when you tried to buy her. I'm pretty sure there's someone else in her life." Carrie blew an exasperated breath from her lips. "Well, I'm not sure, but there's little things I've been noticing."

She looked apologetically at Lev. "Sorry, Lev."

Carrie reached across the table to rest her hand on Lev's. "I think you're a nice guy, I really do, but I don't think Paula is the girl for you. She's not easy to woo, she requires something—well, I don't know. You know what they say about still waters running deep. There's something more to her and if you want her, you have to figure that out."

"She's gutsy," Lev spoke.

"More than that. Paula knows who she is and she knows what she wants." Carrie crossed her arms. "And you know what? She makes me want to be a better woman—to not settle for comfortable." Inhaling a deep breath, Carrie turned to Don, focusing intently on his eyes, searching them. "I think I'm going to do it, take a chance, break out of the rotten routine I've been in."

She looked at Lev. "I'll do the boat thing, for a while anyway. I'll give it a try, see if it's something I like. Hell, it can't be worse than having to put up with customers blaming me for bad food." She raised an eyebrow and smirked.

"And I think you're right, Paula will captain it for me and if she won't I'll find someone else. But this is strictly business and I want provisions written in a contract stating that."

Her lips taut, her brow furrowed, Carrie slammed a hand on the table. "I'm taking a chance, a real chance. You," she pointed to Lev, "have money to fall back on and Paula has family. I don't have a pot to piss in if this thing goes belly up. I'll have to go back to waitressing. I don't even know if I have what it takes to be a fisherman—woman—gal—whatever." She shook her head from side to side. "At least I won't have a bunch of tourists criticizing me."

Don placed his finger aside her chin and moved it to face him. "I like brave women."

"Doing this sounds more like something Mindy would do than me," Carrie sighed.

"I don't know." Don looked to Lev. "Mindy, hmm, that reminds me. She's the one we have to establish as Estelle's first victim. Hank will be harder to prove." Don's interest and gaze shifted to Lev.

"What was Estelle's last name before she married Hank?" Lev asked.

"Reardon," Carrie interjected.

"How appropriate is that," Lev chuckled. "I mean, her ass--"

"Okay, you two are going to talk shop, and I know how you talk, so I'm out of here." She stood, leaned to kiss Don deeply, to run a hand along the inner side of his thigh. "See you later, baby." He watched her move through the glass doors.

"Damn. You're a lucky man," Lev said.

"I know. Maybe I'll get a reprieve."

Lev tilted his head questioningly.

"I got a chance with Carrie."

"You didn't tell her about screwing witchy woman did you?"

"No. But how in the hell did you know?"

"I wasn't sure, but—well, now I am. I figured you might be getting some when you were in

139

New Bern, you certainly had the opportunity. But that night at the restaurant when we all went out and Estelle came by to take the order, she was coming on strong, man, I could feel the mojo. And then you sort of disappeared after we finished eating, sort of rushed us out of there. Paula said you dropped Carrie off, didn't stay with her. I was right, huh? Is Estelle good? Hell, what am I asking for? Of course she is. I can look at her and tell that."

"I guess it all depends on what you call good."

Lev sighed heavily. "So what's next?"

"I'm leaving for New Bern tomorrow, I have to find out a little more about Estelle. She's up to something. Vera might be able to help me out and the V-girls." He laughed.

"Oh yeah, the V-girls. That should be fun. I don't envy you though, they're crazy as loons."

Don shrugged. "I can handle them. I probably won't be up there too long, should be easy getting what I need. It may give me something to work with. You know, I'm Estelle's pet project now."

"How's Carrie handling that?"

"No need for her to know, and I want to wrap things up before Estelle has a chance to cause any more damage."

"Be careful, Don. Estelle will do whatever it takes to get what she wants. She'll either tell Carrie about you boning her or worse—that woman kills people when she doesn't like them."

"You're not telling me anything I don't know. But I have to find things out. I have to have her put away where she can't kill anymore."

"Remember Peterson?"

"Yeah, but I don't want to go there."

"He'd take care of things for you. I know where he's at."

"Don't tell me. And how the hell are you privy to his whereabouts? You haven't--"

"No, I've never needed him. But Dad says he's around if I do."

"He was with you in Iraq, huh?"

Lev nodded. "Yep, right there by my side practically the whole time."

"Are you and he buddies?"

Lev laughed. "Hardly, I don't think I've ever had a conversation with him. He pretty much does what my father asks and doesn't get involved."

"How did your father manage to get him in your platoon?"

"Don't ask, don't tell. Pop has all kinds of friends. Why do you think I took my mother's name? It was the only way I could join."

"He's just looking out for his little boy," Don teased.

"Screw you."

"So," Don drummed his fingers on the tabletop. "I hear you had a visitor the other day."

"News travels fast."

"You should have mentioned it."

"Paula told Carrie, Carrie told you. You see, women are always women, they can't keep a secret. I told Paula it was no big deal, told her not to tell anyone."

"Paula is one of the straightest arrows you'll find, when it comes to the law and one of the most loyal people you'll ever meet. She's not going to let some shyster rummage around for information on a cop and say nothing about it. She told Carrie to tell me. I'm your back, other than Peterson. You have to tell me shit like this."

"Paula is a straight arrow, huh?"

"The straightest."

"So who was this guy that came to see you at the bar? Paula said he was tall, over six foot, skinny, had a little paunch."

"Compared to me he would be gaunt. Tried to pass himself off as a vet. Really pissed me off. He had girl's hands, soft and dainty, made me want to puke."

"What do you think he was looking for?"

Shrugging, Lev continued, "I'm not sure. But he's probably been on the net checking me out. If he's any good he knows by now who my daddy is."

"Moore says Estelle has someone living with her. Sounds like he could be the same guy who visited you. You say tall, thin, walks kind of slumped at the shoulders?"

"What color hair?"

"More gray than anything," Lev paused, "and wide set eyes, brown. Yeah, they looked brown, maybe amber. I couldn't tell in the light. Nervous as hell, though. I don't think he does this kind of thing very often."

"Was he coming on to Paula?"

"I guess, she could have blown him off, but she's dumb about men, how to handle them."

"Already a slight towards Paula. And I thought it was *true love*," Don joked.

"Screw my cat, bastard."

"Eat shit," Don retorted.

"You just watch, after a few weeks of dragging in the dough on that boat, she'll be falling in love with me. You just watch."

"Uh huh. Now, let's assume that the guy that visited you and Paula and the one living with the Estelle are one and the same. Why is he staying with her?"

"Support," Lev spoke.

"Support for what?"

"Finding out info without her having to get her hands dirty."

"Who does she need info on?"

"There's me, you, Paula, Carrie."

"Why does she need info on the girls?"

"A way to get to you or me."

"She already knows Carrie. She already has shit on me. She told me so the night I was over there. She knew about Maggie, my ex—about Phil. And then there was all the crap about Sarah and Reggie and the damn drugs. She knows everything on me. Remember she's sort of blackmailing me to protect her. But I don't buy that. She's buying time. That's what all this protection bullshit is about."

"Buying time for what?"

"Estelle is all about what she can get out of or from people. She's fishing. Hell, she's a better fisherman than Paula ever thought of being when it comes to dirt. She's looking for the next victim to set her hook in—to reel in. And she's got whatever his name is, Graves, John Graves, there because he can offer her something, even if it is some kind of service."

"Stud?" Lev guffawed.

"Who knows? But I doubt it. I don't see her as being with nervous types, and he comes off really nervous, less than confident. She likes John Wayne, a forceful man, a challenge. Then she's going to find his weak spot."

"She found yours, I assume."

"I'm different, her time to use me is limited. My guess is she'll find a way to knock me off or just leave me in her wake. She's using me for time, like I said. She's after the rest of Hank's assets. E.J. has them. Even if Estelle really doesn't want them, she'll be damned if anyone else will."

"So we need to be keeping an eye on that old woman."

"The chief's on it. And I'm going to see if I can talk her into leaving town for a bit. Have her take a little trip up north or somewhere. And we need to know just exactly who John Graves is, if that is what his name is. I have a feeling that it's not."

Chapter Thirteen

Chief Moore had told him to simply give the girls a call, he didn't need to drive all the way to New Bern. But the chief didn't understand the dynamic between the women. The V-girls were totally off the wall and one needed to play their game to get information, needed to crawl into their little world of daytime drama to get the real scoop.

Surely Vera would be easier to gather info from, as long as she was clean and sober, as long as she was walking the path he'd left her on.

He hadn't heard from her since leaving New Bern, but then he hadn't left a number or indicated in anyway that they needed to keep in touch. My god, he hoped she would never call him, despite the fact that he wished her well in her sobriety and her new found life of educating herself to another level.

As for E.J., he was glad she was leaving. She had jumped at the thought of getting out of town for a while. Fate had been living with her, sharing her beach home, having listed his house as a vacation rental property.

Fate liked the idea of getting the hell out of Dodge, at least until all the degenerate crap was over with.

He welcomed the opportunity to take his sweetie to Texas and show her all the places his father used to take him to on visits and vacations. There was history in Texas that sort of called to him, made him lonely for a way of life he'd only heard about from his father—cowboy days, herding cattle from Mexico as a boy, walking across the border to Reynosa for a cabrito tamale.

He'd visited Texas as a boy with his father, Jay, heard the exciting stories of running into Mexico for tequila, rough and tumble episodes with men that still wore guns on their hips. It all sounded so exciting, so other worldly. But he doubted that anyone would be around now, anyone who'd remember his father and family. Still it would be fun exploring those lost days.

A camper was the only way to go. Fate purchased a thirty-foot Prowler and he and Emma Jewel left the island heading southwest. Maybe they'd take in a little of the Florida panhandle, gamble a little at Biloxi and stop at New Orleans on the way down to south Texas. He knew just the spots where he'd like to go—Padre Island, then around Donna, maybe Zapata or as far west as Big Bend. Oh, the places he'd love to go. "How long do you need us to be gone?" he had asked.

"I hope we have this thing wrapped up in a couple of months, just to be on the safe side," Don had replied. "You wait though, till I give you a call."

"I don't need anymore bullshit, nobody trying to take what life I have left from me." He thrust an arm around Emma Jewel who nodded in agreement and listened to Don relate his suspicions to the couple.

"I think we might get married down there."

Fate turned to E.J. "You haven't ever been married have you sweetie?"

She shook her head. "Only one I wanted to marry was you and you never asked me."

"I'm asking now."

Don rose to leave, reassuring E.J. that he would keep her place in New Bern neat and clean and that he would "tidy" up the situation on Topsail.

Breathing in the cool afternoon air, Don slid into the Charger, backed out of Emma Jewel's driveway and headed north into Sneads Ferry. He'd be in New Bern in a little over an hour.

As he drove, he wondered about E.J. and Fate—about their pasts. There seemed to be so much water under their bridges, he dare not ask about their stories. He was sure he'd find out at some point just what those two had endured. Anyone who had been involved with Hank Butler and his family had to have a history, a history steeped in southern mystery and charm that he'd seen in movies and read about in books.

He'd seen some of that when he'd been a young Marine and stationed at Lejeune, visiting the island before it was so deep in development. Now, people like himself were overrunning it, trying to get away from cities and the rush and rudeness of places overpopulated.

He was seeing it himself, northerners coming to the quaint island, forcing their ideas, the things they'd known all their lives upon people who lived life close to the earth, a place his kind of people didn't understand. It had taken him a long time to appreciate the simple, less complicated way of life.

He shook his head slowly and thought, *you don't know what you've got until you don't have it anymore. And now that it's gone, people dress up the newness with old nostalgic photographs, antique shops, and other things as if to pay homage, to placate those who remember the old ways, the simpler ways. Old timers frequent Hardee's and other newly built restaurants and reminisce about dead friends and what used to be, trying to make things matter in a world that has passed them by.*

Time, change and hurricanes were changing the island forever. "Now if I had that boat of Lev's I'd be on my way." He paused, reminding himself that there was no running from things any longer. "I'd be out there fishing every damn day I could." He spoke aloud to himself, "Damn if I don't know why Paula wouldn't take the boat Lev offered. I've seen him buy women cars, and the jewelry he's given. Hell, he's got money to burn."

His old man must be loaded but it's none of my business. If he wanted me to know about his family he'd tell me. Can't be anything too reprehensible about his family, everything must be above board or they'd never let him on the police force. Maybe I need to get on the Internet and check out my old friend.

Don's thoughts moved from one subject to another as he drove northward. Since his youthful days in the Marines he'd found Southeast North Carolina captivating, always feeling as if this was his true home, that Pennsylvania had been some sort of dream.

148

PA hadn't been bad. He couldn't complain about his childhood—it was pleasant enough. He had good parents, a hard working father, a stay at home mom, good friends and good times with family and friends. Maybe that was the lie. Maybe he expected his life to be like the one he'd grown up with.

Then, joining the military seemed the right thing to do. He had no idea that life would take such turns, such intensely cruel turns. At times he had wanted to go back home but on leave he'd felt the distance his experiences had cultivated in him. He didn't belong there anymore. Topsail seemed a place to start anew.

Don sighed a breath of regret as he drove, noticing familiar road signs, billboards, houses and businesses as he entered the town of New Bern. It was sleepy at this time of evening. Juniper and magnolia were the only foliage keeping the town from looking gray and barren.

New Bern was a home, a cozy home, not unlike the one he'd left in Pennsylvania. It could have been an alternative course of action, so to speak. But it was Topsail that drew him and Topsail it would be.

As he drove east, through the town, into the countryside toward Beaufort, he noticed the glaring lights of the bar. It had only been a few months since he'd last been there but it seemed a lifetime ago. There had been changes in his life. His priorities had changed, there was Carrie now.

He pulled into the gravel lot and wondered, the engine of his Dodge still purring. *Be funny if the girls were here, if they're still Madonna-ed, loud and obnoxious.* He laughed softly to himself and turned the ignition off.

"Gran Marnier, ginger ale, twist of lime," he told the bartender. That was Lev's drink and he'd enjoyed it when he wasn't sipping a Bud. Tonight seemed like a good night for change.

Leaning against the bar railing, he perused the dimly lit room, booths, tables; they were mostly filled. He found himself disappointed not finding any of the V-girls. The prospect of having to hunt them down, to go to their residence was not an appealing one.

"Humph." He turned to face the bar, studying the rows of hard liquors before the mirrored wall. He sipped from the glass of Marnier and felt the spicy cognac glaze his throat. He watched as the door to the bar opened letting a rush of cool air and loud voices permeate the room.

"I'm telling you, that's his car outside. That faded gray Charger, it's his. I'd know it anywhere. And looky there, if that ain't his scrawny ass sitting at the bar I'm Beyonce's momma."

Vela strode boldly to where Don sat, wrapped an arm around his shoulders, rubbing her breasts against his side. "Honey bunches of men, I swear if you ain't a sight for sore eyes. Sugar, where in the hell have you been all these months? You left without saying good-bye." She stretched her neck and met his face with hers, thrusting her lips on his, her lipsticked mouth sliding against his, her tongue endeavoring to part his lips.

The overwhelming smell of cheap perfume enveloped him, almost making him gag. Don gently pushed the woman a few inches from him, ran a napkin across his mouth and struggled to find clean air, all while still keeping a hand resting on Vela's. "Nice to see you again. You're looking uh, you're looking *good,* like you always did Vela. In fact, you haven't changed a bit." He turned his head to seek breathable air again. "Wow, that's some powerful cologne you're wearing."

"Oh, you like it?"

Don shrugged.

Vela scrunched her nose. "I found it really cheap at the dollar store." She tousled his hair, "Ooh baby, you are looking good. Just like you always did." She stroked Don's hair with her long painted nails, and then ran a fingertip across the edges of his ear. "You didn't even say bye." She whined and leaned in for another kiss.

"Veda, I didn't even see you there." Don rose from the barstool. "You're looking well, too. Haven't changed a bit either."

"I try to keep up with the other half, you know. We are twins, Vela and me." Placing a hand on his shoulder she massaged the muscle and moved her fingers to his armpits. "You're ticklish I bet." Veda moved her fingers near his pits, he pushed them away and she resumed rubbing his shoulders. "You like that don't you, feels good don't it?" She leaned in next to her sister, both of them encouraging him to sit again in the stool, pressing down on his shoulders, both of them hovering, touching him, stoking his shoulders, his arms, legs—"Ooh honey, sugar, sweetie pie, lover boy."

He felt as if friendly witches were working a spell on him. He felt smothered in cheap perfume and feathery boas, teased hair and boobs, all pressed to his face.

"Okay, okay," he gasped for air. "You two were always so friendly, and I appreciate that, but—"

"There's always a 'but' isn't there, sister?" Vela ruffled her lips.

"And what a nice butt it is." Veda grabbed at his.

"Yep. This one never would take us up on anything. He was sweet on Vera." Veda twisted a long puce fingernail into his bicep, it hurt. "You left her high and dry, good buddy. I don't know what you did to her but ever since you left she's been a different woman. I ain't never seen her like she's been acting in the last few months, she's changed, and I don't think for the good, she hardly has anything to do with us since you left."

He wondered if Vera had gotten off the wagon, was back to her old ways, drinking her self to sleep. Pining over some man. Was it still Hank? He wondered. He hoped it wasn't himself. *No, that wasn't possible. He'd told her about Carrie, exaggerated a relationship with her. Yes, he'd told her he had a girl back home, made sure there was no door left open and he'd surely made no moves on her, he'd always rebuked any advances she'd made. And by the time he'd left he was sure there was an understanding that they were friends, just friends, but you know women,* he told himself, *you're nice to them and they think they're in love.* He rolled his eyes.

"And what's that all about?" Vela snorted. "I saw you roll your eyes." She looked to Veda. "See, he's like he always was, a little snooty—too snooty."

"No, no." Don searched his head for an explanation. "I was just thinking about Vera, has she quit school?"

Vela stepped back, eying Don curiously. "Vera's met her a man at the college. He goes to those AA meetings with her, too. She's all uppity and acting like her shit don't stink."

"But you said she's been acting differently since I left." The words fell too quickly from his mouth.

Vela turned to her sister. "There you go Veda, just like a man, thinks the world revolves around him, like no woman can take a breath, lest she's taking his air."

Veda razed her tongue at him. "You're all up in yourself, always was, didn't fool me none." She held the feathery pink boa, her fingers stoking it lengthwise, draping it across her neck. "Vera is still at that damn community school—college, whatever you call it. And she's seeing that guy, one of the teachers out there. She thinks she's hot shit now. She and him drive around in his little sports car, a pooh joe—something like that. He putts from here to Beaufort and back all the time with our big sister."

It sounded good, good for Vera, and Don relaxed into feeling that his old cohort had settled into some modicum of normalcy. He had wished her the best, recognizing the downward spiral one could get lost in—one that sometimes you needed jolted out of before living life for something better.

If she had a man in her life, well, that was a good thing too. He just hoped it was someone who wouldn't take advantage of her. Maybe he was well off enough to offer Vera a better life. Or at least show her that there were other ways of living.

He nodded to the twins. "Sounds like Vera is doing alright. Hope you two are also." He sipped from his drink. "Glad to see you girls are happy as ever." He had no intention of the statement sounding sarcastic but nonetheless that is how the women took it.

"La-ti-da, always saying something smart. Well, Mr. Don, you look just as happy as ever too." The women turned their heads, swishing the boas around their necks. In unison they chimed, "See ya, wouldn't want to be ya."

Don chuckled, those two were characters straight out of someone's book, reinforcing each other to live in a world they'd created. He called a hearty, "nice to see you again and take care of yourselves" after them and headed for the door.

He drove slowly down the oyster shell driveway of E.J. Rosell's New Bern cottage, it looked deserted. With winter having settled in, leaves had gathered around the walkways, a few stray pieces of trash had blown into the mix. He flipped the collar of his jacket up, there was always a rawness to the winter weather when by the water—the coldness seemed to go right through you.

He was grateful to Emma Jewel for the use of the house and he told her he'd only be using it for a couple of weeks. He hoped that was all it would take to gather the information he needed about Estelle from Vera and her sisters.

****

The light switch was right inside the door, but lower than he expected. Don fumbled searching for it then adjusted his eyes to the dimness; the ceiling lamp needed a couple more bulbs. He walked into the living room and switched on a table lamp, then another. The room lit up to a cozy display of oversized chairs. A faded mauve colored sofa with a multicolored afghan draped across the back sat against the far wall. An oblong cypress knee coffee table with matching end tables parenthesized it. "Now that's something you can't buy anymore." He muttered and padded to the largest of the three bedrooms.

A great iron bed, painted white, stretched its head high toward the ceiling. Don pressed a hand on the firm mattress. "This will do just fine." Already his back felt better, even at the thought of stretching out on it.

Scanning the room he found the closet door, opened it and retrieved a large zip lock bag of bed linens and two more bags of pillows. Off from the closet another door led to a half bath. On a small table, also in zip lock bags, were towels and washcloths.

An older home, and one not utilized very often, E.J. had left the place clean and neat if not up to date on all the latest electronics. The house phone was rotary, the television set was the old box style. The kitchen appliances were at least thirty years old—proof that older machines were built to last.

Don opened a cabinet door above the sink and found old jelly glasses with Bugs Bunny and Daffy Duck staring back at him. He chuckled, recalling how his grandmother had collected the very same Welch's Jelly glasses when he was a boy.

This wouldn't be a bad place to retire to— out here in the boondocks where no one can bother you. He grabbed a beer from the six-pack he'd bought at the little convenience store on the drive down and walked outside following the wooden dock leading to the small pier stretching out into the sound.

Leaning against the railing he rubbed his fingers over the wood worn smooth with time. In the distance he saw the lights of a shrimp boat making its way to the inlet and ocean. It glided silently under a sparsely stared sky.

Running a hand farther along the railings he relaxed into the silken darkness and near quiet of only the rustling of reeds made by marsh life scuttling about at night. Whatever creatures entwined with that darkness, their surreptitious murmurings were calming.

Don sipped slowly from the bottle of Bud and leaned to look over the side of the pier. A dim reflection looked back, he smiled at it and sauntered back to the house and bed.

Morning could have come later but the giggling and banging on the door woke him to frenzied alertness. He grabbed at his jeans and hollered, "What the hell do you want?"

"Sweet cheeks, we thought you might be here."

"And we were right. Honey, you need to either get another car or paint that poor thing. It's bum fugly."

More tittering and door banging ensued as Don struggled with his jeans.

"Oh no," he groaned. "How in the hell am I going to get rid of them?" Barefoot, he walked to the back door, inching it open.

The girls still wore the outdated attire from the night before. "Don't you ladies ever sleep?" He questioned politely, remembering that Vela and Veda were the type who sought retribution when feeling slighted. He'd try the girlfriend excuse again, that always worked with women, they always seemed to sympathize with one another when it came to matters of the heart. "Look, I'm sorry but I promised my girlfriend I'd give her a call at--" he looked quickly at the sky to estimate the time, "eight o'clock. I'd love to chat but--"

Vela pulled the sleeve of her sweater above her wrist, exposing an old style Swatch. "Honey, it's fifteen minutes after eight. You better get on that phone."

Both girls stepped closer, Don held the door firm.

"I'm sorry but I really don't have time. Maybe we could meet for lunch or something."

"We just wanted to apologize for being rude last night."

"Yeah, we talked about it and talked about it and decided that maybe we were too—uh--"

157

"Came on too strong. You know, with you having a girlfriend back at Topsail."

"We'd like to meet her some day," Vela grinned, showing her teeth. "You know, I always like to see somebody in love."

"We wondered, too, if you'd seen or heard anything from our cousin Estelle. We haven't seen her in months."

Don shook his head no.

"We were over by her old place, that little house that dead man left her. I know she's been back there since last summer, 'cause that Bug of hers has been moved."

"Really?" Don asked casually.

"Yeah, it's parked farther away from the house than it was."

"We were just wondering if she might want to sell it or even give it to a couple of relatives." The girls laughed in unison.

Vela batted her lashes. "If she didn't want too much, I'd really like to have it."

"It needs lots of fixing up, you know, with the busted lights and bumpers," Veda added. "Looks like my cousin took a baseball bat to it."

"Won't be the first time she's done something like that," Vela giggled.

"Yeah, she has one kinda bad temper."

He tried picturing the Volkswagen from the last time he'd been at Estelle's. It was damaged but not to the extent the girls were describing.

"No, Vela—Veda, I haven't seen Estelle but if I do, I'll be sure to pass on the information."

The twins took another step toward the door. "Would you like us to make you breakfast?"

158

Don pressed his body against the door. "No, no thank you. I'm fine. My girlfriend packed a really nice bunch of apples and pop tarts for me." He knew it sounded lame. But they seemed to bite.

They giggled again, blowing kisses as they walked toward their vehicle.

"How in the world, why in the world?" He shook his head. "Out of the eighties? Fifties? Gaga—gag, gag," he snickered. He shook his head again. "Watching too many reruns of Miami Vice or Baywatch—or Designing Women—too much T.V."

"The Bug—I'll have to take a better look at that. Thanks girls." He smiled and padded back to bed.

Chapter Fourteen

"Shit, hell, damn, son of a bitch!" Estelle launched a glass across the living room, it shattered upon impact with the wall. Another slew of curse words flew from her mouth as this time an asparagus fern flew across the room.

"Why didn't anyone tell me?" She screamed, the veins in her neck popping forward. "Why didn't you tell me, Theo? I had to find out on my own at that bumpkin's gas station. That raggedy ass clerk said he'd gone to Texas with Emma Jewel! What kind of shit is that? She's supposed to be here!" Estelle scowled sharply at Theo. "What did I tell you to do when I went to Ken—New Bern? I told you to check up on people."

"You told me to check up on those four— Lev, Carrie and the others. You never said anything about Emma Jewel or Fate. Now, you can't blame me for that."

"Well, who am I supposed to blame? It's not *my* fault." She stood, hands on hips, glaring angrily at him. "See, like I'm always saying, you can't think for yourself. Now, take me, if someone asked me to check out the locals, I would have checked out as many people as I could have." Estelle swiped the magazines from the coffee table, picked a few up and began tearing pages.

"Calm down Estelle, you're out of control, you're destroying the place."

"Shit, damn, hell, fuck everybody, I hate everybody and *you,* you are the most stupid person I have ever known." She stopped for a moment, her mouth pursing, she slid her eyes toward Theo and hissed, "That's why you haven't heard from your darling Emily. She finally found out how damn stupid you are. She finally discovered—and *she's* not the sharpest tool in the shed either—that you are worthless, dumb, and no good. What in the hell would a girl like her want to do with a screw up like you? That's where she's gone, Theo. She's gone *away,* far *away* from you. She's probably with someone else right now, a real man, someone with some guts, not some dumbass chicken farmer. You can call her all you want, but she ain't going to call you back. She ain't going to marry you. She doesn't want anything to do with your sorry ass."

Slumping into a nearby chair, Theo bit into his bottom lip. He drew a finger to his mouth and bit the surrounding skin, then held his face in his hands, his shoulders jerking as he sobbed.

Estelle heard the sobs, they annoyed her even more and she wanted to shout more cruel things to him. She wanted to hurt him. She wanted to tell him how she'd killed his beloved fiancée, how she'd lulled her into oblivion with an éclair, how she'd tricked her into liking her and finally how she'd disposed of the plump lump of nothing. That part of disposing of the little mouse had been delicious.

Rather, she screamed, "Because of you, E.J. has left town! I need her here!"

His face red from sobbing, Theo asked, "Why would E.J. leave town because of me? I don't even know her." He wiped his face with his shirtsleeve. "And why is it so important that she is gone? What does it matter whether or not she goes on vacation?"

"Stupid, you don't understand!" Estelle shouted again. "E.J. is Hank's mother-in-law. Don't you understand?"

"Why does that matter?" He asked again.

Her face hot, aching from screaming, Estelle scrambled to untangle the mess of lies—killing Emily, going to Kentucky, the time frame, how she wanted what Hank had left Emma Jewel. It was all a jumble.

Stalling for more time to sort it out, she flung another barrage of criticisms at Theo, berating him over and over. She watched him cringe, wipe tears from his eyes, avoided her gaze— her words like sharpened spears cast into his flesh—then finally the story came together, she presented her best plausible excuse: "Emma Jewel and I were very close before Hank died. She blamed me for his suicide and said I wasn't a good wife. She went to an attorney, you know, those good old boy attorneys; well, she had him take some of the assets of Hank's estate from me."

"Don't you have enough already, Estelle?" Theo looked questioningly at her.

"Really? That's what you have to say?" She scrambled again for a response. "One of the things she's taken from me is the little house were we buried the little Yorkie Hank bought me last year." Her voice cracked as she choked back a sob. "Oh Theo, it was so cute. It was Hank's gift to me and that old bitch won't even let me go on the property." *Will he buy this one?* She thought.

"I didn't know you liked dogs, Estelle." He wondered how much of what she said was true. He had doubts. Emily had doubts, too. Oh how he wished he could talk to Emily.

"I liked this dog, Theo." She pulled a chair next to him and rested her head on his shoulder, her voice quivered, becoming gentler. "This one was special. It was so cute. And Hank gave it to me." She rubbed Theo's arm. "I'm sorry for cussing at you."

He touched her hand. "I'm sorry for all you've lost. I really am Estelle, but it makes me feel bad when you yell at me like you do. You shouldn't take your anger out on me." Theo patted her hand gently. "You can be so cruel. It's hard to forget all the cruel things you say, Estelle. But I forgive you, at least I want to. Just because you say you're sorry, it doesn't make the hurt go away."

He straightened in the chair, and released his hand from Estelle's. "That's another thing Emily taught me, my problems are mine, not yours. It goes both ways, your problems are not mine. And Estelle, your loss of land is not my problem or my fault."

The heat of anger began to swell again but this time Estelle quelled it before it took control. She inhaled, and then exhaled slowly. The tantrum was over, she had found her composure. But things were not right. They would never be right again. Just as surely as

Theo was sitting next to her, he was just as surely gone. She felt it, knew it. He was lost—lost to her. Emily had taken him and though she was no longer an obstacle she had become a barrier. Theo was lost to her forever. She truly was alone now.

The realization brought doubts of security, of her power over the people who were supposed to love her. It was an uncomfortable feeling, one she did not like.

Estelle mustered her fortitude, fought to diminish the insecurities. She studied the man sitting next to her who should have saved her, should have rejected everyone but her. He was no longer that person. He was just another user, another one to be used, just another bump in the road.

The thought flashed upon her like a blast of cool air. She didn't hate him or love him, she was totally indifferent to him now. The feeling, the acknowledgement had come upon her quickly and adamantly, it was true, but she would wait until the tower was finished before she excused him from her life forever.

"We'll go to the tower tomorrow and you can show me how it's progressed and how much longer it will take. You can tell me what you found out about those locals I asked you about, right now, I'm going to bed, I'm tired."

****

The door closed behind her and the bedroom fell into darkness. Standing there, her body rigid, her eyes shut tightly, Estelle could hear the crashing of the ocean waves across from her home. Her head ached, it pounded, each crash of the waves seemed to make it hurt more. Each crash beat against her temples relentlessly.

Her hands flew to her chest, her fingers grasped the edges of her blouse as she tore it from her body.

Inside she screamed, so loudly the vessels in her head seemed on fire. It was all so unfair.

Theo was supposed to fix the tower, he was not to have anything or anyone else in his life to distract him from his task. Estelle needed all of his attention, all of his love. He had always given it, why had he stopped now?

Emily, damn Emily had gummed up the plan.

Everything was going so smoothly till her. It had gone so smoothly since she'd met Hank— seducing him, introducing him to Dilaudid, their marriage, his suicide. And she had the house, the boat, and the property. She would soon have the respect she longed for—the acceptance and clout that went along with being somebody important. There had been no glitches, no mistakes and no suspicions, except for that goofy Detective Don Belkin.

"Aw, he's a piece of cake. I've got that idiot running scared," Estelle reassured herself.

But Emily, she had disrupted things. *It was supposed to be only Theo and me.* "And then he messed things up with her, telling her bad things about me. Choosing her over me—no, that didn't happen. Did it little mouse?" Estelle snickered.

166

Sitting on the edge of the bed, the room still in darkness, Estelle pulled the jeans from her body and kicked them to a corner. She laid back and rested her head on the pillow. Beginning to relax, she reached for the rest of the pieces of the scenario she'd devised—the ones that had not been obscured by Emily and E.J.

"Emily's gone, out of the picture. Theo will get the tower finished by April. E.J. is out of town, now that makes things difficult. I wanted her out of my hair before the tower was finished. Completing the tower will make everyone forget about some old woman who half of the town doesn't even know exists."

Estelle closed her eyes to the darkness. "One, two, three, four, five, six, seven, eight..." to thirteen. "Thirteen, thirteen little spaces." In front of the lines she imagined the number seven, a large seven and then a noose, a little stick figure. "E.J. is gonna sway," she chuckled. "Thirteen, how fitting—E.J.'s lucky number. We're going to play hangman this time."

Glancing at the ceiling, she scanned from one side to the other. "Hmm, how to? I like the hanging idea. It would be so cool to find her hanging from the rafters of the third floor of the tower."

Her mouth opened wide. "Ha, that would be so cool. Maybe a group of tourists would find her there swinging in the breeze." She laughed again, this time louder and longer and opened her eyes. "Hmm, something more meaningful. Let's see...weren't she and that old bag of bones she's living with sweeties back in the

167

day? Hmm." She tapped her chin. "Maybe I ought to off that bastard just for the fun of it. Him first so she can watch. I'd love to see that old bitch squirm, love to see her beg."

Their images grew in her head, she licked her lips and moved her hand to her thigh, rubbing it gently. "Aw, that would be so damn sweet, her begging for his life, him begging for hers. What do you suppose I could get them to do before I ended it all?"

Chapter Fifteen

"Here's the glass he was drinking out of, Lev. I haven't touched a bit of it. Except for this tiny bit. I can even see his finger prints on it." Troy held a slim fluted beer glass by the bottom high above his head to catch the light. "Yes sir, there's gotta be at least three or four good prints on this glass."

"Thanks Troy." Lev placed the glass in a bag then patted the young man on the shoulder. "Next time he comes to the bar keep an ear open for me, would you? Let me know if he talks to any women. Let me know if you hear anything that sounds—different."

"Yes sir, I sure will." Troy nodded eagerly, stepping through the threshold of Lev's oceanfront home. "Sure have a nice place here. Can I ask how much rent you're paying?"

"None, son. She's all paid for. Got a good deal on this place. The taxes may be out of sight but it's worth it, if only for the view." He eyed the youth, he seemed eager, fresh and curious.

"If you ever need any handy work around here, just give me a call. I 'm pretty good at just about anything. I helped them build a few of those houses over at Magnolia Acres in the Ferry."

"Really? So you're a handyman."

169

"I'm whatever I need to be," Troy laughed. "I'm tending bar 'cause some jerk left a drop cord wrapped around a ladder. I missed it and man—went tumbling down, cracked a rib, broke a couple of fingers on my left hand—my nail banging hand."

"Lefty?"

"Yes sir, but I've had to start using my right and I've gotten pretty good. I'm what you might call ambidextrous—I guess. But I'm good to go now. Just looking to get back on my feet, so to speak and start banging nails again. I'm really good at flooring, setting deck—looking to get into boats, there's lots of money in boats. Thing I learned though was you don't work for people with small boats, they don't have any money. I'll only work on yachts. And maybe if I'm lucky some transient coming through will need someone to tag along on a trip to the Bahamas."

"Sounds like a plan," Lev nodded, recalling his own youth, traveling as much of the world as he could on his own dime. Wanting to do as much as he could—see as much as he could.

He figured Troy was in his early twenties, eager as he was at the same age. "Are you living with your parents?"

"No sir, dad kind of kicked me out. Got mad at me because I won't go to college. Says he wants me to learn how hard life can be without a degree."

"Kicked you out, huh? So I guess you're renting."

"No sir, can't afford rent, I'm saving up for a car. Mine broke down and Dad says he's not fixing it for me until I need it to drive to Wilmington to UNCW."

"Where are you staying then?"

"Here and there, sometimes out on the beach or under the bridge but mostly with friends. That's another reason I'm still tending bar, I need a vehicle to get to construction jobs. But it's getting kind of cold to sleep out in the open, so--"

"You're looking for a place, right?"

"Sort of." Troy kicked at the air, stuffed his hands in his pockets.

"I've got an extra room, it's not much, just a spare room. But I'm with your dad. There aren't any free rides, son."

"Did you go to college?"

"Joined the Marines. There's something you can do. The military offers all kind of trades, you can learn a lot. Then if you want there's always the G.I. bill—you can go to college on that."

"I don't want to go to college. There is no way I could ever be cooped up in a building."

"You're cooped up in a bar."

"That's just until I get myself in shape and like I said, I'm good to go—all healed up and ready to start banging those nails again."

Lev thought of the frustration the young man's father must be feeling. He was sure his old man was frustrated with him not wanting to follow in his footsteps—wanting to make his own way.

Yes, this one wanted to live life on his own terms but then again he had wanted that too and things had not turned out so badly for him.

He'd had a good career in the Marines and now as a detective. Life was good.

"I have a little room, not much, just a bed and dresser. Maybe I'll rent it to you in exchange for doing a few things around here. I've been wanting to have a deck built on the north side of the house—need a few trees planted—a few other things that should keep you busy through the winter." He looked at Troy for a response.

"Sounds like a deal to me." The young man reached to shake Lev's hand. "Yes sir, I won't let you down, I'm a hard worker."

"No loud music, no drugs. Got it?"

"Yes sir."

Chapter Sixteen

"This is it, the last remaining tower on the island that hasn't been turned into someone's private residence." Estelle pulled herself up the concrete skirt of the tower and brushed the sand and grit from her jeans. "So far, so good, Theo. It looks almost like it did back in the day—like those pictures you have. I want--" she paused, her thumb resting on her bottom lip. "I want this place to be a gold mine." Her eyes flashed brilliantly to Theo.

He shuffled his feet on the sandy skirt of the tower. "It's gonna be."

"Have you heard from Emily yet?"

Theo shook his head slowly. "No, I'm worried, it's not like her to not return my calls. I think I should go back home, back to Kentucky and see if I can talk to her."

"Not until you finish this tower," Estelle ordered. "She's probably gotten cold feet, give her some time to think about things. If you rush her, you'll just chase her away." She ran her hands across his shoulders. "It won't be the first time something like that has happened."

"Emily would let me know if something was the matter, I know her."

Brushing against his shoulder, Estelle fixed her gaze directly into Theo's obedient eyes. "You know what they say, 'While the cat's away, the mice will play'—maybe your little mouse got really lonely and found someone else to play with, Theo."

He shot her an angry glance then bowed his head low again.

"Well, enough talk about Emily. Let's move on to business. What did you find out about the four stooges?" Settling her hands on her hips she waited for an answer.

"Carrie has two kids in college, divorced from a lazy drunk. Moved here three or four years ago from Florida. You know where she works, that restaurant. But she's fishing now with the bridge tender lady, Paula. Now that one is going to really surprise you."

"Miss Know-it-all. I don't like her, she walks around like she knows everything. What did you find out about her?"

"Never married. No kids, been seeing that Lev guy for a while—sort of." Theo grinned broadly. "Her great-grandma is in the graveyard—kin to just about everybody around here. Her family lost all their land and holdings in '96 when hurricanes Fran and Bertha came through. She went to UNC Asheville three years and dropped out. Did the hairdresser thing for a while and now she works the bridge and fishes."

"Not much, another loser."

"Aw, but you're going to really enjoy the rest of what I found out about Miss Goody-Goody."

Leaning in, Estelle asked, "What? What nefarious thing could she do?"

"She's shacking up with a married man." Theo waited for the shocked response. It never came. Rather, Estelle's eyes squinted in thought.

174

"Who is he? Anybody important, any of the local bigwigs?"

"He's the daddy to that kid that works at Gerard's. I saw the boy there when I was checking out Paula and Lev."

"Got any dough? Is he one of those locals who had lots of land and sold out?"

"Naw. Not a whole lot. He's only got a house here. And has a couple rentals. But he ain't swimming in it like your husband was."

"What else?"

"He lives in Asheville with the wife. Comes and visits his kid now and then, at least that's what the locals think. Really, he's boinking Paula when he comes here. The kid is living with Lev now."

"How do you know all this?"

"The land stuff I found out at Gerard's. You're right about the locals at the bars, they'll give you an earful and everybody was singing this guy Micah's praises like he was some god or something."

"So how did you find out that he's been doing Paula?"

"I followed her to her place—walked through the woods and saw her drive up and this guy Micah, in a big yellow hummer, pull up behind her. Right from the start they were all over each other and then they went inside for a few hours. "

"And?"

"I looked in the window, they were hot and heavy alright. I heard them talking, too. Paula brought you up, said she didn't trust you, didn't like you and that she didn't like his boy, Troy, living with Lev, because he was a cop and was

175

on to you—said she was afraid his boy could get caught in the crossfire—something like that, pretty close. What's she on to you about, Estelle? What is it that they think you've done?"

"Beats the hell out of me. She probably thinks I'm going to try and seduce Troy or Micah or who knows who else. That woman is as ugly as a turd. I mean, who would want her?"

Theo shrugged.

"Really Theo, who would want someone like that? I bet she smells like fish all the time, too. She's a freaking fisherman! Damn—but you say she warned this man about me, really?" Estelle tilted her head, she licked her mouth. "You never know about people, do you?" She rocked back and forth for a few seconds. "Okay, anything else on the two bitches?"

"Nope, that's about all I could find out. But I sure did get some really juicy stuff on the Lev guy. I had to find out about him online, on my computer. Nobody around here knows anything about him. He kind of keeps to himself, doesn't do a lot with the locals."

"Go on. What did you find out?"

"You'll never guess who his daddy is."

Estelle folded her hands behind her back and leaned against the tower exterior. "Who? Some big general in the Marines?"

"Nope, his daddy is Arizona Senator Buddy Worther. He's a big deal. He's the one owned all that solar stuff." Theo paused, "You know, the Icarusaton Project. The federal government bought into it and it went belly up. The bastard made a mint. And Worther's daddy, Lev's grandpa, was supposedly tied to an arms supplier for some of the dictators that cropped up in the Caribbean back in the fifties and sixties. And it doesn't stop there." A broad smile stretched across his face. "And old Worther's daddy, Lev's great grandpa, was a bootlegger during Prohibition. I'd say it runs in the family—corruption, that is."

"Can't be, can't be the right guy. Lev's last name is Gass."

"That's his momma's name—maiden name—his grandma was one of those German Jews, she escaped Germany back in the 1940s. She divorced Worther and took back her maiden name, Lev took it when he joined the Marines and he's kept it. His mother died in a car wreck when he was a teenager and from all I can figure he doesn't have a whole lot to do with his *daddy* but he gets a big check deposited into his bank account every month. He's Worther's only son."

Estelle steepled her fingers and brought them to her lips. Her eyes narrowed as she turned her face toward the rolling waves.

"And Don, well you know nearly everything about him. Grew up in Brownsville, Pennsylvania. Football star, joined the Marines right out of college, married some girl, Maggie—knocked her up, then got shipped off to war and dumped her when he came back. Of course, she was a meth whore by then. The kid—he finally got custody of but last year he sent him off to military school. The detective is another screwed up piece of work."

Estelle flipped her hand in the air. "I don't give a damn about him, he can be taken care of easily." She stepped closer to Theo. "Lev, he's the one I want to know about—and he's loaded, huh?" She nodded her head. "Shorty—never liked short men. It's that Napoleon thing, you know. Have to prove to everyone just how tough they are."

"He's not short Estelle, he's just not taller than you. Most men are not as tall as you—I'm taller--"

Her eyes glared a familiar vehemence, he'd forgotten not to question her authority. Her mouth pursed as she waited for the apology.

Theo nearly gave it too, except the words wouldn't leave his mouth. His lips held tightly, he met her eyes, "Well, it's true Estelle. Lev is probably an average height and--"

"Well," she interrupted, "nice to see you've taken such an interest in the man."

"You did tell me to find out--"

"And you did." Her lips curling at the corners, her blue eyes focused on the bridge between his, Estelle's voice dropped an octave. "You've done a good job—found out what I needed to know." She moved closer to Theo, extended a leg and rubbed it against his.

He stepped back, her eyes now boring into his. "Estelle, you're upset with me, I can tell. Every time I disagree with you--"

"Don't be silly, Theo. You can think for yourself. I'm sure Emily encourages you to do that all the time."

He nodded. "She's always telling me that—to think for myself. I just wish--"

"Oh, you worry too much. You need to call her again. Maybe she's been with friends or maybe she lost her phone or the battery is

178

dead. You know she's so excited about the wedding and planning for it. Maybe she's just been so busy with that, and forgot to call you. You know how women can be."

Estelle pictured Emily sitting cross-legged on the bed, gorging on the chocolate éclair. Then lying motionless next to her.

He grinned. "Yeah, I shouldn't worry so much."

"No you shouldn't." She stroked his hair. "You did tell her that I was paying for the wedding, didn't you?"

"Uh huh." He smiled again.

"And that you and she can stay here together until the tower is finished."

She had considered finishing Emily in the chicken house, maybe burying her beneath the chicken shit and feed but had decided that was too obvious. The body would eventually be found. No, the hog pen was the best bet. After the hogs finished with the pudgy girl, there would be nothing left. Not even a tooth. Emily's body was surprisingly easy to drag there.

He nodded. "Yes. She liked that."

"The best wedding money can buy, that's what I told you I'd give you and you two can have a room at the house all to yourselves. I want Emily to stay with me a while—if you like, before the wedding. You've done so much for me over the years, it's the least I can do for you." Estelle leaned back against the cement face of the tower and smiled gently. *The cat plays with the mouse.*

She leaned Emily's still breathing body against the sturdy fence, and reached into the pocket of her jeans withdrawing the switch

179

blade. Flipping out the blade, she pulled it across Emily's wrists, watching the blood as it poured into the pen. The hogs raised their fleshy snouts into the air.

Estelle propped the body up higher on the wooden slats of the pen and reached to Emily's neck to pull the blade against the skin. Now the hogs were really snorting and grunting. They moved closer as Estelle pushed it to hang half way across the top railing. It had taken more energy than she'd anticipated but finally she shoved the body over into the pen. She watched as the hogs snorted and grunted, sniffing at the body and the wrists and neck where she'd made the incisions.

Recalling the familiar sounds of hogs slopping, Estelle's lips lifted ever so gently at the corners. She listened to Theo as he spoke about the dead woman, the one that would never stand in between her and Theo again.

"Thank you." She heard Theo whine the words.

"Emily was really excited about coming here and said she'd come in a few days but that was Tuesday and I haven't heard from her since."

"She's probably bragging to her friends about coming to Topsail Island and getting married.'" Laughing, Estelle patted Theo's hand. "I bet she shows up and surprises you. I bet she's just playing with you—keeping you on your toes. Women do that—we like to play games with men."

Theo shook his head. "Emily doesn't play games, she's really doesn't have a lot of friends and she's not one of those girls who goes around bragging. I've really started worrying about her."

"Oh, there you go again, worrying too much." Estelle slid her hand to Theo's shoulder, her fingers trailing to his ear, she rubbed a finger along the edges.

That was something the old Estelle would do, he thought; he fought for a moment to shrug the overt gesture from his mind.

"Call her again this afternoon when we get back to the house. I'm sure she'll answer soon. She'll be here soon and then there'll be the wedding and then I'll pay for your flight back to Kentucky when you finish with the tower—my gift to you and the love of your life. I'm sure you deserve each other."

He winced for a second, the last statement grinding against his better judgment. But Estelle stood so casually against the tower, her face awash in kindness, her eyes caring. "Sounds good, I'll call Emily when we get home." He motioned toward the entrance to the tower and waited for Estelle to lead the way up the stairway to the second floor. "So this used to look like this." He sifted through the manila envelope of photos and handed a couple to Estelle.

Studying his face, Estelle lingered on the droop of his lips and eyes, the upward turn of his brows. *You will never see her again. You'll think she's left you for someone. That will teach you to want someone else. I'll teach you to treat me with respect, I taught that manipulative little whore just what real love is all about. That's what I did, and I did it for you.* She reached for Theo's hand. "Oh Theo, I think we can make this place a real gold mind and do the community some good. They'll appreciate refurbishing this back to what it looked like during the 'Greatest Generation.'" Her eyes twinkled as she took his arm and leaned against him.

"I think it's time I got over my mourning and looked for someone to bring new meaning into my life. Hank was such a drag, you know, Theo? People on drugs are always such drags."

"Got anyone in mind?" he asked.

"That Lev fellow, the one that hangs around Carrie and her group of friends, he sounds interesting."

"I thought he might. What about the height, thought you said he was too short for you."

"Nobody's perfect."

Chapter Seventeen

Of course it had been intentional, Lev thought as he felt the jolt from Estelle's buggy slamming into his. Of course, she would be the one to initiate their meeting one another.

He half grinned as the woman stood before him, her eyes locked into his.

"Sorry I didn't see you there." Estelle moved the buggy to the side of the grocery aisle and searched Lev's eyes wantonly.

He returned the gaze, her eyes lingering for a few moments before trailing the lines of his muscular physique.

Of course it turned him on. Who wouldn't be turned on by a woman as beautiful as Estelle ogling him?

She stood at least three inches taller than him; he could feel a predatory aura emanate from her as he stepped back. "You are a tall drink of water." He teased.

"Thirsty?" She giggled.

"You don't waste any time, do you?"

"Why should I? I know what I want when I see it."

She knows, he thought, *that string bean, Graves or Theo, whatever his name is, did his homework and found out all about me. She's coming on strong this time.* He raised an eyebrow. *What games are we going to play now?* "I'd be happy to buy you a drink if you like. Gerard's is just around the corner."

Lev held the door as she walked into the dimly lit bar, she strode ahead, walking directly to the corner most table and slid into the chair.

"You come here often?" Lev remarked.

"Not really, I just prefer corner tables. They're more intimate, more private, you know. We can talk and get to know each other a little better."

Lev ordered the drinks and watched Estelle stir hers. There was nothing coy or mysterious about this woman. She was all about the sex, all about getting what she so conspicuously wanted. He figured that within the hour he'd be between her legs.

There had been times in the past when her type turned him off. Easy was less fun and sometimes a real turn off. He'd always enjoyed the thrill of the hunt even if it turned out to be a short expedition.

But this time sex was just the prelude to the real game. The thought was exhilarating. He reached a hand to touch her index finger. Lev stroked it slowly. Estelle inhaled a quick breath.

She made it seem like a dream. The kind you have about some movie star with the perfect body, the perfect gestures, the perfect responses and words. It was so unreal—it was surreal. Fucking her would be like doing Angelina Jolie, Charlize Theron or Elizabeth Taylor when she was in her twenties—just once, so you could say you had.

It was going to be fun, damn fun, and in the process he'd find out all he needed to know about Estelle. He'd catch her in her own trap.

He was smarter than her. He knew he had more resources. He'd drag the game out longer and play with her for a while.

Wouldn't it be cool if she fell in love with me? he thought. *I could do that. I've made lots of women fall for me.* He thought of Paula and shrugged. *If she'd played her cards right she'd be sitting debt free in that Holland.*

At least he knew what Estelle wanted, money. And he had plenty of that. It wouldn't be the first time he paid for a piece of ass. One way or another, you paid for everything so the question wasn't if you were going to pay for something, it was whether or not it was worth it.

They had a few drinks, explained a little about their lives—at least what they thought the other would like to hear. Then he invited her to his house, Estelle rose seductively from her seat and reached for his hand.

For the next two weeks they saw each other every day.

Chapter Eighteen

"You knew I'd do this, Lev knew I'd do this." Paula pressed the ignition switch. Diesel fumes filled the air for a few moments. Her old boat had been gas powered. She liked having diesel engines, they used half the fuel.

"I think you really wanted to do this all along. Right? Just not with Lev."

"Yes."

"Okay, I understand why you turned him down. But it would have been a lot easier if you'd just written a contract and made payments."

"I don't want to get involved with him at all. I know what he's up to. I know what he is, Carrie. I'm not stupid. If I took this boat from him in any fashion, things would get too complicated and I don't want to encourage it."

"From what I gather, you've been *involved* with him a few times already—I'd say that's somewhat encouraging."

"Humph, so I've been with him a few times. But I don't have any feelings for him, you know what I mean?"

"Ooh, I never figured you for that kind of person, Paula. So unlike you."

"I guess you really don't know me, Carrie."

"It's not like you to lead people on."

"I never led him on. I just gave him what he wanted—sort of. He wants more. I don't. He wants me to fall for him and that's not going to happen."

Paula worked quietly, untying the lines from the cleats, unplugging the electrical cord from the boat. "Hey, if you want to help out and learn something I wouldn't mind. Here." She tossed a line to Carrie. "This boat is your project, I'm just the captain," Paula snapped.

"Tell me what to do. I'm at a loss here, *captain*."

"Coil the lines so we don't get them wrapped around our feet. Take that gaff over there and set it over here." She pointed to the long pole when she recognized Carrie's puzzled look. "A gaff is for hooking a fish when you think it might be too difficult to pull it into the boat. Also, gaffs are good for grabbing lines."

Carrie followed instructions and waited in between them as Paula maneuvered the boat from its slip into the Intracoastal Waterway.

"Today we're going out about forty miles— the Gulf Stream. It's a good day for it, nice and calm. You need to get used to things and learn what fishing is all about. You might decide that this isn't for you and that perhaps you are better suited for catering to the public."

Damn, Carrie thought, *she is definitely all business when it comes to fishing.* She took another look at her friend and wondered just how well she really did know Paula. At Grocery World, they had been friends, but they'd never engaged in much girl talk or went shopping together. Things women or girls usually do. Paula had always excused herself from those activities.

And if the conversation got too intimate Paula always seemed to steer it in another direction.

"We're going to do some trolling and maybe bottom fish a little on our way back. We'll stop along a reef and see what we can catch. To troll you're going to have to rig the lines with spoons and maybe some ballyhoo or other bait."

"Okay, you're speaking Greek to me now."

"Wait till we get through the inlet and out a mile or so and I'll show you everything. But today we will not have a great catch. Today is for learning, it is fishing 101 for Carrie Adams. But you'll learn how to rig a pole, gaff a fish, reel in a fish in and tie on rigging—among a few things."

"What's the difference between trolling and bottom fishing?" Carrie asked.

"It should be self explanatory. Bottom fishing, you drop a line to the bottom, trolling you *troll* through the water—drag the line through the water."

"I understand that but do you catch different kinds of fish when you're trolling?"

"Yes, bigger fish like bait that is swimming away from it—catch my drift?"

"What's the biggest fish you've ever hooked on a line?"

"Caught a two hundred pound marlin once. But mostly when I'm trolling, I'll catch tuna, albacore, mahi, barracuda, pompano—bottom fishing, it's bass, snapper, grouper, red fish and the last few years we've been getting a few lionfish."

"What are they?" Carrie asked.

"Not a good thing, to tell the truth, but they're here, so we may as well eat the bastards."

"Huh?"

"They're not indigenous, they're from the Indo Pacific area, and they're killing our reefs eating animals and plants. They love shrimp and baby fish—so they're really bad for commercial fishermen."

"What do they look like?"

"Like a lion—pretty—it has spines that look like the mane. But those spines will zap the crap out of you. Make sure you have gloves on when you take the hook out."

"This is just what you needed, a bigger boat. You can go farther—diesel engines too, this is exactly what you need."

"Yes, sure is. Maybe I'll buy it from you someday." Paula grinned.

"The money you got from selling your boat could be a down payment."

"Then I'd be in business with Lev. I thought you said you understood why I don't want to be in business with him?" Paula snapped.

"Gotcha." Carrie nodded. "So Lev did a good job picking out this boat, huh?"

Paula shrugged. "I really don't want to talk about him."

Waiting a few seconds, Carrie asked, "You're seeing someone else, aren't you? That's the real reason you don't want anything to do with Lev."

"If he was the last man on earth I would have nothing to do with him. Understand! He is a user, Carrie. I know the type. Now would you please drop it?"

"Geez you can be a bitch."

Paula continued maneuvering the Holland through the inlet.

"Sorry, I don't mean to pry into your life, but I thought we were friends, Paula."

"We are."

Carrie watched Paula as she steered the boat past the last ICW buoy before entering the ocean, the change was dramatic—from tossing and turning to motoring motionless in the blink of an eye. "Come on now, tell me who about the other guy. I know there is one. Who's the man or the men you're dumping Lev for? There's got to be some love, some good old mushy stuff about your life, woman does not live by fish alone," Carrie teased.

Paula breathed in. "There's only been the one. The only one."

"Lev doesn't rock my boat—never did," she tittered. "He was around when I was lonely, I guess, for lack of a better expression. Lev filled a need when I didn't think—when I was too lonely to think."

"Does this guy live around here?"

"Asheville."

"That's a long way a way. How's that working out?"

Paula studied the GPS and turned southward. "He's in my bones. Does that answer your question? Like this ocean. And I don't think I could breath without what he gives me, even if it's not everything or all the time—is that mushy enough for you?" A stark glare emanated from her eyes as she turned to meet Carrie's. "End of subject."

Most of the ride to the Gulf Stream was made in quiet except for the few instructions Paula offered Carrie in the way of tying lures and attaching bait to hooks. She went over the technical parts of fishing and stressed the importance of always wearing gloves because as Paula warned, "Line speeding through your hands can cut the hell out of them and it's easier to tear a hook out of a glove than your skin."

"When we're trolling I have to maneuver the boat so you will be the one reeling in the lines and taking off the fish. You have to be quick about it or you can lose your catch or lose your pole. My rigs range between three and five hundred dollars per pole—I'll expect it in cash, if you lose one.

"I'm set for six poles, the ones on the transom need to be let out to around seventy five feet, the ones on the sides, around one hundred and the ones farther back, the outriggers, should be around one-twenty-five. I don't want my lines tangled, so when you reel in a fish, throw him in the box and reset your line to the same length as before."

Carrie listened intently, half of what was said flew past her; she knew she was a hands on person—she had to learn by doing. There were going to be mistakes, she just hoped they wouldn't be severe.

The part about lines tangling evoked images of bird's nests in the little reels she'd used when fishing with her parents on the Withlacoochee River in Florida. And the thought of tangling the lines of one of Paula's

192

expensive poles left her feeling confused and doubtful of this new venture she'd fallen into.

What have I done? What have I done? She thought, looking to Paula confidently standing behind the wheel on the flying bridge, her eyes scanning the seas. *What in the hell have I gotten myself into this time?*

Carrie felt so inadequate, so ignorant of this new world she'd tied herself to. In a way it scared her. The newness of it was overwhelming. Now, she felt that perhaps she didn't have the tenacity or physical strength to do the job but she did have the poles rigged having learned to tie a lure—loop at the top, eight times around the strand, then back up to thread the end through the loop and pull. Now she had affixed four poles with spoons and two with ballyhoo. She thought she'd done a pretty good job tying the rigs, making the knots. And she was getting used to handling dead fish, the little ballyhoo, the smell had stopped bothering her and she viewed them as simply bait.

"Let the transom lines go," Paula hollered.

Carrie felt the boat shift to a lower speed, she found her sea legs, balancing herself and letting her body move with the ocean.

Pulling a rod from its holder, she hit the release, line whirred rapidly from the reel.

"Put your thumb over the line, don't let it go so fast, control the flow," Paula hollered again. "Remember—seventy-five feet."

How am I supposed to know how far seventy-five feet is? Carrie thought.

"Okay, that looks good. Flip back the release," Paula hollered once again.

Carrie followed the line of monofilament to where it entered the water. She withdrew the next pole from the transom holder and released the line as she had before, approximating the distance, comparing it to the other pole. She did the same with the gunwale poles, estimating one hundred feet and one hundred and twenty-five for the outriggers. Feeling good about her calculations and releasing of line, Carrie relaxed against the side of the cabin. She was catching the breeze as it moved against the little hairs on her arms. She licked her salty lips, giggled and closed her eyes against the morning sun.

She had just settled into a state of relation when ZZZZZZZZZZZT! The sound pierced the calm air before she could take another breath.

"Portside!" She heard Paula holler.

The portside transom pole was quivering in its holder and she rushed to pull it out. It lunged forward, ramming her into the side of the boat. There would be a bruise there, she told herself.

Her arms struggled to keep up with the tug of the line; she scanned the ocean to see if a fish had broken the water. What kind of fish could fight so fiercely? She pulled back as sharply as she could on the pole.

"Don't pull back like that!" Paula's voice snarled loudly. "You'll pull the hook right out of his mouth, make it slow, just reel slowly, then let him have a little line—then reel a bit more."

It sounded so easy coming from Paula. For a split second she resented the fly bridge position.

She reeled what seemed an inch or two, just holding the pole was difficult enough as the fish jerked and strained to stay under water. She felt the muscles in her arms, shoulders and back strain to keep the pole from being torn from her hands—refusing to relinquish any ground to whatever was on the end of the line. She reeled a few turns of the handle, then a few more and pulled slowly, the pole arching gently, then she felt it ease a bit; then there was more tugging, she watched the line zig zag across the water as the fish fought against it.

ZZZZZZZZZZT! The other transom pole sang, bending and quivering in its socket.

What do I do? What do I do? Carrie glanced quickly to Paula.

"Where's your knife?"

Carrie shook her head, confused as why a knife would be needed now.

"Cut the damn line! This fish you have on now, is tangled with the other line, there's no fish on it. Just cut the other damn line. I don't want to lose my rig!"

Carrie reached into the leather sheath on her hip, pulled out the long slender blade, stretched across the stern of the boat and lifted the knife across the mono. The pole twanged against the release. Carrie stretched back to the portside of the boat continuing to reel in more line, then even more line. With each full twist of the reel handle she felt the fight of the fish diminishing. He broke water and her muscles eased from their tenseness as the fish neared the boat.

She could see it now. It was long and fat, torpedo like, and shiny in the water, its sparkles matching the sunlit sea itself.

The metallic blue body, the deep blue, almost black hue near the dorsal fins, the yellow of the fins shining as they tipped from the water—all stood in contrast to the breeze beating against her skin, the salt on her lips and the ache leaving her muscles. Without being told she reached for the gaff and slapped the hook into the body.

"Albacore," called Paula from her perch. "Big one. They like to fight."

Chapter Nineteen

Lev ran his fingers along the inner side of her thigh. Estelle moaned softly.

"I've never seen so many freckles." He leaned to kiss her knee. Straightening the leg, he ran a hand along its length. "You have the longest legs."

"I need you to need me." Estelle wrapped the leg across his back, her hands pressing against his shoulders.

"Oh, baby, I need you, too." He chuckled.

"No, I need you to love me."

"I do love you, baby." He slid his eyes across her body, pulled his to meet her face and cupped her breasts. "I love what you do."

She returned his snide grin, aware that he was not falling for her yet. He wasn't ready to follow her to the ends of the earth, as Hank had said he would, as Jeff had said, as even Theo had.

Her teeth tugged lightly at his lower lip; she wondered if he ever would. She was getting tired of this game with Lev. How many more times was she going to have to screw him before he was compliant? She wished she could simply drug him now and get it over with. But he still had not told her about himself, at least not very much. She wanted to know about the money, what he owned, what his daddy owned. He had to be loaded but so far the only thing he'd bought her was drinks and dinner.

Lev had been evasive about his past, his family. When she nudged a conversation about his parents, he scowled and changed the subject.   If only she could find out more about the old man, the senator.

Maybe she could get Lev to introduce her to Senator Worther, a name Lev had yet to mention. Certainly he had even deeper pockets than his son.

Tracing the rise of Lev's bicep, Estelle faced him. "I want to get to know you better. Tell me about yourself, your family. " She paused and looked deeply into his eyes.

"Not much to tell."

"Oh, come on now. Everybody's got a momma and daddy."

"Sure do. What about yours? What about your momma and daddy."

Estelle turned her head, her eyes slid away from his gaze. "My daddy was a drunk."

"I'm sorry." He grazed a finger gently across her cheek.

Estelle drew closer to Lev, wrapping her arms around his neck. He could feel her hot tears on her skin and he kissed her face softly.

"He used to beat me," she sobbed. "He beat my mother." She held tightly to him.

"I'm so sorry you had to live like that." Lev rocked her body, holding her closely, stroking her hair away from her damp face.

Moving to his rhythm, Estelle let him hold her, caress her. Every few seconds she would release a quivering sigh—Lev would hold her tighter.

So this is what he needs, She thought.

****

"You know what I'd love to do?" She whispered. "I'd love to take a cruise somewhere. I've never been on a cruise."

"Sounds like a good idea." Lev leaned his head against the headboard. "Maybe we should check out Royal Caribbean."

"I was thinking more along the lines of cruising there on our own boat." She waited for his reaction.

"You want me to buy a boat."

"You bought one for Paula. Don't I rank up there with her? Come on now, there is no comparison between she and I."

Lev rolled to his side. "There sure isn't but sweetheart, I get sea sick and I have no idea how to navigate." His hand slid the distance between her breasts and hips. "But if you insist, I'll look into it." He kissed her. "It might be nice, just you and me on the water together—where do you want to go?"

Estelle shrugged. "I don't know, you decide. Just take me away from here. Take me somewhere where you've never been."

"That would be kind of difficult, honey. I've been just about everywhere, except Antarctica. You don't want to go there do you?"

"No," she giggled. "I hate being cold. Take me somewhere warm, somewhere where nobody knows us and we can pretend nothing bad has ever happened."

"You got it, honey." He kissed her again, this time longer.

"I want to feel special, I want you to trust in me, like I trust in you." She kissed him back. "I—I know you think I killed Hank. But you have to believe me, I didn't do that. Really, I could have never done that. I loved him, truly loved him, Lev. He understood me. He never looked down on me because of my background." She shifted her eyes to meet his. "You know, I came from trash, pure Kentucky trash. Pigs used to come in my house and chickens, too. And my father--"

Lev stroked her hair. "I know, I know. Life must have been hell for you." He kissed her forehead. "But why, I don't understand why you would let Theo back into your life after leaving that horrible place—after all he's done to you, too." He shook his head. "He hurt you like your father did, didn't he? Why would you allow him to come here?" He posed the question wondering where it would take him.

Estelle's head dropped to her chest, she sobbed lightly. "I don't know. It's like he's got this hold on me Lev. I don't know what to do, please help me. Help me know what to do. I'm so confused."

Pulling her tightly to him, Lev kissed her face, holding it in his hands, he kissed the tears streaming down her cheeks.

"Please believe me. I could never hurt anyone. I need you to trust me. I need to trust you."

"My father is Senator Worther from Arizona. We rarely speak, but I'm his only son and--"

"I want to know about you—what makes you tic, what you like and don't like. I want to know everything about you. Not just your family." Estelle pulled the sheet to cover her body. "I want to know why you love me." She laced her fingers with his. "And you do love me. I can tell—don't you?"

****

Standing at the kitchen island, Estelle rested her hand on Lev's, tracing the lines of his fingers. "Oh, that was so nice. You can be such a sweet lover." Estelle kissed Lev's cheek then touched a finger to her damp eyes. "I've never felt like this."

"I know, baby. I'll take care of you now." He pulled her close to him and closed his eyes.

It seemed heartfelt as Troy entered from the kitchen. He stood frozen in the threshold, watching as the couple embraced. "Sorry, didn't mean to interrupt."

"No biggie, we're just getting ready to have a drink." Lev spoke. He gave Estelle a swift soft kiss to the lips, she stepped back a few inches and rested against the wooden island.

"Got the day off. Must have screwed up my schedule at Gerard's. I thought I was supposed to be in at three," Troy explained.

"Troy I'd like you to meet Estelle. Estelle this is Troy, my roommate," Lev called.

So I am a roommate, thought Troy, he smiled and clasped the woman's hand gently.

"Make yourself comfortable, Estelle." Lev motioned to the broad cushiony sofa centered in the large living room. "What would you like, sweetheart?"

"Rum and Coke will be fine." She leaned against the arm of the sofa and crossed her legs.

Troy leaned close to Lev and whispered. "Not bad, but what happened to Miss Paula?"

"Aw, she'll come around. But in the mean time I'm not going to be lonely if I don't have to."

"She's gorgeous." Troy gawked at Estelle. "I've seen her a few times at the bar, a while back. She sure is a looker, sure you can handle her?" he joked.

"Oh, I can handle her. I'm going to be really sweet to this one."

Lev mixed two rum and Cokes and walked to the sofa. "You look lovely."

She smiled, held his gaze and sipped from her drink.

"Hey kid, did you say you were off today?
"Yeah."

"Well, the waves look killer out there, why don't you grab your board and spend the day?"

Troy snickered. "Gotcha man, I'm out the door."

Chapter Twenty

Emma Jewel slipped the key into the back door of her beach home and flipped the light switch. She breathed in a long breath thinking of how familiar the smells of her own home were and how pleasant it was to be back.

Fate settled two suitcases on the floor next to the kitchen counter. "I'll get the rest tomorrow, E.J."

She and Fate had been gone for over two months and in that time the local police had not been able to put Estelle away. The last time she and Don had spoken, only a few days ago, they were not any closer in charging her with anyone's murder than they'd been before she and Fate had taken off to Texas.

"They need more evidence, they're this close to arresting her, waiting on this, waiting on that. Shit, how long do those things take?" she mumbled, reaching for a glass and filling it with tap water.

"I don't give a flying monkey about any evidence, they know she did it. So what's the problem?" Fate commented, mumbling in return. "They fiddlefart around long enough and she's going to skip town."

E.J. was glad she and Fate had returned. He was getting antsy about his gas station and in the last couple of weeks had been quite grumpy and short with her. But then, she hadn't been much better, snapping at him for going on and on about Texas and how great it was and what his daddy, Jay, used to do as a boy. All the reminiscing had begun to get on her nerves. The trip back to Topsail couldn't have come quicker. They even planned as they drove through the southern states, to sell the camper and fly anywhere they wanted to go in the future.

"Life is for the living," Emma Jewel snarled at Fate one afternoon after dinner at Sam's in Reynosa. "Your daddy and my momma are dead and gone and until you and I are dead and gone I don't want to hear another damn thing about what they used to do."

"Aw come on, it is kind of interesting," Fate commented.

"Yes, it is darling, but now that we've talked about what our parents did and how good the good old days were, for the umpteenth time, don't you think we ought to just move on with our own lives?"

They headed back after that discussion and after a short talk with Detective Don Belkin.

No warning, no amount of scare tactics designed to keep them away from Topsail was going to work. Home is where they wanted to be.

"And if that bitch tries to harm one hair on your head I'll blow her brains to kingdom come or back to wherever she came from." Emma Jewel pulled a pink handled Lugar from her handbag. "I'm not putting up with this shit. I'll go get her myself."

****

Sitting, her hands relaxed on the steering wheel of the faded red1990 Chevy truck, E.J. watched for Estelle to exit the sliding doors of Grocery World.

She'd come for a bag of puppy pads for the rescue dog she and Fate had picked out the other day in Jacksonville.

It was cute, and according to the paw size, looked as if it might grow to sixty or seventy pounds. In fact, E.J. guessed taking into consideration the pup's one blue eye, that husky was the breed most prominent in the blonde and white pup. "Maybe a little Burgonese and Retriever in there," she'd remarked to Fate." As she combed her fingers through the thick fur of the dog's neck.

Fate thought there was more collie than anything and teased that he might call the dog Lassie.

E.J. remembered rolling her eyes at the suggestion. She was still a little pissed that they'd gotten a puppy and that it had taken so quickly to Fate. "Maybe I'll just go back to the pound and get a dog of my own." She blew a frustrated breath as she watched and waited for Estelle.

"I need a bag of chow, too," She said aloud. "Wish that witch would come on out so I can see which car is hers and so I can get my shopping done."

Earlier, when pulling into the lot, she had seen Estelle pushing a buggy toward the entrance. She wasn't about to go into the store and risk the chance of running into her.

Perhaps Estelle didn't even know she had returned from Texas. Emma Jewel surmised that she probably didn't. And then again, maybe the witch didn't even care. But E.J. doubted that. She was aware she was on Estelle's "to do" list. And that Mindy had been a mistake. "I was the one meant to be on the end of her knife."

Drumming her fingers on the steering wheel, Emma Jewel sipped from the bottle of water she always kept in the cup holder. "Yutch, I need to wash that bottle out and put some fresh water in there."

Her eyes peeled, E.J. waited for Estelle to exit. She thought of the new puppy, partially dreading having to take the energy and time to housebreak it. It had been years since she'd had a young dog. Nickie had been with her for nearly twelve years. "Twelve years makes a difference, I don't know if I have the energy to keep up with a pup."

She and Fate had talked about getting another dog after Nickie passed away, and they'd decided on an older dog, one maybe one or two years old—one already house broken. But Fate had been a sucker for the little mixed breed sitting alone in the corner of the wire kennel. Her head held high and her eyes sort of saying, "I'm the best one here." She lifted her furry head, breathed a heavy sigh when she'd caught Fate's eyes then blinked and lowered her head. Other puppies scurried about, whining, stretching their bodies against the cage begging for attention.

This little girl set herself apart, raising her head once again to look directly at Fate, she blinked again.

"Just like a woman," he scoffed jokingly. "That's the one I want."

And that was the one they got. From that moment, when he set her in his lap and petted her, the dog was his. They were smitten with each other. "Nadine. That's going to be her name, Nadine."

"And I know why, you sly old coot, you can't get anything over on me."

Fate slid his eyes to meet her and chuckled. "You sure do know me, don't you?"

"Kim Basinger, 1987, the movie, Nadine."

"Most beautiful woman in the world." He slid his eyes to meet hers. "Except for you."

Emma Jewel winked. "Yeah."

"She was young and soft and feminine and this little gal reminds me of her, coy, girlish— pretty. With her long blond hair and pretty white crest and paws. This girl is going to grow up to be a looker."

Emma Jewel laughed thinking of the new dog and Fate. With them her house was now becoming a home again.

Those few years since Emma's death had been lonely and reclusive ones, where she pulled herself away from everyone, succumbing to old age. How glad she was that Fate had opened that door and walked back into her life. She wasn't dead yet and didn't want to be. In fact she felt like the years had only been a mirage and that life now, with its happiness and promise was what was real-- except for Estelle. She was the fly in the ointment. But E.J. would take care of her and her murdering ass. "Live by the sword, die by the sword—you fucking bitch. I'll run your ass out of town or find some way of getting rid of you. You're not going to ruin this last chance at happiness that I've got."

Taking another swig from a bottle of water, E.J. watched the doors of Grocery World slide open and Estelle saunter from them. Her hair was tucked beneath a ball cap, tendrils fell from the sides. She wore jeans with designer rips about the knees and thighs. Her shirt was of a thin and gauzy, designed to hug the body. And it did.

"Slut. Her figure alone is enough to make me hate her." E.J. chuckled. "Why do all the nasty bitches get great bodies?" She thought of her Aunt Ellie, remembering her in her youthful days, boobs up to her neck—and the curves. Even when she gained a few pounds, the curves were still there. "Never was fair," E.J. groaned as she watched Estelle walk into the crowded lot of cars. She heard the "ping ping" of the keyless entry device and watched as she opened the backdoor of a maroon Chevy Tahoe to deposit the three bags of groceries.

E.J. slid down in the seat as Estelle backed the Tahoe and drove past her, exiting the parking lot.

"Cuntusabuntus, the queen of mean, Whorella de ville. I'll get you, you bag of worms. Now that I know what you're driving. I'll follow your ass around—see what your ass is up to," Emma Jewel sneered. "How in the hell have they not arrested you yet? Probably too busy banging you—men."

She knew every inch of the island, every path, every stand of trees, every hammock, every place where sand dunes used to be. And she was a damn good shot with a rifle.

Even if it was only a twenty-two, maybe it was enough to scare the hell out of the monster Estelle.

If she thought someone was after her, really on to her and wanted to hurt or kill her, maybe she'd get the hell away from Topsail. At least that was the way Emma Jewel figured things. Most bullies bully because they can. When someone comes back at them, calls them out, they tend to back down. Or in this case, as E.J. hoped, run away—*crawl back under the rock from whence she'd come.*

It was dusk, growing darker as E.J. blended well in her khaki colored shirt and trousers, lying in the dune. The tall beach grasses completed the camouflage and she lifted the rifle to her shoulder, cradling the stock to fit comfortably. She looked through the scope, scanned Estelle's house looking for her through the curtainless windows.

She found her, leaning against the kitchen counter in an oversized tee shirt. In one hand she held a long thin knife and the other a cucumber. Estelle slid the knife easily from one end to the other, gliding just beneath the green skin, removing it ever so delicately.

One of her bare feet was on the tiled floor, the left one rested on the calf of the right. To Emma Jewel she looked like a flamingo. "Poop," she snorted and drew her attention to Estelle's head where her luxurious hair lay stacked loosely.

A head shot, she thought. And it would have been a clean shot, right at the base of the skull. E.J. lowered the rifle, moving it toward the left shoulder blade. There it would pierce the heart and send her victim slumping forward, eventually sliding to the floor.

E.J. drew the barrel of the twenty-two down, she shook her head. "No need to bloody up the place. I'm no Hank, I'm no Estelle, I'm sane."

Aiming for the window just below the kitchen sink, she squeezed the trigger. Thup. It whizzed past Estelle leaving a hole in the glass. Thup. Another bullet whizzed past, just as Theo entered the room.

Chapter Twenty-One

"Got the prints, our friend John Graves and Theo Cornby are one and the same. But I think we already knew that." Holding the phone to his ear, Lev thumbed through the spiral tablet lying on the side table. "The rest of the stuff I found out about him is interesting though."

"How interesting?"

"You tell me? He's from a long line of farmers. His family goes way back in Kentucky—middle class, did okay with chicken and hog farming until around the nineties when there was some kind of freak accident in a grain silo—big explosion and his parents bought the farm. He got the farm—ha, ha, his parents *bought* the farm. Get it? Theo gets the farm."

"Yeah, I get it. What else?"

"He was the only child and he makes it easy on himself, doesn't have to hardly lift a finger, he goes with Tyson, you know, those big chicken corporations are taking over the business—chicken business anyway," he laughed, switching the phone to his other hand. "The hogs he keeps as pets, so the neighbors say, never takes any to slaughter, just feeds them every day. The grocer out there says he comes at least three times a week to get old produce."

Don nodded. "Chicken farms, there's a lot of farmers doing that these days. The big corps are taking over everything." Don settled himself on a bar stool and motioned to the bartender for a draft beer.

"Seems our friend has a soft heart and when he was a teenager he befriends this old drunk that lived on the other side of his parents' farm. While they were still alive he was over there all the time helping with the man's daughter. There was no Mrs. Drunk. Well, he kind of becomes a surrogate father to the girl since the old man is wasted all the time. He dies, drowned in a mud puddle, just when the little girl turns sixteen, and not long after that is when the explosion happened killing his parents.

"Well, our boy Theo tries to adopt her. By this time he's thirty one or so—his parents are dead, her pa is dead but the state says she's too old for Theo to adopt, she's sixteen and in Kentucky she can do whatever the hell she wants."

"Convenient."

"Yeah, makes you wonder," Lev answered.

"Did she stay in her father's place after he died?"

"No. She moved right in with Theo. Now, before her old man died and before the Cornbys got blown up she was over there off and on. It wasn't till after everybody is dead that she moved in full time and she and Theo have been living together ever since, except when she's shacked up with some other man."

"You think Theo was in on it?"

"Naw, everybody around there says the family was decent, that the boy—well, I guess he was a man by then but that there was never anything odd or disruptive going on over there, except that he's not the sharpest tool in the shed. Well, he's not stupid, just—like I said," Lev answered.

"It all sounds sort of strange to me."

"Sounds that way, but I'm not sure. I don't think they've, you know. Maybe she still sees him as her father. From what I gather, he's the only parental figure she's had in her life. But then get this, he got hurt on a job, or so he says, a decade or so ago—hurt his back and sued the company. He gets a chunk of money every month deposited into his bank account, plus he's got the fifty acres and the farmhouse and he gets the dough from Tyson. Never has to do much of anything, just putters around the farm, feeds the chickens, feeds the hogs— that's about it. He never ventures far from his farm except when he goes to a doctor up around Altonville. That's around every other week or so, he's got Crohn's and some depression issues. He doesn't bother anyone, doesn't cause any trouble. Most of the folks around his place say he's a nice enough guy, keeps to himself, but that he dotes on the girl."

"I assume the *girl* is Estelle."

"None other."

"You think she could have done the killings all on her own. Killed her father and caused the silo explosion?"

"Possibly but there was never an investigation."

"Wonder what brought her down your way?" Lev questioned.

"Her cousins?"

"Yeah, but what prompted her to move away from Theo and the farm?"

"Good question."

Silence ensued for several seconds, Don moved to a near by booth and propped his feet up. "So, anything going on, any dire straits going on at the beach?"

Not much going on, I'm with wacko woman now. She bumped into me at Grocery World."

"No kidding."

"No kidding. And string bean, Theo spends a lot of time down at the tower. He's moving right along, too. Looks like he knows what he's doing, too.

"I'd like to see that. Hope he gets it completed before we have to arrest him," Don snickered.

"It's like you were saying, she's going to have it modeled like it looked in the forties—Operation Bumblebee. Theo's been talking to the museum, studying old photos. Somebody from the paper had pictures of it, they did a big write up on what it used to look like and Theo commenting on how he's working to fix it up. Even Estelle had some shit to say. Man, she sounded like she really cared about the place, like she was doing it all for the community. She sure does pour it on thick."

"Really."

"Oh yeah, forgot to tell you. This should clarify everything between Theo and Estelle."

"What?"

"Theo has a girlfriend, Emily something or other—can't remember her last name. Anyway, he met her at his doctor's office."

"What's her problem?"

"She lost a child to SIDS, sudden infant death syndrome, a while back. From what I hear she was a real basket case."

"No shit. Sounds like they make a good pair."

"Don't be so judgmental," Lev chuckled. "Everybody needs love."

"You're somebody to talk about that, Casanova."

Lev snorted and ignored the slight. "She sort of lived with him off and on at the farm and now that he's here, she's moved in fulltime. I'm telling you, his neighbors sure do like to talk. Most of it's good but I got the feeling from Mr. Tucker, the man on the next farm over, that he and Theo don't get along too well. Everybody else sang his praises on how nice and honest a guy he is. But Tucker, no way. Something about the damn chicken feathers blowing onto his land—going to give him COPD.

"Anyway, Emily is supposed to come for a visit sometime in late winter or early spring. Seems he called her up and wants her to come on out—at least that's what Tucker said, and he also said something about the two of them getting married."

"Hope I'm there to see that," Don added sarcastically.

"Yeah, bring the V-girls, we'll make it a real party." Lev chortled. "So how's it going with those V- girls?"

"The twins are around, nutty as ever. They mentioned the Bug in the backyard; I'm going to check it out again. And Vera, she's doing well—talked with her for a few minutes the other day. I was worried she may have started drinking again, but no, she's still in school and she's seeing someone."

"Did she give you any background on her cousin Estelle yet?"

"Funny thing is, this man she's seeing is one of Estelle's old beaus. That's got me a little concerned. Anybody who has been involved with Estelle is questionable."

"Including you?" Lev laughed.

"Pot calling the kettle, jerk off." Don cleared his throat. "Never have felt quite clean enough since her—even thinking about it makes me feel dirty. How about you? Able to wash off the dirt?"

"Nothing like a good roll in the mud," Lev joked.

"Enough about her, what's interesting is this old beau of hers—and isn't that what you are now, her new beau? Isn't that how they refer to boyfriends around here—beau," he chuckled. "For Estelle to be interested in a guy, to be seeing him he's got to have some dough and got to be spending it on her."

"Maybe she found out the old beau didn't have as much dough as she liked."

"Maybe—whatever the case, if he's been involved with Estelle, he's suspect. So, I'm being careful. When I was talking to Vera the other day, Ruben, that's his name, was sitting right there. I wasn't sure just how I should proceed, tried feeling him out. And according to him, he had very little to do with her. Says he saw her a couple of times and then she cut it off—acted like he had leprosy. It looks as if she dumped him about the time Hank came into the picture."

"Maybe it's true. Maybe he's the one that got away unscathed. Lucky guy, if you ask me."

"If he's telling the truth," Don sipped from his beer, "then he is lucky." He turned toward the door and watched as it opened. The twins entered wearing matching chubby faux fur jackets and in their overly teased hair were matching oversized bows. "Ah shit, Vela and Veda just walked in and Vera's on her way. These two are going to screw everything up."

"Buy them a couple of rounds, maybe they'll get drunk and bother someone else."

"Now that's an idea. There's always a fool around here that thinks he'd going to get lucky—at least long enough till Ruben and Vera show up. Vera said her boyfriend would keep the twins busy while she and I talked. They should be here anytime. I'll let you know how it turns out."

"You do that. Damn, I wish I was there to enjoy the show."

"Hey, you watch it with Estelle, buddy. Don't get caught in her claws, she's deadly. You ought to know that."

"Don't worry about me, I know exactly what I'm doing. In fact, I'm pretty sure it's she that's falling for me."

"Yeah sure," Don chuckled. "Watch it anyway. Look, gotta go, the twins are moving in."

Don heard the laughter from the phone and rolled his eyes before hanging up. Forcing a grin he watched as the twins made their way toward him.

"Sorry about the other day." Vela puckered her lips and blew a kiss his way.

"Yeah, we've been kinda—well, you know how women get when it's our time of the month."

Wincing, Don reached for his beer. *Gross, TMI.* "No problem, I understand completely." He eyed the chubby style jackets and wondered if they were newly bought from a retro shop or if the women had fished them out of their mother's closet. Either way, they added to their nearly comical appearance. He fought the urge to comment.

Vela stepped back, eyeing Don openly. "How's that girl you got back at Topsail, did you have that little talk with her the other morning?"

"Sissy said you and she never got it on because of her. What's her name?" Veda giggled.

Don ignored the question.

"But I don't believe it." She batted her lashes and ran a finger along the rim of Don's beer glass.

"Hey," Vela pouted. "It's not like you to not offer to buy us a drink, Don. Me and Veda are sort of thirsty and I know you like taking care of the ladies." She leaned in closer.

Oh my god, if she tries to kiss me again, I swear I'll throw up. He waved to the bartender, holding up two fingers.

The bartender nodded and chuckled. He knew the V-girls and their routine and the poor patrons they pressed for drinks. He couldn't remember a time when the women had paid for

218

their own. "Here you go," the bartender chuckled, winking furtively to Don. "Enjoy."

"Ooh Bobby, we sure will enjoy," Vela cooed after the young man, turning to her sister as he walked away. "He just doesn't know how I could rock his world."

Don rolled his eyes and watched the women pull the drafts to their lips. There wasn't any pretentious lifting of little pinkies or dabbing at their lips after a brief sip. No, the V-girls were real swillers and drank to nearly half empty then settled the glasses on the bar.

"Beer has never been my drink of choice," Vela blurted, suppressing a burp.

"Rum and coke. You could cough up a couple of rum and Cokes for us, couldn't you Don?" Veda inched closer to him, thrusting her cleavage nearly into his face.

"Gosh, he's so good looking." Vela breathed into his ear.

"Oh, I know. If that gal at Topsail doesn't want you, I'll take you sweet cheeks." Don shuddered. They had him boxed in, one on either side of him, their cheap perfume overwhelming his nostrils, their thick and fuzzy jackets bunched up against him, making him perspire.

Don glanced in the mirror at the image of himself and the V-girls, smothered by too much of everything. In a way it was funny. He grinned to himself then breathed a sigh of relief as he noticed Vera and Ruben walk through the door.

"The cavalry's here." Ruben stretched his hand out to shake Don's. He leaned in to whisper, "Hard to get away when they ambush you like this, huh?"

The men exchanged knowing glances. Ruben snagged the bartender and called, "Two rum and Cokes, two ginger ales and fill this guy's glass for him."

"It doesn't bother you to come into a bar?" His eyes met Vera's.

"Nope. Me and my man here come all the time. In fact, we like coming, it reinforces our determination to take one day at a time."

"And Frick and Frack," Ruben nodded to the twins, "rub in our faces what we used to act like when we were drinking."

"Screw you, buddy," Vela hissed. "But thanks for the drink." She winked.

"Boring!" Veda rolled her eyes.

"Yeah, come to think of it you have gotten pretty boring big sister." She crossed her eyes and stuck her tongue out at Vera.

"They are sooo boring. Just pains in the ass since they got together—absolutely no fun at all," Veda barked.

"But then Miss Prim and Proper started being boring when *you*, Mr. Detective, came to town last summer." Vela wiped a drop of spittle from the corner of her mouth as she watched the bartender set the drinks on the bar.

"Let's get a table," Don encouraged as he grabbed the glasses and made his way to a far corner. He watched the twins relax into their chairs and curl their fingers around their drinks, comfortable on a path that would lead them to nirvana. Ruben nodded to Don as if he understood his job—keeping them occupied while Vera and he found another table where they could talk. Don nodded back in appreciation.

"Tell me about your cousin."

Vera sipped from the ginger ale. "My, just cut to the chase. No 'you look nice, Vera'—no 'glad you've found someone to love.'" She glared.

"You look nice, Vera." Don patted her hand and chuckled. "You always look nice. And yes, I'm glad you have someone now."

"Thanks." She paused, then blurted, "I'm so happy, Don. I don't think I've ever been happier. Ru is such a good man. He keeps me on the straight and narrow." She leaned over to kiss Don's cheek. "Thank you so much for everything. If it hadn't of been for you I'd have never started going to AA or enrolled in school." She paused watching the expression of humility pass over his face. "What is it? Are you the Lone Ranger or something—just passing through to do good deeds?"

"Ha. Good deeds—yeah. I'm one of the most selfish people I know."

"No. I never met that guy, the selfish one. If that had been the case then you'd have had your way with me and dumped me like every other jerk I'd been with. But you didn't do that."

Don shrugged. "I dragged you off to where Hank was living, used you to get info on him."

"Ah, you could have still taken advantage and gotten the information. Nope, you're a good man—you helped me make amends with myself."

Pressing the beer to his lips, he shrugged again.

"So how are things going with the woman you used as an excuse not to bed me?" she laughed.

"Her name is Carrie and things are going well. I guess you could say I've made amends with myself, too." He met Vera's eyes.

"Guess we all have demons, huh?"

"Yep."

"You'll have to tell me about yours sometime, friend." Vera squeezed his hand in hers. "Now, talking about demons, let's talk about Estelle, my dear cousin. That's what we're here to talk about, right?"

"Sorry to say, but I think your cousin is Satan incarnate. I think she's involved with Hank's death and with the murder of another person. Only thing, she hasn't been charged with anything and it doesn't look like she's going to be."

Vera drew a deep breath, "She's bad, Don. Really bad. I never realized how bad. I heard about Hank dying. Couldn't believe it. A part of me says no way and then I think—yes, yes she could. Estelle was always mean as a snake and sneaky as one too."

"She's good with a knife, isn't she? I think she likes carving on people."

"Wow, you're talking like she's a monster." Vera rubbed her fingers across her lips, her eyes drifted toward the ceiling. "I never really thought about her doing things like that but come to think of it, that little house she has in New Bern—she got that from some old boyfriend. He died—left it to her in his will. Do you think she killed him?"

"Possibly—there's other things, too—her father. What do you know about her father?"

"We really aren't blood related. He was my daddy's stepbrother. My daddy grew up with him but when they were teenagers they had a fight—at least that's what I heard—they were in their teens, anyway, one went one way and the other went the other. Her daddy ended up in Kentucky. They came and visited a few times when I was a kid and then I didn't even see her until a couple of years ago when she suddenly appeared."

"Did she ever tell you what brought her?"

Vera's brow crinkled, she brought a finger to her mouth. "Come to think of it, she was all antsy and excited—said she always wanted to live near the beach." Vera lifted her eyes upward once again. "I came to find out that wasn't true. She could care less about the ocean. Anyway, when my daddy passed he left my sisters and me a few properties—you've been to my house. Well, the twins have one like that except a little bigger. Personally, I think my lovely cousin came here to see if we had a bunch of money 'cause she wanted some of it. At least, that's what I've learned about my dear cousin, she's in *anything* or in *anyone* for the money—and you know all about that—about Hank."

Don nodded. "That's all you know?"

"Estelle never confided much in me except for telling me that her father had died—that he was a drunk—of course she didn't just call him a drunk—he was an F-ing drunk. And she had a few other choice words for him. Said she was glad he was dead. I never asked her much after she said that. Seemed like she had a bad time of it so I didn't ask anything more and then, of course, back then I was drinking and was drowning in my own swill."

Tapping his fingers on the table Don sighed. "I was hoping you knew more."

"That's it. Nothing earth shaking, except maybe the house in New Bern."

"The one the dead guy left her."

"Yeah. Come to think of it, I remember meeting him. What was his name? Hmm."

Don watched Vera rub her forehead and purse her lips.

"Jeff Bunion," she tittered. "I remember that because Estelle was always making foot jokes about his last name. Jeff, he was a nice guy. Had a couple of little girls at home and a wife. He was gaga for Estelle—most men are. At first he was all giddy about her. Couldn't keep his hands off, left his wife for her and followed her around like a little puppy and then the last time I saw Estelle with him it was she who had her hands all over him and him not looking too pleased about it."

"How'd he die?"

"ODed on something."

"Did he have a funeral?"

"His wife, the one he left Estelle for, had him buried—no funeral—put him in the ground really quick, too. That was the first year Estelle was here. I wasn't aware of her evil ways." Vera scowled. "But I learned pretty fast. She dragged me to the funeral, insisting that it was his ex-wife that drove him to kill himself. Talking trash, that's all she was doing, but I believed her then. What an idiot I was. And there they were, that poor family—the mother and those two little girls, they couldn't have been more than six or seven years old. Estelle glared at them the whole time." Vera shook her head. "Lord, how I wish I could apologize to that woman right now. I know she had to have gone through hell."

"How long ago was this?"

"About three years ago—something like that."

"Where is he buried?"

"At cemetery in New Bern."

One of the first things he would have done was to have Jeff Bunion's body exhumed.

Chapter Twenty-Two

He'd been in New Bern nearly two weeks, met with Vera a few times. The info about the old boyfriend, Jeff Bunion, was interesting. It could turn out to be something of value.

And he'd been out to Estelle's old beat up cottage once—hadn't found anything interesting there though, nothing concrete to compel him to stay further. Why wasn't he on his way back to Topsail and Carrie instead of driving toward Estelle's old place again?

He pictured the curl of Carrie's lips as she spoke, the subtleties of her face as she gestured. He had called Carrie nearly every night since he'd been away—loved hearing her voice—its reassurance. He missed that.

This new leaf he'd turned over felt good. He wanted to go back to that right now. Yet, there was an uncertainty, an underlying feeling he was missing something here in Carteret County. Bunion could be the nail in Estelle's coffin, he hoped so, but then he may pan out to be nothing at all.

Don wanted, no, he needed something else. There *was* something else, some illusive clue, some simple article, or something—there was something missing. He could feel it.

Whatever it was, it was somewhere, just below the surface or just out of reach. He just needed to find it. He couldn't justify leaving until he found it or until the uncertainty proved futile.

Don pulled down the long rutted road to Estelle's old cottage, parking in the back, just behind Estelle's red Volkswagen. It sat, still parked and trashed even worse than last summer, just like the V-girls had said.

Maybe vandals had done more damage— maybe Estelle had taken a bat to it. Either way, there were more dents than there had been before. The rear bumper hung loose, the eye lashes that had flirted so gaily last summer were in bits and pieces on the ground; the side mirrors were gone, too. "Maybe I missed something inside the car," he said aloud. "Wackadoodle may have left something incriminating in the Bug." *But I went over that thing with a fine tooth*comb. "Humph." He eyed the car curiously as he passed and walked to the empty house and entered. It was not locked.

It was as if no one had ever lived there, emptiness palpitated everywhere and with the cool of the year, the building felt a barren wasteland. Don pulled his jacket collar up, stepping deliberately from one room to another.

In the bedroom he studied the curtainless windows—last summer there had been towels nailed over them. Standing before the rear window, he studied the Volkswagen again—*I must have missed something.* He pictured himself rummaging through it several days before—there had been nothing. He brought his fingers to his chin and scratched at the two days growth there. *I really don't want to have to*

228

disassemble that thing—would be a real pain in the ass.

A bed sat squarely in the center of the room against the back wall. A closet door was open revealing emptiness, a single dresser sat against the wall next to the closet. He'd already opened all its drawers; he did it again and searched the closet again as well. He lifted the mattress, skewing it, and searched beneath the box spring, pushed against the frame and examined the flooring. All this, he'd done before—nothing.

The living room was the same, barren. The couch where Estelle had lain sprawled last summer, teasing him, looked worn and dirty. The coffee table—the same. He walked into the kitchen. The refrigerator door was shut; he opened it to a gagging stench and held his hand over his mouth. Perusing the contents he had seen a few days before, he moved the slimy head of lettuce aside. Nothing had changed. What had been green was mush now and what wasn't supposed to be green, was.

What was it with Estelle and leaving bowls of food around? Several bowls sat willy nilly on the kitchen table (an image of Estelle flashed in his mind) flies buzzed around whatever was left inside. Estelle was a pig.

He stepped through the back door and slowly walked toward the VW. It looked just like it had the other day. But last time he hadn't moved the car. He stretched a leg in and pressed on the clutch, then moved the gearshift to neutral. Stepping to the rear of the Bug he pushed. The vehicle rocked forward and back into the ruts it had created over the last several months. Don pushed again, harder and the car moved out of the soft earth. He leaned his shoulder against the sloping rear and pushed again, moving it a good two feet, it rolled another three.

Resting his hands on his lower back, Don straightened and felt his tightened muscles. Already they were sore. He grimaced in pain, regretting having moved the VW. "Shit, I'll have to see the chiropractor for this." He rubbed the sore spot, closing his eyes to the sensation. He turned his neck from side to side, heard the few cracks and opened his eyes to the ground where the car had sat and to a cylindrical metal object half hidden in the earth. He flipped it loose with the toe of his shoe.

"What the hell?" Don flicked dirt from the electronic cigarette—that is what he recognized it to be, as he continued wiping. The faded pink color was mottled somewhat with rust, but there was no doubt in his mind as he held the apparatus, that it had at one time belonged to Mindy.

"Why in the world would Estelle bring that thing all the way up here?" He asked aloud. "And what the hell was it doing under the tire?"

****

Ruben shook Don's hand vigorously, "Good to have met you. Keep in touch."

Don nodded, he had a good feeling about Ruben. He hoped he was right. Smiling to Vera he spoke, "Glad you're doing alright. Call me when you graduate, I'll try to make it."

"You want to hang around for a few minutes more? Vela and Veda are due in any minute," she giggled.

"That's alright." He winced. "You give them my good-byes." Reciprocating the hug Vera offered, Don felt a sense of pride—a sense he hadn't been used to in a long time. He was happy to see Vera straighten out her life, happy that she'd found someone patient and understanding, who seemed to care deeply for her. He thought of Carrie and how maybe the world was a good place after all.

Stepping into his faded gray Dodge, he turned on the ignition and studied the clock on the dashboard, the incorrect time flashed against the dimming light of day. He pushed one tab to correct the minutes and another to correct the hours and nodded as he pulled away from Vera's home, a grin still on his face from the warmth he'd encountered. *Maybe the world is a good place,* he thought again. He glanced toward the glove compartment where the vape lay cradled in a plastic bag and his grin disappeared.

****

Meanwhile, on Topsail, Emma Jewel has been following Estelle's movements. She's aware of the younger woman's routine and bides her time in an oak hammock just south of one of Hank's old rental houses in Sneads

Ferry. The low set trees create a sense of safety; the cushiony palette of leaves are like a carpet as E.J. steps along to a small oak and relaxes. Leaning against the mossy coat, she anticipates Estelle's entry into the scene before her.

The Castles, a couple who'd been renting from Hank for several years, have been to talk with E.J. to complain of how Hank's widow keeps nagging them about the rent.

Hank always waited for the Castle's rental payment, their social security checks didn't come until the third Wednesday of the month, sometimes that was on the fifteenth and sometimes that was on the twenty-first but Estelle was not as patient as Hank had been and insisted that payment be made by the fifth of every month. After that she charged a fee for everyday the rent was late. The last few months she'd begun coming to the residence to demand payment.

Emma Jewel snuggled against the tree, her hand holding the rifle as she waited for Estelle to drive into the leafy driveway. She sighed, recalling how when she was a girl she used to climb the old scrub oaks with friends and how there had been one tree stretching out over the water with a long rope tied to it.

She could see herself and Vickie and Bonnie in their two-piece bathing suits and Randy and Kenny in cut off jeans, clinging to the rope and swinging out over the sound, releasing their hold to splash into the water below. "Damn, that was a long time ago," she whispered and sighed again more lightly this time then cocked her head to hear the crunch of foliage as tires pulled from the hard road to the driveway.

She caught Estelle in the crosshairs as she exited the vehicle—again, it would have been so easy. "Kabam." Estelle imagined pulling the trigger. "Shit," she mouthed. "Why am I so good?"

E.J. would settle for scaring her, she wanted to see the reaction this terrorist Estelle would have once she suspected someone was after her. "The shoe's on the other foot," E.J. whispered.

It couldn't be just some pot shots taken at her, E.J. realized she had to be careful, she certainly didn't want to get caught she just wanted to see if she could scare her away. Today she had to make sure Estelle was in front of the sound where the bullet would travel. She was not about to leave anything behind, nothing lodged in a tree or car or body that might lead to her. The best place for a bullet was in the water where no one would ever find it.

Estelle was alone, and the look on her face would have scared an ogre. That was one thing Emma Jewel had noticed since her return from out west—Estelle was a shapeshifter. That's what she called her, a shapeshifter. One day or at one time Estelle might look beautiful, almost caring, gliding sensuously as she moved. Another day, one when nobody was around, she had the look of a shark—her eyes lifeless and mechanical. And the way she walked, well, to Emma Jewel, Estelle looked territorial as she clomped along, like some animal stalking prey.

Drawing the rifle once again to her shoulder, Emma Jewel flashed back to when her uncle Phil had taken her squirrel hunting in these very woods when she was young. She giggled lightly, so grateful that he'd taught her the stealth movements of a hunter and equally as grateful that he'd taught her to shoot clean and quick.

Emma Jewel followed her prey as it moved toward the front door of the little cinderblock home. She waited for her to hesitate, as everyone did as they opened the little white gate, then she squeezed the trigger. Thup. she watched Estelle flinch as she recognized the same sound she'd encountered only a few nights before.

Thup. Estelle whirled, her eyes scanning the brush and trees around the clearing and house. "Who the hell?" she hollered. "What the hell is going on? Now, if you wanted to hit me I know you would. These shots are coming too close." She whirled around again, her face red with anger, her fists balled striking at the air. "Who in the damn hell is shooting at me?"

Rattling the gate, she stomped the ground and screeched, "What do you want?" Estelle's face, red now, eyes bulging, her teeth barred screamed again, "Face me, show me, dammit!"

"What the hell is going on out here?" An elderly George Castle called from the doorway. His bent and lanky frame toddled out onto the stone path. He hollered again, "What is your problem lady? I told you you'd have your money by this Wednesday. Now what's a couple of days? We've been living here for nearly fifteen years and we've never welched on the rent."

"No need yelling—no need ranting and raving like some spoiled little brat out here." Gwendolyn Castle joined her husband on the walkway, her stout frame a good eight inches shorter than her husband's. "Why do you have to make such a fuss?" She wiped her hands on the tea towel in her hands, and then flung the cloth across her shoulder. "We talked to E.J. just the other day. She said not to worry about a few days, and to do just like we've always done when Hank was alive. Now you just get on out of here or I'm calling the police."

"You talked with E.J.? When?" Estelle asked curiously.

"Just a few days ago, maybe on Friday or Saturday. And she said not to pay you no mind, that she was going to have a talk with you as soon as she had the time."

"So she's back here, back from her little trip?"

"Yes, she sure is and I'm going to give her a call about your nasty behavior and your screaming out here. You got some nerve."

Chapter Twenty-Three

"Your two weeks are up." Chief Moore leaned back in his chair, propping his feet high on the desk before him. A grin stretched across his face as he interlaced his hands behind his head. "Hope you got something."

Don tossed the plastic bag holding the electronic cigarette onto his desk. "Got that. Got Jeff Bunion."

Moore eyed the bag and smirked, "Who's Jeff Bunion—foot doctor?"

"Ha, ha. He's some jerk Estelle was banging in New Bern. He left her a run down house in the middle of nowhere. I don't know if it was like that when Bunion died or if Estelle trashed it.

"That Bug she used to drive is parked out back. I found that," he nodded to the vape, "under the back tire. Still can't figure out why she took it up there and why it was under the car."

"Maybe she dropped it."

"Maybe. That's good—simple—but good and probably right."

"Sometimes it's as plain as the nose on your face. What's the vape got to do with our lovely lady friend?"

"It was Mindy's or at least looks like the one Mindy used to use."

"You'll need a DNA on that."

"Yep. Can I get one?"

Moore picked up the bag, ran his fingers over the vape. "Mindy's huh? That was an odd little gal. Sweet, but odd. But then she was a millennial and they're all goofy." He lifted his feet from the desk and sat forward. "Sure would like to find her killer."

"Me, too."

"I'll see what I can do about the DNA." Moore paused for a moment more, still rubbing the vape through the bag. "And who is this Jeff Bunion—not a name easy to forget especially if you've had one of those things on your foot. Erica had one last year. I told her she needed to quit wearing those tight pointy toed shoes."

"Bunion is the guy who left Estelle the house in New Bern. He was originally from Beaufort. Left his wife and two young kids to be with her."

"Did he marry her?"

"No. But he left the residence to her in his will. His ex-wife had him buried at the cemetery in New Bern. I'm thinking we get the body exhumed and find out what he had in his blood stream."

"You thinking poison?"

"Drugs, and I bet its Dilaudid. That's what Hank had in him. And you know Hank didn't do any drugs. Estelle was probably feeding it to him as Tylenol or something. Had him out of his mind. I'll bet she did the same thing to old buddy boy Bunion."

"Why didn't she get him to marry her?"

"Beats me. Maybe she hadn't perfected her technique yet. Maybe Bunion was just for practice. Who knows? The bottom line is, he's dead, Hank's dead, Mindy's dead and I'm beginning to think that the bitch offed her old man and Theo Cornby's parents."

"Theo Cornby—the man living with her."

"Yes, John Graves, whatever name he's using now. But Cornby is the real one. He's from Kentucky—chicken farmer. He helped raise Estelle. I don't think he's a wack job like her. I don't think he's the sharpest tool in the shed but he'd not the dullest either."

"He's working on that tower nearly every time I drive down that way."

"Yep. I'm curious to see how that's coming along."

"I know, I stopped and had a little chat with him the other day. He seemed all excited about re-doing the place to look like it did seventy odd years ago. Showed me old photos and the designs. It looks pretty good, pretty authentic. Says he likes to build things. Then he went into telling me about his girlfriend and how he hoped they could get married on the beach in front of the tower, use it as a reception room and as a grand opening gig all at the same time."

"Fixing the tower is going to take a long time. How long is he planning on staying here—you ask him?"

"He thinks he'll have it completed by spring—couple of months. Some days he's got a couple of other men working on it with him. Most days he's by himself."

Don nodded. "Maybe he can get it done. I know I'd like to see what one of those towers looked like back in the day."

"Pretty cool," the chief agreed.

Pushing his hands deep into his pockets, Don asked, "You think we can get Bunion exhumed?"

"Dilaudid, you say?"

"That's what we're looking for." He paused for a moment and added. "While we're at it, I'd like to see if the Cornbys in Texas or Estelle's father—Reardon is the name, were buried. If they were, maybe we could get them exhumed too. Maybe they have Dilaudid in their systems, too."

"You better find out how long that stuff stays in the body before I move on that. It may be gone by now. How long ago did she off Bunion?—if she did."

"Year and a half ago. Just about the time she met Hank in New Bern."

"And the people in Kentucky?"

"I guess three or four years ago, something like that."

"Moore nodded his head. "I'll look into it. Do you know what county? What part of the state?"

"I'll get that to you ASAP."

****

"Missed you." Don grabbed the belt at Carrie's waist and pulled her to him. Pressing his mouth over hers he let his hands caress her shoulders and back.

"It looks like it's going to be a nice day today. The weatherman said it was going to be in the sixties."

"Hope sixty hurries up, it's chilly this morning."

"It's around forty now," he said, his hands reaching for a large Styrofoam cup of coffee— he offered a sip to Carrie.

"Thanks." She held the cup in her hands, warming them. "Nice of you to volunteer your time to help Paula and me today." Carrie leaned into his chest, snuggling against its warmth.

"Think nothing of it, just wanted to see what you gals do everyday. Can't be too difficult if two women can do it." He teased, cutting his eyes slowly to meet Carrie's.

"You've got a lot to learn," she retorted.

Don studied the layout of the boat. The traps stacked one on top of the other in a corner of the deck and the long poled buoys attached by long coiled lines to each one. He'd never done any commercial fishing before, though he'd enjoyed casting a line now and then.

"Hope it's not rough," Don said as he watched Paula switch on the diesel engine. Fumes filled the air for several minutes until the engine settled into a steady purr.

"Want a cup of coffee?" Paula called above the low rumble of the engine, she held up a thermos as she stepped up the ladder to the flying bridge. From there she would utilize the Cuda fish finder and from the vantage point decide just where the traps would be placed as the boat motored through the water.

Carrie held the steaming cup Don had handed her up high. "Already have some, thanks."

"Where we going?" Don asked, tugging at her thick flannel shirt. "You won't be needing this in a few hours.

"Fifteen mile rock, there's an artificial reef about fifteen miles south of here. Usually there's pretty good fishing there. Paula's the one that knows all about that stuff—finding the fish, knowing where reefs are. I'm just the lackey, the laborer."

"She just drives the boat? What about all that?" He gestured toward the traps and buoys.

"Yep, she just drives the boat but then I don't know diddly about boats or reefs and until I came along she did all these things by herself."

Don glanced to the flying bridge to study Paula, a look of stern concentration on her face as she rested her elbows on the fiberglass counter.

She glanced down to catch his gaze and quickly turned back, calling down to the couple to cast off the lines. "Let's get the hell out of here," she snapped.

"Is she always in such a good mood?" Don asked sarcastically.

"Last couple of days she's been in a horrible mood. I think she's seeing someone and things aren't going so well."

"That was quick, just a couple of weeks ago she and Lev were hot and heavy."

"According to Lev?"

"Okay, I get your point."

"This other guy has been in her life for a long, long time. I think he comes and goes and she waits around for him. I just think Lev was McDonald's and I think she's decided she'll do

242

with peanut butter and jelly, at least for a while."

"What?" he laughed.

"Peanut butter and jelly. It's something I've heard E.J. refer to—her way of keeping it clean."

Don nodded. "Sounds silly to me."

"If I'm hungry I can always stop at McDonald's for something to fill my stomach but why spend the time or money when I can go home and fix myself a peanut butter and jelly sandwich? At least with peanut butter and jelly I know I'll always be satisfied because I know just how much of what I need to make a good sandwich. And I can enjoy it without having to deal with someone else—a sloppy cook, uncaring cashier—no wondering if someone's feelings are going to get hurt. Lev was McDonald's and I think he thought he was lobster and artichokes."

"This is getting to convoluted—lobster and artichokes? Explain that one."

"Lobster—the finer food. Artichokes—one has to strip the leaves away to get to the heart, the sweetest part."

"Okay," Don chuckled. "It's an okay analogy. I think Lev thinks he's lobster to all the women and it's always been easy for him to pick up girls, especially if he threw a little money at them—bought them a few things."

"Didn't work with Paula. She'd rather settle for P.B. and J because what she really wants is lobster and artichokes."

"And that's what the other guy is?"

"Yep."

"And this comes from E.J.? That old woman is full of surprises." Don stepped back as the boat traveled through the inlet, the rhythm-less rock and sway of the waves forcing him to lean against the gunwale beneath the flying bridge.

Carrie stood on deck facing him, her legs tensing and releasing with the rock of the sea. "Come here." He grinned lasciviously. "You look sexy in your Sneads Ferry Sneakers."

Carrie kicked at the short white, rubber boots and brushed aside a stray hair with the back of her hand. "They are quite fashionable, aren't they?" She giggled. "It sure doesn't take much to please you." She strode playfully toward him and relaxed against his body.

He kissed her deeply; his hand sliding into her jeans, caressing her, feeling her soft skin, its smoothness.

A long breath blew from her mouth as she circled his neck with her arms. She slid one across his broad chest and down to his thigh, rubbing gently.

"Hey!"

The couple heard the call from atop the boat and feeling like teenagers caught by their parents they both scurried to the rear of boat where they could look to the flying bridge where Paula sat.

"Yeah?" Carrie called back.

"I hope you're getting that mullet ready for the traps," Paula growled loudly.

"Crap," Carrie sighed and moved to the buckets lined next to the transom fish box. "You came to help, right?"

Don nodded.

"These fish go into those traps," she pointed. "And down the center cage and then you throw trap, buoy and line out when Paula calls to us."

Selecting a metal trap, Don opened the latch to the middle compartment and slid two fish inside.

"No, you have to twist the fish until they burst open—don't just stuff it in there. All the guts and stuff is what attracts the bass, black bass, that's what we're fishing for. She demonstrated, holding one of the pop-eyed mullet in her hands she twisted until the middle burst spewing innards. Something red and squishy landed near her cheek bone. "Hell, I forgot to put on my sunglasses." She reached in the pocket of her flannel shirt and slid them on. "Hope you brought a pair."

"On the console." He reached for them and following Carrie's instruction began twisting fish and stuffing them into another one of the traps.

"Now what?" Don asked.

"When she calls out, the trap, buoy and line all have to be thrown at the same time. Then wait for her to call out again. Make sure you toss it all away from the boat. We don't want anything to get tangled in the prop."

"All the traps?" Don questioned.

"All the traps, and Paula will make a big circle, could be a couple of miles in diameter, and then we go back to the first one and pick it up." She nodded to the gaff. "Snag the line, pull it in, wind it on the winch, it's a lot easier than trying to grab it hand over fist. When you have the trap up, empty it into the box—and so on

245

until all the traps are in and then if there's time and space we do it all over again."

They sat down on the transom box, waiting for the call. Carrie somewhat self conscious of her appearance, wondering if any fish guts or scales were plastered in her hair or on her face. At least working at Grocery World or The Upper Deck she looked clean and neat with a dab of make up and lipstick.

She looked at her hands, her fingernails were short and unpainted; there were a few scratches along her hands. *And he thinks I look sexy in white rubber boots.* Turning her head just a bit to catch Don in her peripheral vision, she noticed the intensity of his gaze at the horizon. His long legs seemed already accustomed to the sway of the ocean. Damn, he looked good. "Sort of mesmerizes you, doesn't it?" She bumped against his shoulder.

"Um." He nodded.

Tonight it's black lace and eye-shadow, Carrie closed her eyes, felt the breeze and grinned.

Paula's voice rang out and Carrie watched her wave her arm, an indication to drop a trap.

Don flung the first one out and watched the line hover in the air until the trap sank beneath the water pulling the line with it. The buoy, bobbed along with the water movement, its flag flapping in the breeze.

He stood straight, body keeping time with the boat's sway, poised to cast the next trap.

"It will be a few minutes." Carrie nudged him. "Can't put them too close together."

He smiled. "So now is a good time to bait another trap. Right?"

246

Already the second and third traps were baited; she and Don took turns casting the traps and baiting them. They even developed a rhythm, moving past one another to gather gear and fish.

Don strode about the boat as if he'd been born to it, He felt pumped with the salt air sandpapering his skin to smoothness, his lips dry and hair tangled by wind and water. He could feel his thigh muscles moving as they hadn't in years—his leg muscles in constant response to the sea.

He knew his back and arms would ache later. But what a lovely ach it would be. "This is hard work," he called to Carrie. "And you like this?"

Chapter Twenty-Four

"Regulations, that's why nobody can make any money, especially the small guy," Paula explained.

"It's the permits that will kill you," Carrie interjected. "They're ridiculous. They cost thousands of dollars. It's as if the government is deliberately trying to run fishermen in this country out of business. It's as if they want China, Japan and those South American countries to make all the money."

"They want all fishing to cease. Their objective is to have seafood come from farms," Paula snarled. "And guess who is going to run them? Big corporations."

"It's a mess, just another example of the big guys carpet bagging the little ones. Just like using traps for fishing satisfies the conservationists. You don't have to worry about sea turtles or smaller fish or dolphins. But to use traps the government requires the fisherman to buy not one but two permits. They're over twenty thousand dollars apiece. The regular fisherman can't afford that." She shook her head in disgust. "There are just too many regulations."

"You have the permits?" Don asked

"Yes, stupid, I wouldn't be out here if I didn't."

They'd spent nine hours on the ocean and made two passes with the buoys. All eighteen of the traps had been half to totally full of black bass both times. It had been a pretty good day. The transom box was full of fish and after wading through the overflow, they'd packed seven crates of fish.

His body ached, he could feel the soreness in his back already. Just how does she do it? He thought as he looked at Carrie. *This is hard work.*

Catching his gaze she winked, lifted her arm and made a muscle, as if she'd read his mind. "After a while it gets easier and you realize you don't have to be a he-man to chuck out the buoys, a nice toss will do. You learn to rest in between throws, hydrate your body more. Little things like that."

He nodded and turned to Paula. "I would ask why do you do it, but after going out with you and Carrie today, I can see why. I guess it's in your blood."

"My family has been fishing for generations. I'm the first woman to go for it though. I got a lot of flack about it from my parents in the beginning but the times they are a changing," Paula chortled. "At least I'm doing something I love, though I still have to supplement my income with a second job."

"I've really enjoyed this. Thanks for inviting me out to see what the 'real men' do," Don snickered. "I have new respect for fishermen now." He looked at the two women, Paula, her hands resting on her hips, a stern but proud expression on her face, and Carrie, the exhaustion showing on her face. He clapped his hands together and said, "How about me treating you ladies to dinner tonight at the Bistro? You deserve a treat after all this work."

****

"You never got mad when we worked together at the grocery store. I never saw you lose it with a customer," Carrie said. "And some of them could be real assholes."

"No, I'm not an egg crusher or bread squeezer like you were, Carrie. I got used to the tourists, I've been dealing with them my whole life. After all, this is a tourist town, and then I have an outlet, too, a real one, fishing." Paula settled the napkin in her lap and straightened the silverware next to the salad. "Thanks for inviting me along for dinner. I didn't expect it."

Carrie rubbed a hand with her fingers, feeling the still creamy lotion she's slathered her hands with—noticing how the thin scratches from fishing were still noticeable.

She'd worn her most frilly blouse and the blue skirt with the slit up the side. After fish guts and wading in several hundred pounds of bass they'd caught that day, she wanted to feel like a woman. Her eyes lifted to study Paula as she and Don talked about regulations and fishing.

Paula wore no make-up, not even lipstick, but she had pulled her short curly hair back and fashioned it somewhat to look stylish. She wore jeans, but Paula always wore jeans,

251

these were clean and cut lower to rest on her slim hips. Carrie envied those, hers were broader, the kind her ex had remarked were made for birthing babies. And the tee shirt Paula wore had a scoop neck that on Carrie would have shown cleavage

She liked fishing or maybe it was going out on the ocean she liked best. It was, for lack of a better term, soul food. But she knew she'd never have the penchant to be a real fisherman like Paula. She'd decided she'd give it a year or so to help Paula out. Maybe by then her friend would take over the payments, maybe she wouldn't hold such animosity toward Lev by then. In the mean time, she'd be patient— anything was better than catering to rude tourists.

Patient, that was the word. She'd been learning lessons in patience since working on the boat and now she knew that was where Paula had garnered her patience.

There was no way to make a fish bite the hook, no way to tell a fish not to zig and zag across lines to tangle them, no way to tell the ocean to calm and no way to stop the wind from blowing. Yes, she'd learned to wait and accept what ever came her way, not to anticipate, not to expect things to turn out as she wanted. Letting things be, that's what she was learning. Now she understood the mentality of the fisherman and by God it was a great way to be.

Carrie smiled to herself, still watching Paula and Don discuss the ins and outs, the technical details of fishing.

They seemed rapt in conversation, their voices rising and falling as their repartee became more heated, less heated—discussing the politics of fishing. It was sad to her that something so simple had been reduced to politics.

She watched Paula's eyes lift from the conversation as two men walked into the dining room. Troy, the young one, was familiar. Yes, he was the boy who worked at the bar. The older man beside him held a strong resemblance, she assumed he was Troy's father.

Paula leaned back a bit in her seat. Though still conversing with Don, her eyes studied the man until he caught her gaze. He held it for several moments, and then Troy motioned toward a table. They adjusted their direction to one several spaces away from where Paula, Don and she sat.

They know each other, Carrie thought. She watched Paula's eyes shift back to Don, she nodded as he talked. Then her eyes lifted once again to scan the room, she noticed how Paula toyed with the napkin in her lap.

Carrie noticed how her friend reacted when she found the man again, her lips smiling ever so lightly and her eyes closing for a split second.

The man smiled at her and nodded.

This is the man, the one. This is the one she's in love with. Carrie thought as she studied who must have been Paula's lover, facing them in the table nearest the center of the room.

"No Dad, I'm telling you she came on to me. I was lying on the couch sleeping. Hell, I'm always falling asleep on that couch, it's too comfortable. Anyway, she walks in and starts kissing me, takes her cloths off and damn, it happened before I knew it."

"Really?"

"I am twenty-one." Troy puffed his chest, "Can I help it if I'm irresistible?"

"Son, that type of woman is bad news, she's playing with you. She wants something from you and for the life of me I don't know what it could possibly be. I'm just warning you."

"Look, Daddy-o, I bet in your day you'd have wanted some of that, too, so don't preach to me about who I sleep with." Troy pulled the glass of iced tea to his lips.

"Your roommate, the cop, Detective Gass, is not going to like you messing with his woman. I don't care if she's the one who started it. I don't care if she grabbed your dick, Lev is a tough guy, he'll knock the shit out of you and then he'll kick you out of his house. Then what are you going to do? Where are you going to live then? I've told you before, you're not living off of my dime anymore."

"That's the beauty of it, Dad, she swore she won't say a word. It's like she thought I was Lev. That's what she said, and once we were— you know, man does that woman like to dig her nails." Troy pulled up the sleeve of his tee shirt,

"Look at that." He smiled broadly. "Yeah, she's an animal, Dad. I've never—"

"I doubt very seriously if she mistook you for Detective Gass. You're built entirely different from him. You're over six feet, lanky. He's stout, thick. Boy, I'm telling you she knew what she was doing, the only question is why."

Chapter Twenty-Five

"They're exhuming the body tomorrow we'll know something pretty soon. The DNA from the e-cig should be in any day. I called Raleigh and you know how that goes, 'any day, any day.' So I'm telling you just what they told me, any day." Chief Moore stood next to his desk, obviously perturbed about the delays in the tests he'd ordered. "Just because we're small down here, doesn't mean we have to be ignored or put on the damn back burner."

"I think the exhumation is our best bet."

"After we get these tests, assuming they're as you suspect. What makes you think it will be easy to pin everything on Estelle? All she's got to say is that Bunion was in a state of depression. This doctor Bledstone wrote him a script, it looks legit." He shook his head, "Damn, Bledstone—all the way in Kentucky, seems to have patients everywhere. But just how in the hell did someone from New Bern become a patient in Kentucky?"

"That's bullshit." Don scowled.

"I know it's bullshit and you know it's bullshit, but a jury may not. You're going to have more than circumstantial evidence to pin this on that murdering bitch."

"So now you're calling her the murdering bitch. So now you believe me."

Chief Moore nodded. "Yeah, I got a call from Kentucky PD. Seems somebody found a hand with a ring on it. Inside the band it read Theo and Emily forever. Some man by the name of Tucker, from the farm next to Cornbys, was over there. Said he hadn't seen Theo's girlfriend for a while, she's supposed to be taking care of the place while Theo's away. And the grocer said this girl Emily hadn't been in for a while to pick up the old produce they use to slop the hogs. So Tucker and the grocer went over there sniffing around and found a hand just outside of the hog pen. Looks like there isn't going to be a wedding after all.

"Are they sure the hand belonged to Emily, the girlfriend?"

"Yep, already got the DNA back." Chief Moore shook his head. "Even Kentucky is faster than us." He snorted then added, "Of course there wasn't a body, the hogs took care of that. I guess they could gut them and see if there are any remains inside but my guess is all that is left of that gal is that hand and hog shit."

"Has Cornby been notified of this?"

Shrugging, Chief Moore walked toward the door to his office. "I told Kentucky PD I'd do the dirty work for them. I wanted to see just what kind of reaction Cornby would have when I gave him the news. For all we know he could have offed her himself."

"Man, you're one cold bastard."

"That's my job." Moore bit on a fresh cigar protruding from the corner of his mouth. "Come on, this should be fun."

****

258

"Wonder if the tox report could tell if there was any Dilaudid in Emily's system?" Don asked, his elbow propped on the open window.

"Depends on how long ago she took it. You think Estelle went all the way to Kentucky to kill this woman?"

"It would be interesting to find out if there is any Dilaudid. That's Estelle's M.O. That would nail her for sure," Don added. "We need to check and see if she went out of town for any length of time. Theo would know that."

"Maybe Theo was in on it, too." Chief Moore rolled the cigar to the other side of his mouth.

"What would motivate him to kill? From what I've seen of him, he doesn't seem the type. I just see him as Estelle's lackey."

"When it comes to Estelle it's always money, power—same thing to her. This Emily person, did she have any dough?"

"No, according to the chief over there she was pretty much on her own. No family, no friends, lost a kid a while back. Baby daddy skipped out on her."

"Rotten luck."

"Rotten life," Chief Moore scoffed. "Piss poor rotten life—a shame and a waste."

Moore drove slowly south toward New River Drive. If Theo wasn't at Estelle's he'd be at the tower, working, refurbishing the old structure. He was curious as to just how far Cornby had gotten with the reconstruction and how authentic it looked. He'd seen the pictures and he loved history.

"I don't see the truck, Theo's truck. From what I understand Estelle bought that for him for Christmas," Don said.

"Must be nice." The chief pulled into Estelle's driveway, both men exited the car and moved toward the stairway. Before reaching the first step, Estelle appeared on the porch. She wore a flowing brightly printed mau mau, her hair was stacked atop her head. Her face was grimaced into an expression that made her looked much older than her thirty-something years.

"I want something done about whoever is shooting at me," Estelle's voice boomed from the upper level of the house.

"First I've heard of it," Chief Moore retorted. "Have you called the station, made any complaints?"

"Hell no, it doesn't do any good to complain to any of you good old boys. For all I know it may be one of you." She arched her back and dug at the air with long fingernails.

"Calm down, nice kitty," Chief Moore muttered to the detective. "What a frigging cat this bitch is."

"Who's been shooting at you?" Don called.

"That's what I want to know, aren't you supposed to be protecting me? Wasn't that the deal?" Pacing back and forth across the upstairs porch Estelle tossed her head as she screeched, her hair tumbled down about her face. "You know, Detective Don, we did have a deal and the nice police chief is right here. I want something done now!"

Don reached the top stair and reached to grab her by the arm. "Listen bitch, I've already told the chief everything. I don't give a flying fuck what you do. And if I wanted to take shots at you, you'd be dead."

She pulled away from him, rubbing her arm. "Police brutality." her mouth drew into a straight line as she slid her eyes over the detective's face. "No, you wouldn't be shooting at me." She turned sharply to face him directly. "And that old bag, why didn't anyone tell me Emma Jewel was back in town? I feel like I'm being plotted against—like you're against me, trying to frame me for things I haven't done."

"You sound paranoid, Ms. Reardon." The chief pulled the cigar from his mouth and rolled it between his fingers. "You seem nervous. Usually you're a very calm individual."

"Screw you, and it's Butler, Mrs. Butler," Estelle spat. "I just want to know what's going on."

"We'll look into it. Where were you when someone took shots at you?"

Leading the way into her home, Estelle pointed to the hole and shatter marks in the window. "There, and the other day when I went to the Castles to collect some late rent somebody took a couple of shots."

Chief Moore bit down on the stub of cigar in his mouth. "File a report, you know where the station is Ms. Reardon."

She slid her eyes over the officers. "Why are you here? What brought you here in the first place? This isn't a social call, is it boys?" Estelle purred and leaned forward, exposing her cleavage.

"The Castles called," Don lied. "Said they heard gun shots when you were out there bugging them about the rent."

Her mouth pursed. "They need to pay on time."

Holding a lighter to his cigar, Chief Moore sucked on the tip, waiting for the tobacco to come to life. "We'll be in touch but if you want anything done about this you need to file a complaint. Otherwise, it's out of my hands."

****

His hands trembling, Theo dropped the hammer and leaned against the coolness of the tower. A scream reverberated within the walls as he slowly slumped to the floor.

"I wish there was a kinder way of telling you this." Chief Moore settled a hand on the man's shoulder. "We don't know much right now. Maybe she was feeding the hogs and fell in or-
-"

"She wouldn't have done that. You don't need to do that. All you gotta do is throw the food out of the bucket." Theo screamed again, knocking his head against the cement wall.

"Whoa," Chief Moore ordered.

He nodded to Don. "Call the paramedics, he's going into shock." Chief Moore squatted next to Theo, cradling his head against his chest. "Sorry man. So sorry. We'll find out how this happened."

Chapter Twenty-Six

It couldn't have been a more beautiful day for surfing. Troy would have loved to been out in the water. But first he was obligated to do a little work around the house for Lev, his new roommate or landlord, whatever he was. All he knew was the cool guy he was sharing a house with was easy going. He had the suspicion though, that if he screwed up or slacked off his duties Lev could be a real ball buster. He didn't need that, there was ball busting enough to go around from his dad.

Finishing his herbal tea, he rinsed the cup out in the sink and settled it on the drain rack. "Damn, I wish I could get out there right now," his eyes drifted to the view from Lev's kitchen nook window once more then turned and headed to the upstairs bedroom.

"If he wants more closet space, I'll give him more closet space. He studied the small space, figuring how to design extra shelving. Hadn't Lev said he wanted lots of spaces for extra storage?

Pulling out lidless boxes stacked one on top of the other, Troy fidgeted with the loose papers, endeavoring to keep them from falling. "Shit." Standing still, he watched as unkempt notes and envelopes flowed waterfall-like to the floor. He groaned and settled the boxes on the carpet, bending to pick up a few of the scattered papers.

He hummed leisurely, slacking into his usually relaxed self, selecting envelope after envelope, loose notes and pages of scrawled lettering, type written pages of what looked to be upon first glance, legal documents. He recognized that type of correspondence from the one time he'd needed his own lawyer to get him out of the scrape with the law—an ounce of coke. That one time was enough to scare him shitless. He hadn't done that stuff in over a year.

Troy had no interest in the bits of paper, the documents, not at first, it was none of his business and secondly, he didn't give a damn. Nope, he didn't care one bit until his eyes caught the words "ungrateful snot nose brat" scrawled in bold letters on one of them.

His dad had called him that a few times. But then he was beginning to believe his father was right about the ungrateful part. Cut off from the old man, he had come to realize that money didn't grow on trees.

"Is Lev the ungrateful brat?" Troy guffawed. "Man, the guy is an iron horse, he looks like he could squeeze your head off. Who in their right mind would call him an ungrateful brat?" He scanned the paper quickly, looking for clues as to whom the words referred. It was dated September 27, 2001.

"You ungrateful brat. I've given you everything you wanted and now for the life of me I don't understand why you reenlisted. I was hoping this little stunt of yours would end once you had to march to the tune of the military, and the Marines of all branches. It is the most dangerous and with the World Trade

Center bombings earlier this month all hell is going to break loose. Bush will have us in the Middle East as soon as he gets congress to fall in line with his agenda and from the looks of it that won't be long. You'll be right there in the middle of all that bullshit those rag heads have been fighting over for the last five centuries.

Peterson has enlisted and I pulled a few strings to have him stationed at Paris Island. He'll do his best to keep you safe. Damn it, things are going to get tough now. You'll think living with me was a piece of cake. You'll think Paris Island, South Carolina is damn Tahiti compared to the hell you're going to go through now.

Son, you've never been in a real war before. You've never seen your friends blown to pieces. Shit, you've never been shot at.

Write to me. Peterson's scribble is unintelligible. And I want to hear from my only son."

The letter was signed, Your father, Senator Steven Price Worther.

Troy settled the page back on top of the box from which it had blown. Senator? Worther? That name sounds familiar. Shaking his head he continued to move the boxes from the closet to the floor. *So I'm not the only son whose father thinks he's a loser.* He shook his head. "And look at Lev. He's no where near being a loser. If anyone's got his shit together, it's him."

Chapter Twenty-Seven

"She knows you're a cop," said Don.

"By now she knows I've got money, too. You think I'm stupid enough to think she'd give me the time of day if I didn't? Last year when she was working at The Upper Deck she saw me—acted like I didn't exist.

"String bean did his homework and found out I'm loaded. I always wonder how long it will take people to figure out who my old man is. As soon as they do, man, do the attitudes change." Lev leaned back in the desk chair. "She knows I'm a cop but she thinks she's got it all figured out in that little psycho brain of hers. She knows that despite you promising to protect her from the local police that I'm sniffing around her for one reason—to pin those murders on her."

"What are you going to do?"

"Don't know yet. I'm just playing along right now, and she's playing me, waiting for me to profess *my love.* That's her thing, you know." Lev grinned. "This one likes the game. She likes it better if she can string things along, play with her victim. You know, the old cat and mouse crap. I'm safe right now."

"Tough job, huh?"

Lev grinned broadly. "Sometimes I just love my job."

"It's all too weird. She knows you're checking up on her. You know that she knows it, yet you're doing it."

"I told you, it's a game to her. She likes living on the edge, that's part of the excitement. Estelle is so convinced she's totally irresistible, that she believes I'll keep her safe, that I'll switch to the *dark side*." He chuckled. "As for you, my friend, your days are numbered."

"What do you mean?" Don asked.

"Protection. Remember you were all about protecting her? That's what she wanted from *you*. She doesn't need you anymore, *I'm* her protector now."

"I don't think she's going to mess with me."

"Why not? Oh yeah, you're broke, man." Lev chuckled.

"I guess right now being broke has its advantages."

"Yeah, guess so. But damn it burns me that she offed Mindy, poor little Mindy. She never had a chance. That was by mistake—right? Estelle thought she was offing Emma Jewel."

"Kind of throws a wrench into our theory. Mindy had no dough."

"A mistake, remember?"

"Right, and what about Bunion, the Cornbys and her father?"

"They got in her way." Lev chuckled. "She's jealous of anyone who has someone to love them."

"What about Theo?"

Lev shrugged. "She was soiled by the time he got to her, already messed up. And Theo is a naïve fellow, kind of goes with the flow. I don't think he ever understood what Estelle is all about. I'm telling you, she's not playing with a full deck—she's, a serial killer. Maybe she was born that way, maybe her old man screwed her head up big time. Same old thing, nature verses nurture. Me? I'm all about the nature thing. Too many friends of mine grew up in shitty circumstances and moved past it. But who am I to judge?" Lev shrugged. "Theo just happened to get caught up in her web, so to speak. And inadvertently helped her become what she is. No, she never really wanted him. But she wanted you just so she could have something to store in her little box of horrors for later use. She'll use it against you sooner or later, watch and see. Have you told Carrie about being with her?"

"No."

"If I were you, I'd go ahead and do it. If you don't, the shit is going to hit the fan when she finds out. And unless Estelle's dead, she's going to find out."

He knew Lev was right. And he'd been so honest with Carrie about everything—Iraq, Maggie, Phil, Sarah and dealing. He'd told her everything, everything except Estelle. Why was telling her about that so hard?

"You're good," Don smirked. "You know, I think you're right on the money—right about Estelle, her motives her damn psycho shit. You're so good at stuff like that, even when I first met you, you had that damn *I got your number* look in your eye. But hell if you aren't crappy with women."

"I get women." Lev grinned lasciviously.

"Yeah but you can't keep one."

Lev shrugged. "Maybe I don't want to."

269

"Yeah, right."

"Maybe Paula. She'd make a good," he chuckled, "wife."

"Wife?"

"I really like Paula."

"You really like *lots* of women. But none stick around for very long. What's up with that?"

Lev shrugged again. "It's too easy or something like that. I've always had women swarm around me. It's the one's that don't want to hang around that I find interesting."

"Like Paula."

"I guess. She is different, there's something though—"

"Are you going to give it another try with her?"

"She'll come around after a while when the money rolls in."

"You're so full of shit. You're just saying that. Now, if you really want her, asshole, you have to woo her. You have to make her feel special. Money is easy. Look how easy it's been for Estelle. She sees it, she wants it, she gets it. It's the other stuff, the time, patience, trust—stuff like that, women want."

"No they don't. They like jewelry and a nice car, a fine house. That's what women like and want."

"How's that philosophy working out for you?" Don asked sarcastically.

"You heard Carrie the other day. Paula's into somebody else. I don't think it matters what in the hell I do or don't do. I'm not the one."

"Wonder who it is."

Lev slid a sardonic glance Don's way. "Who is lover boy?"

"The guy is a foreign spy," Don laughed.

"She's ashamed of him," Lev smirked.

"He's kinfolk," Don chuckled.

"All joking aside, I know the answer, he drives a yellow Hummer. And I'll bet you he's married."

"Stoic Paula, I don't see it. She plays by the rules. I don't see her stealing another woman's man." Don shook his head.

"Maybe she's just borrowing him for a while. You know, the heart wants what the heart wants."

Chapter Twenty-Eight

"Hell, what happened to you?" Don studied the gauze bandage taped to Lev's hand.

"Things got a little rough last night at her place. You ought to know how Estelle can get."

"Yeah." Don touched his left thigh, slid his eyes disapprovingly to Lev and snickered. "I know what happened, you two were making a romantic dinner, she was chopping the cilantro and the knife just happened to slip."

"You're getting better; it was something like that. She was making this soup she raves about and was chopping celery, I reached for a piece and she slices my hand then jumps on the island. Hell, she didn't even bother to move the food out of the way—and orders me to do her."

"You're going to get the clap," Don joked, reaching into the refrigerator for a bottled water.

Lev motioned for his friend to hand him one as well.

"Naw, she only screws the men she kills."

"What about me?" Don chuckled.

"It's not over yet, my friend." He gulped thirstily.

Don rolled his eyes.

"By all accounts that would make her having been with, counting you, how many?"

"That would be Bunion and—you think she did old man Cornby?" Leaning against Lev's kitchen counter, Don drew his lips tight, he crossed his arms. "What are you going to do? Keep seeing her until she gets you hooked on something? She's going to put something in your food or in a drink. Hell, she could switch out the Tylenol for something else. But sooner or later she'll slip something inside you and bam! You're hooked or dead. When are you going to quit fooling around? She's not fooling around with you. I can guarantee that. You are on the agenda, my friend."

"It's the only way she's going to let me hang around." Lev paused for a moment. "She likes sex and she likes dough, doesn't mean a damn thing to me. I've had money my whole life. It's new to her, and I can manipulate her with it." He smirked. "Thought I'd take her shopping tomorrow and see just what kind of things turn her on."

"She ever ask for anything?"

"Not yet. She hasn't shown any interest in the financial side of me, but I know it's there. I catch these looks and little hints she drops. No, she never asks for anything. In fact, she bought the groceries last night and bought me this cool Guy Harvey shirt." Lev flicked his fingers across a shoulder of the fabric. "She says I look good in blue—goes good with my soulful gray eyes."

"Soulful my ass. Don't tell me you're falling for her shit."

"Do you take me for an idiot?"

"Sounds to me like you're drinking the Kool-Aid."

"Yeah, right." Lev guffawed. "She says I ought to quit my job, she wants me to go to

Costa Rica with her. You know, the living is cheap down there. She says we'd live like royalty."

"You going? Giving up on Paula already?"

Lev leaned back, twirled the bottle of water in his hand. "Drove by her place down that little dirt road before I went to Estelle's. The yellow Hummer was parked there again—some guy from Asheville."

"You checked out the tags?"

Nodding, Lev lifted a shoulder. "I'm always compelled to check things like that out."

"Sorry about that, buddy. But like you say…"

Squaring his shoulders, Lev nodded. "Yeah, it's just the way it is."

"So, you think you and wackadoodle will go to Costa Rica?"

"Yeah, sure," Lev scoffed. "It's uncanny. We both know what's going on. I can't figure her out. Maybe we've been looking at this all wrong."

"What the hell are you talking about?" Don turned, shaking his head. "I knew it, I knew something like this would happen. Man, she is playing you and doing it so good."

"I know what I'm doing. I'm in control of this. Not her."

"Then where's this evidence you're supposed to be finding. I haven't heard a damn thing about evidence since you've been playing this game. Come on now, Lev, the sex is good but it's not worth dying for."

Rising from the couch in the adjacent living room, Troy rubbed his eyes, "Oh yes it is. Good sex is always worth dying for."

"What are you doing there?" Lev asked angrily.

"Long night, late night. Let me tell you about this chick…"

"I don't want to hear about any chick." Lev growled. "I don't like you sleeping on my couch and I hope you didn't have that *chick* on it last night. You have a bed, you have a bed*room*." His eyes hooded as he moved toward Troy.

"It won't happen again, Lev. Promise. I was just so tired—sat down for a minute and the next thing I know I hear you two mumbling in here about knives and killing people and yeah, what's this about a yellow Hummer? My dad drives one." Troy rubbed his eyes and sat, turning toward the kitchen. "What's going on? Are you working on some kind of case? Ooh, sounds ominous—sounds cool."

"You need to forget everything you heard."

"Does it have anything to do with the finger prints, the bottle of beer I gave you, the one from that Theo guy?" He tousled his hair. "And the Hummer, where did you say you saw it? I didn't get that part. Could have been my dad's."

Chapter Twenty-Nine

What a shame, Lev thought as he watched Estelle move from the bed to the kitchen. One of the most beautiful women I've ever seen— and fantastic in the sack.

"Black coffee, that's the way you like it, isn't it?" she called. "Want any French toast? I'm in the mood for something sweet this morning. How about you?"

"Sounds good to me," he called back. Rolling to his side he pushed aside a glass dolphin and reached for a small pad on the nightstand. He flipped quickly through the empty pages before settling it back in place. Gently he pulled the nightstand drawer open. There wasn't much inside, only a few tissues, fingernail file, and a small note pad. Lev slid his fingers to the pad and pulled it from the drawer. He flipped open the cover and thumbed quickly through the first few pages.

She's not a bad artist, he thought as he studied the profiles and scribbles. There was a drawing of a round girl, with limp looking hair. Her features were drawn all too closely together. In place of eyes were two exes, he shrugged, thinking of how they reminded him of old cartoons depicting dead characters.

There was another drawing of a body laying prone, another of what could have been Theo, the resemblance was blatant. He had little exes over his eyes, too. "Her little book of wishes?" He asked himself silently.

Lev flipped a page over, *Hangman, so she's playing hangman now. Humph,* He counted the lines—"Thirteen, thirteen letters. Now what could they be?"

He studied the figure hanging from the giant seven, the scaffold—it was female, that much he could make out. Estelle had drawn breasts and longish hair. And whoever it was had a wrinkled face. "E.J.?" he said the name almost too loudly.

He studied the letter game again. *E.J.* His mind raced, devising sentences, letters or whatever might fit into the empty blanks.

"Do you want powered sugar on yours, my love?" Estelle called from the kitchen.

"No," he called back quickly, scurrying to replace the pad into the nightstand exactly as it had been before he'd taken it out.

Chapter Thirty

"It looks like Mindy's but I couldn't say for sure." Carrie felt the coldness sift through her body as she touched the electronic cigarette through the plastic bag—evoking a chill from another artifact of death. "Poor Mindy. Why? And you think it was Estelle?"

"I'd bet the farm on it," Don answered.

"Why can't you arrest her?"

"No evidence. I've got to make sure I have something that will stick."

"DNA?"

"Working on that, it takes so damn long. And once we do have it, that still doesn't tell us who killed her."

"But if you found the e-cig at Estelle's in New Bern, shouldn't that be enough to arrest her?"

"Maybe—depends. I'm waiting on Bunion's body. His wife and he were in the process of getting a divorce. It's gotten sticky. She's all for it, his family says no. So we're still trying to figure out who has power of attorney to exhume it."

"First Hank, as if that's not weird enough." Carrie leaned into Don. "I'll never forget that. I don't understand how he could do what he did. I can't believe I let myself get suckered in by him."

"That's what killers do, Carrie. They certainly couldn't ply their trade if they walked around being mean and nasty. They pull you in with charm—find your soft spot—what you need or want and then they do their thing." He paused for a moment, breathing in a deep breath. "I need to tell you something—Estelle and--"

Her gaze was soft, full of empathy, she smiled gently and nodded. "That's enough. You don't have to say another word. I kind of suspected it anyway."

"I'm sorry."

"Yeah, I know you are." She slid a hurtful glance his way. "She's a witch, a manipulative witch. She does that poor pitiful thing, I want to be your friend thing. She had me going for a while, acting like she wanted to be friends back last summer."

He nodded. "My head wasn't right."

"Sick world."

"Yes."

"Just wanted you to know before the shit starts. Once we get the DNA and we start moving in on her, no telling what she'll say or do to manipulate people."

"Um, I understand." She paused, searching his eyes. "You're forgiven." She took his arm and wrapped it around her. "Never again."

"Never again."

Chapter Thirty-One

The girls were enjoying another beautiful day on the ocean trap fishing. Paula had pulled to her familiar ledge about fifteen miles out. The Loran read well for the black sea bass they were after.

Already they'd worked the traps once and were bringing in the second go around with only four more to go when the winch busted.

Paula stepped down from the flying bridge, "Damn, I knew that sooner or later this thing was going to go."

"So what do we do now?" Carrie asked.

"We do it the old fashioned way, hand over hand." Slipping on a pair of gloves, Paula grabbed the gaff and reached for the buoy near the boat. "Here." She handed the gaff to Carrie. "Make yourself useful and help me pull this trap in, it's heavy."

"Damn, I wish this thing was empty." Carrie whined, pulling against the pressure of the ocean. Her back strained, her arms burned.

"Don't wish that," Paula scolded. "We need the money."

"Ugh," Carrie complained.

The women worked silently, expelling grunts and moans as they fought to bring the traps to the water's surface.

Carrie glanced occasionally at her friend, who seemed tireless, strong and full of energy. *Just how does she do it?* She thought. Again she noticed the rhythm Paula had established, even in pulling line. She wondered if she would ever attain that place where it came naturally. "Don told me about Estelle," Carrie blurted.

"Really? And did you tell him to take a hike?"

Carrie shook her head. "He's been through hell, Paula. And he's trying. Iraq did a number on him."

"No need to explain. My brother went over there. Not so much changed when he came back but a different dimension to him and he was hard to live with. His wife left him, she couldn't take it."

"How's he doing now?"

"He found a better woman, got himself together, for the most part. He's a fisherman, like me. I think that helps, to tell the truth. My brother's a good guy."

"I'm glad for him," Carrie responded recalling the time a couple of years before, when she'd had dinner at Paula's parent's home and met her family.

"You know, last summer I sort of got suckered into Estelle's web. She was trying to be friends when we worked at the Upper Deck. Or so I thought."

"She's a user, knew that the first time I saw her."

"How? And why didn't you tell me?"

"It's in the way she walked, the way she talked to you that day at the coffee house. And you wouldn't have believed me if I'd told you she was bad news. You had to find out for yourself."

"I'm a schmuck."

"No, you're not. You're just a nice person, trusting." Paula winced as she pulled a trap from the water. "There's all kind of people in the world, most of them I don't want to know. They'll use you just to satisfy their own agenda, that's Estelle. People like that don't care what they say or do."

Carrie nodded. "That's a fact." She continued studying Paula as she worked, then said, "I don't understand how you do it alone. I could never do it alone. I like having someone in my life, a best friend, who thinks I walk on water." She laughed. "But you, I mean, there's Lev. Now, you've gotten rid of him. And you were so vague about some other guy. Aren't you lonely?"

Paula slid an uneasy glance and grinned. "I like being alone." She paused as she brought a trap to the side of the boat and motioned for Carrie to help unload the nearly full trap.

"The thing is, and you're going to laugh about this--"

Curious, Carrie leaned against the trap, waiting for Paula to continue. "Yeah?"

"Hank, you know, me and Hank several years ago, hell, he's my cousin—was my cousin—third or fourth, but still kin." She laughed. "After I broke up with this man I'd been seeing forever, well, cousin Hank healed my wounds."

"Hank? Damn."

"That was a long time ago, I was in my early twenties and it was before Hank went nuts. Back then he wasn't such an arrogant bastard; Hank was a pretty cool guy. He was sweet and always made me feel like I was special. And back then I trusted him. He told me how men were, how he was, he was honest with me, maybe because we were *family*." She laughed again. "He said that it was all about ego—that men don't care or don't even consider that all their wooing makes a woman fall in love with them, because to them it's all about sex, all about feeding their ego. He told me to quit giving of myself so much."

"Maybe that was just him. Don's not like that," Carrie said.

"Well, it seems like it's been that way for me."

Carrie nodded. "Yeah, sorry. You have trust issues then?"

Paula shrugged. "I don't know. Things are just the way they are."

"What happened to Hank? Why did he change?"

"He fell head over heels for Emma, E.J.s daughter, his to be wife, and well, you know the rest. I'm telling you, after that, after his parents died, after losing the land and especially after Emma died, he was different, really different. Scary even. We got together again sometime after she died and well, it just didn't work. He was gone by then, if you know what I mean."

"So, who's the guy?" Carrie tittered. "Who are you seeing now?"

Paula pushed the boat into gear and motored to the next buoy. "The same man I broke up with when I was a kid, Micah Conway. I've known him my whole life. We were going to get married then we had this huge argument and broke up. He got married to some rich bitch from Wilmington and moved away." Paula shrugged. "It broke my heart, Carrie. I couldn't understand after all those years how he could dump me like he did.

"I didn't see him for years, avoided him when he came to the island. Then a few years ago." She turned away. "Things happen."

Carrie grabbed the gaff and pulled in the line. "You've been seeing him since?"

Paula nodded as she tugged on the trap line. "Yes, and before you ask anymore questions, I'll tell you that he's still married."

"So you're in love with a married man? Damn Paula, you're setting yourself up, you know."

"Maybe."

"You don't think that maybe Micah is like Hank said, in it all to feed his ego? Maybe he's just using you."

The color left her face as Paula unlatched the wire door to the fish trap. "I just can't believe that. Not Micah, he's always meant so much to me. He's like the ocean, always there for me."

Carrie held the coiled line in her hands, listening to Paula. She hadn't expected such an explanation to the question--*who are you seeing?* What she had expected was a flippant non-answer or some kind of illusive response typical of Paula.

But instead her friend responded as she pulled on the line. "Micah, I surely can't take him home to mom and dad," she snickered. "But we come out here and we go places. Last year we took a trip out west, saw the Grand

Canyon and Mount Rushmore—had a blast. I live for those times."

"What about his wife?"

"Helen." Paula raised an eyebrow. "Helen was always snooty. I never understood why Micah married her." She paused. "I don't know. I guess there are things but I don't ask anymore."

"What about Lev?" Carrie blurted.

"Every once in a while I get lonely," Paula sighed. "And Micah and I did have an argument the last time, about Troy. I hadn't seen or spoken to him in over two months. I was miserable."

"Oh."

"Lev is a player. I knew that the first time I met him. I knew he was after me and I knew what he wanted. He got it and he will get over me if he hasn't already. I think he was in awe of me for a while, the idea of me, the independent earth mother or something along those lines." She grinned. "He couldn't have me, couldn't have me adore him. That's why he bought the necklace, bought the boat—it's just another business venture for him and he's all about business and material things. Most people are, especially women. But that never works out for me. Besides, Lev has all the women he wants."

"But you're cheating yourself."

"I don't think so. I'd be cheating myself settling for someone like Lev. I can't pass Micah up. I've always loved him. It's out of my hands." Paula shrugged. "I don't think I could ever love anyone like I do him."

Paula tinkered with the electric winch. "I hate this thing." She breathed in and turned to Carrie. "Life's too short to pass up the good." She turned back to the winch. "It's always falling apart. Guess I'm going to have to cough up some money for a new one, this one is shot." She jerked sharply on the trap line. "Let's get these things up. I'm ready to go in and take a bath."

Chapter Thirty-Two

"We've got it," Lev spoke into the phone. "We've got the DNA on the e-cig. It was Mindy's. Now you tell me how in the hell did Mindy's vape got all the way to New Bern—all the way to Estelle's place?"

"Yeah, I'd like to hear just how Estelle is going to twist this one around. She's pretty good at doing that. But we both know how Mindy's vape got there. Now we just have to prove it." Don slammed his car door and started the engine. "Who's going to question her, me or you? No, don't answer that, you're at the office. I'm on my way over there right now." He backed out of the driveway, slid into second and cruised along New River Drive to the county line, speeding up to 55.

A scenario of him confronting Estelle with evidence played in his head. "*I have no idea how that thing got under my tire. Maybe Mindy was snooping around my place. Maybe Mindy had a thing for Hank and was stalking him. You know how she was always sleeping around with everybody.*" Yeah, he thought, she'll gaslight the thing. *Piss on my head and tell me it's raining.*

He felt his jaws tighten, the thought of Mindy burning into his head and how Estelle had gotten away with murdering her.

"To hell with Hank, good riddance to that bastard. But Mindy—no, no, that shouldn't be.

This one's history. One way or another, she's going down." The anxiety and anger mounting, Don pressed harder on the accelerator.

"Shit." *relax, don't work yourself into a frenzy.* Consciously he worked to calm himself. He was learning all about that in EMDR, calming yourself, drawing from positive images. That was supposed to help. Wasn't it?

He blew a long slow breath from his lips, relaxed his body into the seat and made an effort to lower his shoulders from the tense high point they always gathered to when he was angry.

There was time, Estelle would not be ready for what he was going to hit her with. The ball was in her court now, and she had no one to throw it to this time.

Once again, things felt too easy. He was going to nab her before she murdered again. This time things would turn out the way they should—the bad guy wasn't going to win again.

Estelle hadn't hurt anyone yet, as far as he knew. Well, there was the cut on Lev's hand. That should have been a warning to his friend. It surely was to him, Estelle was in pain mode, beginning to manipulate. But this time she wasn't going to finish the job, he'd stop her this time. Finally some good was going to be done before anymore bad.

The wheels turned in his head. He was glad he'd gotten E.J. out of town, at least for a while. And he was glad he was spending most nights with Carrie.

He slowed even more and turned right then eased the Dodge into Estelle's driveway. He noticed the yellow truck parked near the dunes across from her house, and assumed it belonged to a random beach walker. They did it all the time, parking where they weren't supposed to.

From Estelle's open windows he could hear music. This year there had been hardly a winter at all and he brushed the small beads of sweat accumulating on his brow aside with the back of his hand.

"That was quick." Estelle stood, leaning over the banister, her hair flying about her face wildly.

"What do you mean?" Don asked.

"I just put the phone down, just now."

"You called me?"

"I called the police station."

"Why?" Don didn't like the feeling. Something was wrong. She'd done something, hurt someone, or worse. He heard the sirens as they approached and stood numb as he watched Lev exit his car.

"You know anything about this?" Lev asked.

"Just got here, three seconds ago. I haven't even had a chance to--" Don raced to the stairway, taking the steps two by two. He pushed aside Estelle, glaring at her and entered the living room, scanned it then walked hurriedly into the bedroom.

Lev followed slowly and reaching the porch, stood facing her. "What happened?" His attention drifted for a moment as a litany of curse words flowed from the bedroom.

"I didn't mean to do it, Lev. I just wanted to scare him. He was standing there and I woke up." Her face scowled. "You know somebody has been taking shots at me. It's happened

291

twice. And I've been on edge—I thought--" she shook her head. "I didn't know who he was. I took the gun out of the night table and shot. What else was I supposed to do?"

In the bedroom Don looked at the man lying on the floor, he recognized him from the restaurant several nights before. Wasn't he the bartender's father? He bent down and placed his fingers on the carotid artery, feeling for a pulse. Pulling his phone from a pocket, he summoned the ambulance.

"Shit," he cursed aloud. *If I hadn't of slowed, if I'd kept my foot on the accelerator.* "Lev, get in here."

"Is he alive?" Lev asked, peering at the body on the floor. "That's Troy's dad. What the hell is he doing over here? Estelle!"

"His name is Micah. Micah Conway. He's got a place here on the island, his family is one of the originals," Don spewed the information.

"What in the hell was he doing over here, Estelle!?" Lev cried again.

Breezing into the bedroom, Estelle frowned. "Don't look at me. I've never seen the man before today in my life. Believe me, Lev. This man means absolutely nothing to me." She watched the two men bending over the body. "Is he dead?" She raised an eyebrow. "I wasn't trying—I'm not very good with a gun. He was going to attack me. Is he dead?" she asked again.

"What was he doing in your bedroom?"

Cocking her head, Estelle shouted, "What do you think? I certainly didn't ask him to come in." Her voice grew louder, "Is he dead? Why won't you answer me?"

"No, not yet." Lev moved aside as the paramedics came into the room.

Don stood, scowling at Estelle. "Fucking cunt. What are you after now?" He stepped toward her, his fists clenched.

Resting a hand on his shoulder, Lev shook his head, "No not now."

Her head swiveling from Don to Lev and back, Estelle raised an eyebrow. "Not yet? What are you two up to? I never saw this piece of shit stalker before in my life, not until just a few minutes ago. I tell you, he scared me. I've been being shot at. Didn't you know that? I told you and Chief Moore about it the other day and I called it in to the station, just like he told me. Someone shot at me once over in Sneads Ferry and once here. Go check out my damn kitchen window." She glared at Lev. "Look at the fucking hole in it. Now, what the hell do you expect me to do when I find a stranger standing over me?" She stood, her hand on her hips, her face thrust forward, twisted into anger.

"You didn't let him in your house, he just walked in?"

"I never lock my doors, not in the daytime, Detective Gass," She spat the name. "And what's it to you if another man is in my bedroom? After screwing you, anything is better."

Lev balled a fist, he wanted to hit her, too. He *really* wanted to hit her. His jaw clenched and he stepped away. "Get the hell out of my sight."

Estelle stood shaking, her lips trembling. "Is that what you want, are you sure that's what you want Lev, Detective Gass?"

"Yeah, bitch. I want you out of my sight. You disgust me. Your days are numbered." He turned to Don. "You were right, she makes me feel dirty."

Facing her, Lev steeled his eyes, gazing into hers. "We're getting a search warrant, that will be easy." He nodded to Estelle. "All kinds of little tidbits all over this place, I imagine. You like writing things down, don't you honey?" He gestured to another officer. "Take her in for questioning."

"There's the gun," Estelle yelled frantically, pulling her arm away from Officer Scaggins. "There's the damn gun, right on the nightstand. I put it down right after I shot him." She moved toward the stand.

"Very cool, Estelle, you're always so cool about killing your victims."

"Prove it, who else have I killed?"

"This man."

She looked at Micah, being lifted onto a gurney. "I thought you said he wasn't dead."

"He probably will be soon."

"I hate you!" She screamed, the cords of her neck protruding, her face brilliant red. "He was an intruder, he could have killed me or raped me! But then you don't give a damn about that do you?" She spat in his face.

Lev wiped the spittle away with his fingers. "Take her, now," he ordered Scaggins.

****

Her hands cuffed, Estelle held them calmly in her lap. Her mind raced between the pad in the nightstand and the events leading to the shooting: He, Micah, had parked near the dunes, crossed the black top and taken the stairs to her home, rapidly, cursing as he stepped. He was angry when he stood at her opened door.

His voice ordered vehemently, "Leave my son alone. Understand? You can screw anybody you want, steal whatever in the hell you want and from what I understand—kill—no, I'm not going there, you sorry piece of trash. That's what you are. I see right through you. What have you got up your sleeve you white trash whore?"

"What the hell are you talking about?" She eased toward the man, as if he was another seduction, then turned, stepping further into the living room. Micah followed. "And besides, your son is such a pretty young man."

"Too young for you and too naïve to understand what type of woman you are."

Her brow pinched, Estelle asked, "And what type is that, asshole?"

"Whore, user, manipulating black-widow. You name it, any piece of slime there is, that's you. You think he's got dough. Whatever gave you that idea beats me. But that kid hasn't got a dime unless I give it to him."

"Maybe I just like the way he looks or maybe I like his daddy." She moved toward him again.

"Stay away from me. I know what you are and I wouldn't dirty my hands with you. Maybe Lev needs to know about you, oh, that's right. He does know about you. *You're* his job. Somebody's got to do the dirty work. Doing you is something the police department is paying him for, bitch."

She cocked her head to the side, drawing her lips tight, pursing them. Her eyes scanned his body. Then she laughed. "You and the fish lady, you suit one another."

Micah waved the comment away. "I don't give a damn what you think of me, I'd have to respect you for that, and I have more respect for a sewer than I do for you."

"Really?" Estelle stopped, sliding her eyes vehemently at him. "How about I just happen to mention to that beautiful young son of yours, Troy, that you've been screwing that smelly old fish lady, that ugly, tit-less, cunt? I know all about her, about you and her. You need to get a less obvious vehicle."

He breathed in heavily, and ground his teeth. "You leave Paula out of this."

"Why should I?" She strode easily into the bedroom.

Hesitating at first, Micah followed her to the doorway.

"How about I tell that pretty little surfer boy that you're screwing the fish lady? How well do you think he'd take that?" Estelle sat cross-legged on the bed. "Does his momma know you have an extracurricular activity on Topsail?"

"He's over twenty-one, time he found out what the real world is like."

"You think that epitome of the American youth and naiveté is going to understand? Shit, he brags about what a pillar of society you are. He's talking about you when we're lying in bed doing it. He ain't half bad for a boy."

His anger building, Micah stepped a few feet closer to Estelle. "You are a real piece of work, you know that? Now what good is it going to do you by telling my son that I'm cheating on his mother? Just what do you think is in it for you? Paula and I are friends, that's all."

"Does Paula know you're *just friends*?"

"There's an understanding."

"Yeah, I bet."

"What are you threatening me for? I don't have a lot, not as much as you think."

"Oh, things always come up. I always like feathering my nest with favors, with little tidbits of information I can call on later."

"That's what I figured, I figured you screwed Troy for a reason. I certainly wasn't because you mistook him for Lev."

"Not hardly," she smirked.

"You know what? I don't give a damn if you tell him or not. Maybe it's about time I let him know about my life. I don't give a damn what you do, you worthless piece of shit."

Estelle picked up the glass dolphin on her nightstand and threw it, missing Micah by inches.

"You're crazy, too. Bats in the belfry."

Estelle's face burned hot red as she reached into the nightstand, drew the pistol and fired.

Chapter Thirty-Three

"It's her word against his," Chief Moore explained. "And he's not talking yet—if he ever does at all. I'd love to keep her locked up but I can't. She walked about an hour ago."

Cursing aloud, Don shook his head, "That sucks. How's it going with Conway?" he added.

"Shot twice, once close to the heart, missed it by an inch or so. Shot once in the head. But that one is the lesser of the two. It just grazed him, took off part of his ear though."

"Wonder what he was doing there?" Don asked. "Have you talked with his son yet? Maybe he knows why."

"Can't find him. Don't know how to get a hold of his wife either. But Paula's at the hospital now."

"Paula? Hmm. Have you talked with her?"

"She's not talking. Can't or won't, but she hasn't uttered a word. She just sits there in the waiting room last I saw her, waiting to get a chance to see him. Not being kin, well, you know how that goes."

Don nodded to Chief Moore, then strode from the office to his vehicle. A trip to Wilmington would take around thirty minutes. Pulling his phone from a pocket he dialed Carrie. "Are you there, how's she doing?"

"Like a rock, she sits here like a rock. I haven't seen a tear, a frown, but then, she's not talking either."

"I'm coming up. See you in a few. Love you." He slid the phone into his pocket and stepped into the Charger.

****

Her mind racing, Estelle flung a duffle bag from a cabinet to the bed. She pulled open drawers, the closet, filling the bag with essential underwear, jeans and a few tops. Then toothbrush, soap, lotions, shampoo were added along with a towel and washcloth. She slid on her Merrill sandals and stuffed a pair of tennis shoes atop the bag. Scanning the bedroom she moved to the living room and kitchen, scanning them both as well.

"I gotta get out of here," She said. "I gotta get the hell out of here!" She repeated, this time screaming the phrase. "Theo, damn Theo. Where is he? I need him to help me! Shit! Fucking shit!"

The bag thrust over her shoulder, Estelle grabbed her keys and raced down the stairs to the Tahoe. She backed out of the drive and headed toward the tower.

Theo stood on the skirt of the tower near the ocean side entrance. His face, tear stained, looked haggard. He turned as Estelle pulled roughly into the parking area spewing sand and gravel.

"What the hell are you doing?" She rushed at him. "Geez, look at you. You're crying. What kind of man cries?" she spat. "You're no man. No wonder Emily didn't want to be with you."

300

"She dead, she's gone. My Emily is gone. She was killed, somebody murdered her." He walked inside the tower, letting the tears fall, his trembling lips barely able to speak.

"Get over it. So she fell into the hog pen, so the pigs ate her--"

"How did you know that?" Theo turned facing Estelle, his vacant stare questioning her.

Estelle flipped a hand in the air. "What does it matter? She's gone. She ain't coming back. I'm here, that's what matters and somebody's been shooting at me. You were there when they shot at me the first time." She leaned against him, her demeanor changing from frantic to timid. "Oh, Theo. I'm so scared. I don't know what to do. Help me. Help me get away from here."

He looked curiously at her, as if seeing her for the first time.

"What?" She paused, returning a defensive gaze. "This man, the one who was in my house." She grabbed at her hair, frantic once more. "He didn't die, he didn't die!" She closed her eyes then opened them widely, "He was in my bedroom, and he is going to lie about me. I know it."

"Nobody knew how Emily died. I never told you how they found Emily." Theo pulled away from her.

"Huh, what are you talking about? I'm being hunted like an animal and you're all wrapped up in that little duh, duh, dumb bitch," Estelle barked. "I need you. I need you now to go with me!"

"What? Go where? What about Emily? Answer me about Emily." Now Estelle looked as he had never seen her before--frantic, confused, so unlike the confident person he'd known since a boy. For the first time, she looked vulnerable.

"How did you find out about Emily?" He studied Estelle, her eyes bouncing from one object to another.

"Answer me. How did you know about Emily?"

"Get off of it! You told me. The cops told me. Hell I don't know. It doesn't matter. Now, listen, Theo, you need to come with me now." She grabbed for his arm.

He pulled away. "The police asked me if you'd been gone for any amount of time in the last few weeks." Theo paused, "I said no. But you were gone. You went to New Bern for three days." He held her by her arms. "You did go to New Bern didn't you? That's were you went to try and sell that little house, wasn't it?"

Estelle pushed angrily against him. She balled her fist and thrust it into his stomach. "Aaah!" she screamed, screeching, she raised her hands to Theo's face and drew her nails against his cheeks drawing blood.

Holding her hands from him, he moved his face inches from hers. "You didn't go to New Bern at all did you? You went to the farm. I'm going to tell the cops to check my farm for any evidence of you being there. I bet they find it. I bet your DNA is all over the place. I bet you killed Emily! I bet you killed Emily! I bet you killed her because you like bossing me around! You don't want anybody in my life. You want to control me, make me your puppet."

He pushed her hard against the wall of the tower, her breath escaping loudly from her lungs. "I hate you. Emily said I was your puppet, that I jumped when you said to. She told me that you were jealous of her, but that she could make you like her. She wanted me to be better, to say no to you, not kowtowing to you all the time. She said she knew you were nuts. That's what she said, but she put it nicer. 'She's emotionally unbalanced,' that's how she put it. And I believe her now. You are sick, a real sicko piece of shit." Releasing her hands, Theo turned and walked toward the doorway of the tower.

Reaching into her jeans, Estelle pulled out the switchblade, she flipped it open and rushed at Theo, thrusting it into his back, beneath the ribs. She twisted it. Theo's hand reached behind to his back. Estelle withdrew the knife and pulled it against his throat, slashing it open.

"Estelle," he gurgled.

Chapter Thirty-Four

Don walked into New Hanover Memorial Hospital, made his way to the elevators and pushed the button for the tenth floor. He wondered, as the car stopped at each floor to unload and load occupants, how Paula was involved in all this. Then he recalled the yellow truck parked near the dunes and her house. It was a Hummer. Hadn't Lev said there was a yellow Hummer parked at Paula's a few days ago?

He exited the elevator as the door slid open and walked to the waiting room. Expecting to find both Paula and Carrie there, he noticed Carrie, alone, flipping through the pages of a Cosmo magazine. She lifted her head as she heard the footsteps.

"Just trying to remember what it feels like to be a girl—you know, the dresses, frilly underwear, something besides Sneads Ferry sneakers and overalls."

Don grinned. "You're a girl, no doubt about that, my love." He leaned to kiss her and settled in the adjoining chair. "Where's Paula?"

"Everyone around here is related," she smiled. "She has a cousin who just came on duty and she signed Paula in as a relative."

"So Micah Conway is her squeeze. He's married, you know."

"Uh huh, she told me. I try not to judge."

"Whatever floats your boat," Don smirked. "I try not to judge people either, not with my track record."

"Did y'all finally put Estelle behind bars?" Carrie closed the magazine and threaded her arm in Don's."

"Ha, fat chance. That woman is the snakiest person I've ever met. She ranted on and on about the shots being fired at her and being afraid, and there were shots, Theo corroborated that. And there is no proof that Micah wasn't an intruder, at least not yet. And we can't find his son, Troy."

"What good would he do?" Carrie asked.

"He could give us a reason, possibly, as to why his father was at her house." Studying her face, Don reached a finger to move Carrie's hair behind an ear. "You look pretty with your hair back."

Carrie closed her eyes briefly, "Thank you." She sighed heavily then said, "Paula didn't talk at all while I was here with her. I held her hand, she nodded an appreciation. That's about all I get out of her when she's wrapped up in something. Then a nurse walked in and introduced herself as Paula's cousin; she and Paula headed down the hall." Carrie shrugged, "I have no idea what is going on."

"I'll tell you what's going on." Paula stood behind the couple. "He has a very good chance of making it. The bullet was not as near to his heart as they first thought. He has lost lots of blood and part of his left ear though. But plastic surgery can fix that." She beamed, tears trailed from her eyes to her chin. She sniffed back

306

snot and reached for a tissue from the box on the table.

"I need to see him," Don spoke sharply.

Paula nodded. "Let me call Nancy back, she'll let you in for a few moments. Not long though, he's in Intensive Care and needs his rest.

"I don't need long, I have only one question for right now. And then if the answer is what I think it is, Estelle is going to get picked up for attempted murder."

****

The answer was as he expected. Micah had not entered Estelle's home to harm her or her property in any way. He was there to tell her to leave Troy alone. She never told him to leave and he had never threatened her or laid a hand on her.

Breezing through the waiting room, Don blew a kiss to Carrie. "Got to go, the game is afoot," he mimicked a Sherlock quote.

She nodded.

"Catch you later, Babe."

Carrie reached for Paula's hand. "I'm glad he's going to be all right."

"He's not quite out of the woods yet but it's looking good. More optimism than not. And knowing my man, he's going to pull through."

"What about Troy?"

"I've been trying to get him on the phone all day. He's probably surfing somewhere." Paula grinned.

"And Helen—"
"I called her, too."

Chapter Thirty-Five

When he pulled into the drive, it looked like half the force was there. One of the officers was pulling prints. Lev was there with the warrant, he held up the notebook from the nightstand and waved it at his friend.

"Got this. And I've got surveillance on Emma Jewel. Nobody is going to mess with her."

"What about Estelle. You got her behind bars yet?"

"She's gone. Looks like she took a few things and split," Lev answered.

"What about Theo? Is he anywhere around?" Don climbed the stairs slowly.

"He's not here. I was just getting ready to drive to the tower to see if he's there."

"That should be interesting."

"I imagine the two have fled. I don't see her allowing him to stay behind."

"Yeah, she sure as hell isn't going to let him do that." Pausing, Don stopped on the stairway, turned and jogged toward his vehicle.

"Where you going?"

"What if he didn't want to go with her?"

"Oh shit!" Lev clambered down the stairs to join Don.

****

"Frigging hell, look at the damn mess." Lev kicked a ghost crab away from the body. A few gulls were hovering at the entrance, he shooed them away and cursed again.

"I think we have all the evidence we need now." Don bent to check Theo's pulse. "He's been here a while, maybe a couple of hours. Looks like she stabbed him in the back."

"You could say that," Lev sneered.

"Then slit his throat. She definitely was mad."

"Impulsive, why does she have to kill him twice? Stabbed in the heart and sliced open the throat. How much more dead would he be?"

Studying the scene, Don walked through a scenario, "Stabbed him in the back and then he reached behind and she finished him off. Man, this bitch likes cutting people."

"She probably came here to order him to come with her. For some reason he wouldn't, so--" Lev ran a finger across his throat and cracked a slicing sound. "And she's gone now." Lev blew a sigh.

"New Bern? Kentucky? Where do you think?"

"Who in the hell knows?"

****

"So Paula's been fooling around with a married man all these years?"

"It's not as simple as that. There's history."

310

"Honey, if she's with him and he's married, it doesn't mattered if there's history or not. Paula is being a fool."

"I hope not. She's such a nice person, so sincere. I hope she'd not going to get hurt."

"My guess is that it's too late for that." Don turned on his side and gazed into Carrie's eyes. "But then, none of that is any of my business." He chuckled. "I guess if you were married I'd find some way to sweep you off your feet, steal you away from whoever--you'd leave Brad Pitt for me. Wouldn't you? You wouldn't be able to resist me."

"Brad Pitt? Maybe. But Benedict Cumberbatch, no way," Carrie giggled. "I'd resist you, if I'm married, I'm married. Not even your animal magnetism and charm could sweep me away."

"Ha," he teased, "You wouldn't be able stay away."

She pursed her lips, "Men, you all think you're so irresistible."

"You'd want me—you like me." He grinned. "You waited for me," He kissed her forehead, "till I got my shit together."

"So you're together now?"

"You're the glue, baby. You're the glue."

Carrie slid her feet close to Don's. "My feet are cold."

He pulled her closer; kissing her lips softly, "I love you. Thank you for being here for me."

"That's what friends are for, we wait, we trust."

"Why? Why did you wait?"

"After Hank—I was so screwed up. You could have taken advantage of that or you

311

could have not bothered with me at all. But you did the right thing. You helped me clear my head. You didn't use me, you were true." She held Don's face in her hands, stroking his lips and the creases by his eyes, "I knew you were good. I knew behind all the garbage in your life, you didn't want to hurt anyone. Most people don't care if they do or not."

It felt as close to good as he'd known in a long time, maybe forever. It felt nice. He sighed into the peace the thought brought him and nuzzling Carrie's neck he relaxed into the newly acquired comfort.

Oh, there would always be bad people, people who use and manipulate, people like Estelle who don't give a damn about anything except what they can get. Maybe they weren't all monsters like she was, but make no mistake, they were there—people who wouldn't think twice about hurting or even destroying another person.

"Tell me you love me." Don moved a strand of hair behind Carrie's ear.

"I love you," she whispered back.

He'd always heard that people are attracted to their own kind and if that was true, he was safe now.

Made in the USA
Columbia, SC
04 July 2021

41288179R00190